HOW
not
TO FALL

HOW
not
TO FALL

EMILY FOSTER

KENSINGTON BOOKS
www.kensingtonbooks.com

KENSINGTON BOOKS are published by

Kensington Publishing Corp.
119 West 40th Street
New York, NY 10018

Copyright © 2016 by Emily Nagoski

All Kensington titles, imprints, and distributed lines are available at special quantity discounts for bulk purchases for sales promotion, premiums, fund-raising, educational, or institutional use.

Special book excerpts or customized printings can also be created to fit specific needs. For details, write or phone the office of the Kensington Sales Manager: Kensington Publishing Corp., 119 West 40th Street, New York, NY 10018. Attn. Sales Department. Phone: 1-800-221-2647.

Kensington and the K logo Reg. U.S. Pat. & TM Off.

eISBN-13: 978-1-4967-0419-1
eISBN-10: 1-4967-0419-3
First Kensington Electronic Edition: July 2016

ISBN-13: 978-1-4967-0418-4
ISBN-10: 1-4967-0418-5
First Kensington Trade Paperback Printing: July 2016

10 9 8 7 6 5 4 3 2 1

Printed in the United States of America

*To the women who had tea
with me at Dawes House,
April 2014*

Chapter 1

Go with Your Gut, Girl

My lips are dry and my heart is racing and he's not even here yet.

This guy. He's the postdoctoral fellow in my psychophysiology lab. Tall. Blond. English. A *rock climber*, for crying out loud. And he graduated from Cambridge University's MB/PhD program when he was only twenty-three. Translation for civilians: he's a *fucking genius*.

The man is a dreamboat. We're all kind of crazy for him, all us undergrads in the lab—even Margaret, and she's a lesbian. And I'm the craziest of us all. In fact, this is how crazy I've gotten: I've asked him to meet me for coffee.

The coffee isn't crazy. We've had coffee before, he and I, to talk through papers or data or research projects. And the dry lips and racing heart are nothing new either—pretty much every time I see him (or, in this case, fail to see him), I feel this way.

But . . . I *may* have slightly led him to believe I'm struggling with some data, and that's why I want to talk with him. (The data are fine. My senior thesis is practically done, and it has gone more smoothly than I ever expected.) In fact, what I'm going to tell him is—and see, I've got it all scripted in my head, so I don't screw it up—"Charles: you know this is my last semester in college, and then I'm leaving for grad school. I think you and I have

A Thing and so I would like to engage in a physical relationship with you before I leave Indiana. What do you say?"

This is as straightforward as it gets, right? I for one would love it if people approached me this unambiguously.

As I sit waiting for him, I consider including in my proposal a list of attributes I think make me a highly promising sex partner—the way you would in a cover letter for a job. Those attributes are, in descending order:

(1) My brain. An asset for every other complex task I've undertaken, and I see no reason why it won't come in handy for this one.
(2) My athleticism. I don't know exactly how this will help me either, but I'm sure I've heard the phrase "athletic sex," and I'm sure I would like to try some.
(3) My enthusiasm. I feel confident it's better to have sex with someone who's really, really glad to be there with you than with someone who isn't.
And possibly also (4), my unblinking willingness to look like an idiot in public.

Am I a beauty queen? I am not. My nose has a great deal of character. My hair has some interesting ideas about its place in the world. My body is built more along the lines of a wristwatch than an hourglass—flat yet bendy. It works for me—I am my body's biggest fangirl—but I recognize where it falls short of the culturally constructed ideal. Specifically, right around the place where my breasts aren't.

Still, having talked this through with Margaret, my labmate and roommate, we've concluded I should lead with my strengths.

I've just told you a slight lie. I said "we" concluded I should lead with my strengths. In fact, the conversation went more like this:

ME: I'm going to do it for real. I'm going to ask Charles to have sex with me.

MARGARET: *laughs uproariously.*

ME: *completely straight face.*

MARGARET: *abruptly stops laughing.* You're serious?

ME: As a hemorrhage. (NB: I didn't really say this. It's the kind of thing I *imagine* myself saying. I think I actually said something pithy, like, "Yes." Also, don't be fooled into thinking I actually know how to spell *hemorrhage.* That baby is all spell check.)

MARGARET: But why not just ask him on a *date?*

ME: I don't have time to date! I'm only here for three more months, and I've got a thesis to write!

MARGARET: *staring mutely, in stunned disbelief.* And . . . when are you going to do this?

ME: Right before spring break. I figure if it doesn't go well, we can avoid each other for two weeks and then come back and pretend it never happened.

MARGARET: Dude. What are you going to say?

ME: Dude, I have no fucking clue. (NB: This is word for word what I said.)

We tried googling "how to ask a guy if he'd like to have sex with you," but we found little of value. There was a lot of "how to tell if he *likes* you," but I already know he likes me—he just thinks of me as his duckling. Professor Smith is the Poppa Duck, Charles is the Momma Duck, and all of us undergrads are the ducklings, quacking and waddling our way through the lab, with somewhere between a third and a half a clue what we're doing.

I did not attempt a search for "how to convince your academic Momma Duck that you're not a duckling after all—you're a sexy-times lady who wants sexytimes with him."

Margaret's conclusion, having thought it through, was that I should not say anything.

"I wouldn't do it," she said. "It'll be awkward."

"I'd rather be awkward than never try," I said. "I really think he and I have A Thing."

And she said, "But maybe trying will actually make it less likely to happen, you know?"

I didn't know. I don't know. All I know how to do is try and keep on trying until I succeed, and then I usually try some more until I get good at whatever it is. That's how it works, isn't it?

So here I am, complete with dry lips, racing heart, and a coffee going cold in front of me. Because I decided it's fine, either way. It's no big deal. If he says no, he says no. We finish the semester, we go our separate ways; no harm, no foul. It won't change anything. Whatever happens today, I'll still graduate in May, wrap up my dance classes, go to the World Congress on Psychophysiology conference, and then go home to New York City to accept free food and lodging from my parents for one blissful month.

And then I'm off to Boston, to begin what can only be described as the Harvard/MIT MD-PhD program.

(I know, right? I kind of impress me too.)

And nothing Charles might say or do will change any of that.

I just want to pause for a minute and say, for the record, I applied to the Harvard program basically *as a joke*. Like, doesn't everyone apply to Harvard? Isn't that just what you do? I applied for undergrad and didn't get in, but last year I was looking at graduate programs and I thought, *Do it*. It's not like you have to take a whole separate MCAT; it's just one extra program to apply to, one extra essay to write. And the program is *a-fucking-mazing*, which is why everyone applies. But nobody gets in. You get rejected by Harvard, you go wherever you're accepted, it's fine.

Besides which, I spent my entire life expecting to go to Columbia University for med school—apart from a few lost years when I thought I'd be a dancer, but let's not talk about that. My parents both got their medical degrees at Columbia. They met there. They fell in love there. I'm a Columbia baby. It was my destiny. Until I got the letter from Harvard.

It's an embarrassment of riches, I know, and I am genuinely

appreciative of all the opportunities I've had. It goes to show how little I have to lose right now. The day the letter came, I sat on my bed, surrounded by my various acceptance letters, and did the only thing I know to do under these circumstances: I Skyped my parents.

I pressed my palm into my forehead and told them, "It's Columbia . . . or Harvard. I don't know."

My dad was like, "You gotta make the choice that's right for you, Anniebellie." (My name is Annabelle. Dad calls me Anniebellie sometimes. He's been doing it since I was born. I have no expectation that he'll ever stop, no matter how often I roll my eyes at him.)

And Mom was like, "Go with your gut, girl."

In other words, they were no help. So I went for a run through Bryan Park, and when I got back to the apartment, all sweaty and panting, I Skyped them again.

"It's Harvard," I told them. And then for no apparent reason, I burst into tears.

My dad sighed and said, "We're so proud of you. But you know what?" And he stopped for a second and sniffed. "We'd be proud of you if you lived in the basement apartment and worked at Starbucks for the rest of your life, because *who you are* is what matters, and you are a kind, beautiful person, Anniebee. You deserve it."

This next part is embarrassing, but I want you to understand my state of mind. All I could say in that moment was, "Daddy," as I sobbed in the direction of my laptop.

And my mom said, "Oh, eHug, honey. Hugs on electrons." Which is the kind of thing she says. She's maybe a little awkward.

So I laughed through my sobs and said, "I love you too, Mom."

Right? I'm lucky. I'll need to grow up eventually, I know; one day when I have a tough decision to make, I'll have to call someone other than my parents. But you know what? That day isn't here yet, and I'm not in a hurry.

Anyway, that was last week. And now here I am, still in undergrad, still at Indiana University. And even though, just at the moment, the idea of living in my parents' basement and working at Starbucks is sounding pretty attractive, I know that in actual fact there are no consequences of rejection I can't cope with. I've been rejected plenty, and accepted plenty too, and I'll be fine.

And oh fuck. There he is.

Chapter 2

Put It on the Table

He sees me right away when he comes in the door. I wave. He puts a hand up in return while he pulls off his hat—it's still cold for March—then he points between me and the counter, eyebrows raised. Do I want a coffee? I raise my cup and mouth, *I'm good*.

See, he's *thoughtful*, as well as a dreamboat.

I try not to watch him too closely as he orders his usual flat white—steamed milk and *four* shots of espresso! *How is that healthy?* He is totally unaware of me, though, so I kind of stare. I stare at the line of his jaw, the curve of his bottom lip, the movement of his larynx when he orders. There are laugh lines just beginning to be visible around his eyes—I can't really see them from here, but I imagine I can, behind his glasses. He's wearing his shitty beige duffle coat, his hat stuffed halfway into the pocket. The ducklings have decided among ourselves that his coat used to be the color of baby puke, but years of neglect have left it somewhere between the color of baby puke and rainwater in a ditch.

But I'm telling you, it is a mercy to the world that the man doesn't try to look good, because even with his shitty beige duffle coat, eyes are turning to watch him. It happens every time. Does he know this goes on? Does he hide it on purpose?

We ducklings have speculated that under the shitty beige duffle coat and inevitable—and inevitably wrinkled—blue Oxford shirt is the body of a Greek god. We're pretty sure this is true. We have no evidence, but we're pretty sure.

When he gets to my table, he puts his stuff down, hangs his coat over the back of his chair (revealing the wrinkled blue Oxford shirt—it's the stripy one today), and sits down opposite me.

"Sorry I'm late. You know how Diana gets. How are you, Annie?"

Of course I know it's just polite to ask someone, "How are you?" at the start of a conversation. I do *know* that. It's just, when Charles asks you how you are, he's really asking. My pulse accelerates by about fifty beats per minute, I fight off a stupid grin, and I debate just spilling my guts right then. *As a matter of fact, Charles, lustbucket of my loins, I have been masturbating to fantasies of you for a year and a half, and if I graduate without at least trying to actually be naked in a bed with you, I will live with that regret for the rest of my life.*

But with my heart now pounding audibly in my head, I opt for the slightly more conventional, "I'm good. How are you?"

I am a conversational goddess, weaving a magical spell. No, I'm not. Headdesk.

"Good, good," he answers. "You're having difficulty with your data?"

So we're getting right to it, are we, Charles? No gentle buildup, just straight to the data I don't need to talk about?

And this is the moment. This is when . . . I chicken out completely.

Instead of confidently propositioning him, I pull out my laptop and mumble something about variance to cover the awkwardness as I open a spreadsheet full of correlations.

"Uhhhh . . ." I say persuasively. "Not so much difficulty as I'm just feeling uncertain about whether I saw everything there was to see. I'd just like another pair of eyes to go over it and see if maybe there was something I missed." I'm making this up as I go.

"Sure, glad to." He pulls my laptop to his side of the table and runs his eyes down the columns. "Not like you, eh? Usually you dot every *i* and cross every *t* and never look back to consider whether one might have slipped past you."

"Well"—I shrug into my coffee—"they kinda never do slip past." This is not arrogance; it's just true. I am detail-oriented. Even Professor Smith says so.

What a shame that skill is of no help to me in asking a man to have sex with me.

He grins. "True enough. The pink cells are the .001 significance?"

"And the yellow are .01, yep." I nod. I am an abject coward. I am a groveling little troll. Ass balls fuck.

He says, "Hm. This is interesting. . . . How much time have you got?"

"I have class at three," I say.

"Well, it won't take that long, but let me . . ." He's copying an array from the raw data and pasting it into a new spreadsheet. He saves it to our shared Dropbox (we share a Dropbox, he and I. No big deal), then pulls out his own computer and opens the file there with the statistical software. "This'll take a moment," he says. As he labels variables, he says, "Feeling a little unsure about the thesis?"

"No, not really," I say, and it's true.

He raises an eyebrow at me, skeptical. "You're looking a little rough around the edges, if you'll forgive me for mentioning it. It's normal to feel anxious about a big project. I was a wreck when I was writing my senior thesis."

He's being so nice, I can hardly stand it.

"Dude, you were, like, twelve when you were writing your senior thesis."

"Eighteen," he grins at his screen.

"Same difference! Everything causes anxiety when you're eighteen."

"As opposed to the confident, striding age of twenty-two. So, not the thesis then. Personal? Should I not ask? Boy troubles?"

"Um, not as such," I say.

"Girl troubles, then?"

That makes me laugh. And then I decide to tell the truth—most of it. "It's a man, not a boy, and it's not so much trouble as . . . a profound *lack* of trouble, when I would like very much for there to be trouble."

"You're not going to tell me you've got a crush on a professor, are you?" he says, teasing.

And there it is. My window of opportunity. I can let it pass, or I can step through into possibility.

With my throat thick and my heart racing, I step through.

I look right at him, lick my dry lips, and say, "Not a professor."

He looks up from his screen and blinks. As my meaning settles into his brain, he flushes pink, the way he does when anyone compliments him or thanks him for anything.

"I . . ." he says.

"You . . . er," he continues.

"That is . . ." he concludes.

Oh, this is way worse than I expected. So. Much. Worse. But what *did* I expect? Was there any point at which I really imagined him saying no? Saying yes? Saying anything? Or did I only think as far as the asking?

I shake my head and wave the subject away. "Don't worry about it. Forget it."

"Okay," he says with immediate and mortifying relief, and he looks back down at the screen, where new analyses are running.

And I think to myself, *But . . . just ask and let him say no. You'll never regret asking, and you'll always regret not knowing for sure what could have happened.*

So I say, "It's just . . ."

He looks up again with the expression of a man facing a firing squad.

"You don't want to hear this, so I'll just say it fast and get it over with and then we can forget it. The thing is, I think you and I have A Thing, and I know if I don't at least put it on the table, I'll always wonder 'what if,' and so I'm just . . . putting it on the table, you know, and leaving it there. Like bread. For sharing."

"Bread?" he asks, looking no happier.

I give him some side eye and say tentatively, "I'm talking about sex?"

He's nearly fuchsia now. "Jesus," he says weakly.

"Feel free to say no! Honestly! I won't take it personally—I mean, even if you mean it personally, I'll just chalk it up to a boss-student thing."

"Exactly," he agrees. "A boss-student thing. So. No. Er. Thanks."

And that was my window.

It has closed.

It is officially time to let go.

But instead I say, "If it's a boss-student thing, once I'm not a student, that's not a thing anymore, and I'll be in Bloomington until early June. . . ." But his eyes are on his screen.

"You did miss something," he says abruptly.

"What?"

"In your data. I can't tell for sure what it means yet, but I think it might actually be quite important. Do you want me to show you, or do you want to find it yourself?"

"*What?*" And by *What?* I mean: *Fuck you, Charles Douglas!* I am done with the analysis! I am writing up my results and discussion! I am presenting these data at a conference in three months! You just turned down sex with me, and now you're finding *errors in my analysis?* I repeat: *Fuck you, Dr. Charles fucking Douglas!*

"I'll save the SPSS file to our Dropbox so you can see how I found it," he says. "But it's there to find in your spreadsheet. Look at it by stimulus."

I take my computer back, and I look. It takes me a few minutes, and Charles sits, patiently drinking coffee while I search . . . but then I see it—the pattern I missed.

Oh fuck.

"Oh fuck!" I say, looking up at him in horror and despair.

"Sorry," he answers, and he really does seem sorry.

But then. Then he fights a grin and loses. I watch a smile spread across his face, and it's like watching a glass of red wine fall, in slow motion, and spill all over a tablecloth.

"I am sorry, truly!" he says. "It's just that this may be the most awkward conversation I've ever had—and I'm British, so that's saying something."

I smile too, but as his eases to a warm little smile directed right at my humiliation, my chin wobbles dangerously, and my eyes fill with tears.

"Shit," I whisper.

He looks at me sympathetically, but he doesn't tell me not to cry or not to worry about it. He says, "I cried almost every day for the last month of my undergraduate work. I'd lock myself in the lab overnight and alternate between data analysis and weeping."

"Did you fuck up this badly?"

"No," he says, but kindly. "Next time ask for a second pair of eyes sooner. Nobody sees everything."

I nod, causing one tear to drip down my cheek, and it just makes me angry.

"Well, I guess I've got some work to do," I say gruffly. "I better get back to the lab." I shove my stuff into my backpack. Charles starts packing up too.

"Me too. Want me to wait here and let you have some time on your own, or may I walk with you?"

"No, we might as well show up together." I start toward the door, and we make our way out into the cold March sunshine as I add, "That way when they see I've been crying, they'll think it's your fault instead of mine. 'Charles, what did you do to Annie?' And you can be like, 'I pointed out an obvious error in her analysis, but only after turning down her highly inappropriate offer of sex.' And Professor Smith'll be like, 'Oh, well, that explains that.'"

He laughs. "As offers of sex go, I'd say it was as appropriate as it could be. Which is to say, not at all, but at least you made an effort not to sexually harass me."

As we cross Indiana Avenue onto campus I whine, "Man, what am I gonna do?"

"About your data or about sex?" he asks. He's teasing me now, and I respond by *thwapping* him on the arm with the back of my hand. "You'll work your arse off and get the work done," he says easily. "I hope you didn't have plans for spring break."

I had planned to go home.

That is not going to happen.

When I get back to the apartment that night, I lie on Margaret's bedroom floor and tell her the whole story. She listens sympathetically as she tries on outfits for tonight, nodding and furrowing her brow as appropriate, with the occasional "No, you didn't!" and "Oh my god, Annie."

"And now not only am I not going to get laid, I've embarrassed Charles, *and* I have a fuck ton of new work to do."

She doesn't say anything; she just gives me a hug.

"Is it because I'm not cute?" I whimper.

"You're totally cute," she contradicts. "You know, for an androgynous white girl."

Margaret's girlfriend, Reshma, is Indian and femme, and Margaret is in love, so anyone who isn't South Asian and into dresses and makeup doesn't look cute to Margaret anymore. Margaret herself is Thai American and also femme, and when the three of us go out, it's like Kelly Kapoor from *The Office* hooked up with London Tipton from *The Suite Life of Zack & Cody* . . . and they're being followed around by Bobby frickin' Brady. I stopped feeling cute a long time ago.

I ask, "Is there some book I could have read that teaches you how to find out if someone would like to have sex with you without completely embarrassing yourself and them?"

"Probably."

"It's not even the rejection I feel bad about, it's how uncomfortable I made poor Charles. He doesn't deserve that. I should have thought of that."

"What was it he said about sexual harassment?"

"He said at least I made an effort not to sexually harass him. I think he meant it was better that I was just like, *Hey, you wanna?* instead of trying to flirt with him or something."

"Annie, you are many things, but a seductress is not one of them."

I wrap my arms around my head. "Quite the opposite, in fact."

Chapter 3

My Sort Is Still in the Lab

A month passes.

I'd tell you all about it, but here's what it would sound like:

I wake up, go to class, go to the lab, teach my dance class at the community center, go back to the lab, go home, and go to bed. Then I wake up, go to class, go to the lab, teach . . .

Except the weekends. Here's how the weekends go:

I wake up, go to the lab, go to the library, and then I go home and go to bed.

Occasionally I don't even make it home but just fall asleep in the lab, and Charles or whoever will find me there in the morning, passed out on the couch in the ducklings' office, my face pillowed on an open book. A few times Margaret and I manage to hang out—as my roommate and fellow duckling, she would usually hang out with me every day, but she's not writing a thesis. She has a job lined up at a pharmaceutical company in Indianapolis starting in May, and until then she's basically coasting. She's *enjoying* her last couple of months in school, socializing, doing all the things we love doing, one last time before we go.

Not me. I'm the thesis-writing, doesn't-understand-her-data zombie who wanders in at night, stares at the TV for ten minutes, and drops into bed without even taking off her clothes. And then I'm out of the apartment in the morning before Margaret wakes up.

So a month passes.

On one of the last go-back-to-the-lab nights, I'm sitting on the ducklings' couch, reading a psychophysiology paper. I've been here for about ten hours, and everyone has come and gone for the day. There's no one else in the lab—probably no one else in the building, since it's Friday night. So when the door opens, I startle and gasp.

It's only Charles.

"Hey," I say.

"Hey," he says. "What are you working on?"

"Noncoherence in anger," I answer, taking off my glasses. I put the paper down and wipe my hands over my eyes. "Anger as an approach motivation, sure, but at which levels of analysis? Basically just anger. From a theoretical point of view, anger is a complete mystery to me." I put my glasses back on. "Still."

And he says,

> *"Rage is the shortest passion of our souls,*
> *Like narrow brooks that rise with sudden showers,*
> *It swells in haste, and falls again as soon."*

I look at him. "Huh?"

"Nicholas Rowe," he says. And then in a soft, high voice, he adds,

> *"I swear I could not see the dear betrayer*
> *Kneel at my feet, and sigh to be forgiven,*
> *But my relenting heart would pardon all,*
> *And quite forget 'twas he that had undone me."*

And before I can react, he pulls a white paper bag from his satchel and says, "I brought food. Take a break?"

"Oh! You didn't have to do that—that's so nice!" He hands me a bottle of water and a warm, foil-wrapped sandwich that smells like a cheeseburger. I take it with a smile but don't unwrap it.

He sits at the far end of the couch, puts another foil-wrapped sandwich on the empty cushion next to him, and then starts rummaging through his bag as he says, "Annie," and then clears his throat. After a pause he continues, "I wanted to say how impressed I've been with you these last few weeks. At first I was impressed at how well you took my criticism. You didn't argue; you just looked at the data and saw the truth." He pulls a bag of miniature Snickers out of his satchel. "But I've been even more impressed since then because your original analysis wasn't wrong, it was only incomplete. You could have kept it as it was, and only you and I would have known the difference. But you weren't satisfied with that; you're committed to understanding your results more thoroughly."

"Thank you," I say. I roll and unroll the corner of the foil between my fingers.

"And I want to tell you that I think the world is going to be a much better place because you are in it and doing good work," he says. He rips open the bag of candy and drops it on my side of the empty cushion. Then and only then does he address his own burger. "But I'd like to present you with another criticism, and I hope you'll take it as well as you took the last one, even though I don't have any data to back it up."

"Okay . . ." I say.

"The world can only be a better place because you are in it, if you are in fact actually *in it*. If you keel over from lack of food, sleep, sunlight, and basic human contact, all of us miss out." And he looks directly at me for the first time. "Will you please eat that burger?" he says.

I raise my eyebrows apologetically and say, "I don't eat red meat."

He presses his lips together, takes the burger back, and says, "Neither do I," and he hands me his own sandwich. "Veggie burger."

"I can't take your dinner."

"So help me, god, I will brace your mouth open like it's *A Clockwork Orange* and jam the bloody thing in if I have to. Eat."

I take it, and he pulls fries out of the bag and starts eating those, so I feel less guilty about taking his food. I unwrap the veggie burger and take a bite—and suddenly I am ravenous. When is the last time I ate? Did I have lunch today? Breakfast? I remember now: I had coffee, and I decided that putting cream in it counted as a meal. Dinner last night? Not that I recall. Lunch yesterday? Nope.

My mother would have my head if she knew.

"Have you read Carver?" Charles says in his I'm-giving-you-a-hint voice.

"Boy, have I read Carver," I answer through a face full of food.

Charles chews thoughtfully on some fries. I take another huge bite.

"What time is it?" I say, realizing all at once that it's fully dark outside.

"After nine," he says.

"Fuck. I should go home."

"Yes, you should," he says, nodding and chewing. "But you should finish that before you go."

Obediently, I take yet another huge bite.

"Thanks," I say again, mouth full.

"Least I could do," he says. "I've felt rather guilty about it, in fact."

I shake my head and swallow slightly too much veggie burger. "I'm glad you caught it. Imagine how I would have felt if I had caught it later and didn't have time to fix it."

Through another mouthful of fries, he says, "There aren't many like you, Annie."

I don't know what to say to that, so I just say, "Can I have some fries?"

He hands me the container and says, "Have the rest. I had dinner out. I was only eating to be polite."

To make conversation I ask, "Where'd you go?"

"Nick's," he says. "The 'English Hut.'"

He says the last words with irony. Nick's is neither English nor a hut. So I ask the obvious question. "Why?"

"There was a graduate student get-together there. I thought I'd spend some time with my own sort."

I nod and eat.

He clears his throat and shifts in his seat. "But the whole time, I kept thinking, 'These aren't my sort. My sort is still at the lab.' And so I stopped at Kilroy's for the food and came to the lab on the off chance you were here." He turns his face to me. "And you are."

He holds my gaze for a second, and the corners of my mouth lift.

"There you go," he says. "Haven't seen that in a while."

I look down. I have a little veggie burger left, but I don't feel as hungry now. As I wrap up the last of it in its foil, I say, "Thanks for this."

"My pleasure," he says. I meet his eyes again, and he says quietly, "No one has what you have. The drive. The curiosity. The powerful intelligence. Diana is lucky to have you in her lab. I'm lucky. We don't tell you often enough."

I'm exhausted. I'm full. And, oh yes, I'm *exhausted*. I feel the burning behind my eyes and say, "Don't make me cry again. You'd have to live with that forever, you know, the guy who made Annie Coffey cry *twice*." I open the bottle of water and take a long drink.

"Do you think we could be friends, Annie?" he says. "I've known you for a year and a half, and I hardly know anything about you, except that you're very bright—and, apparently, wanted to go to bed with me, which, I'll be honest, seem like mutually exclusive facts. Though I expect that second thing isn't even true anymore, now that I've ruined your semester, eh? Ah well. These things do happen."

I choke a little on the water. "I'd like to be friends."

"Let's go climbing," he says. "Why don't you take tomorrow off, get some sleep, and then we'll go rock climbing Sunday."

I shake my head. "I already took yesterday afternoon off for the prairie vole talk, I can't spare two whole days—"

"You can; you *should*. You'll come back to it thinking more clearly. You're stuck because you're sleep deprived. Look, trust me on this one. I spent two weeks banging my head against a wall over a design flaw in the blood pump." (He invented a medical thing. I don't quite understand what it does, but I love what he calls it: the blood pump.) "Then I spent one weekend in the woods, and I woke up with the solution."

"Yeah. You're probably right. Okay." Rock climbing. Absolutely. Fear of heights notwithstanding. Whatevs. It's fine.

I put the remainder of the veggie burger into my bag, and Charles says, "Take the candy, too."

"Thanks," I say, and drop the bag of Snickers on top of everything else.

"How are you getting home?"

"Walking—or there's probably a bus."

"I've got my car. Let me give you a lift." He takes my bag from me—and drops it to the floor. "Jesus Christ, what have you got in here?"

"Seven medical textbooks," I say apologetically. "I'll carry it." But he keeps it, and we go out to his car. It's only a couple of miles, but it feels luxurious just to sit there and let a combustion engine do all the work. In a few quiet minutes of inattentiveness, my brain is growing bleary.

As he drops me off, he says, "Get sleep. I'll pick you up at two on Sunday."

"Okay, see you then. Bye—and thanks again."

I notice through the deepening haze that he doesn't drive away until I've opened the front door and stepped inside.

As I close the front door behind me, I hear music playing upstairs. Margaret is getting ready to go out. I haul myself up the stairs and poke my head into the bathroom, where she's putting on eyeliner.

"Annie!" she says brightly, and then, "Oh my god, Annabelle, you look like hell." She turns off the music.

"I feel like hell. I'm going to bed. Have fun tonight."

"Wait, have you eaten today? There's pizza."

"Yeah, Charles brought me Kilroy's, actually."

She blinks. "That was nice of him."

"It was. He was very nice to me." I blink slowly, my exhaustion growing. "He seemed to blame himself for me having to, like, redo six months' work in one month."

"Aw!" Margaret says, but I'm already on my way to my room.

I barely get my shoes off before I fall into bed.

Over the next thirty-six hours, I sleep for twenty-four of them.

I go for a run, too, I take a shower, and I spend a little time with Margaret—she tells me about her girlfriend, about her apartment hunting in Indy, about her fun and exciting life.

I used to have a life. Now I have a thesis.

By Sunday, though, I feel a lot better. Better enough to recognize I'm having Some Feelings about rock climbing with my, um, new friend.

When Margaret makes her way out of bed and into the kitchen around eleven Sunday morning, I am making pancakes.

"Coffee," she grumbles, her hair in her face. It's nice to be the alert one for once.

"French press," I say, mimicking her tone and pointing to the pot on the table.

"Rock star," she answers in the same voice.

"Yes, I am," I grumble back.

She sits at the table and pours coffee into a waiting mug, then sits sipping it while I flip pancakes. It's a little like watching a person-size balloon inflate, seeing Margaret caffeinate herself in the morning. By the time she gets to the bottom of her first cup, she's almost human.

"Are there pancakes for me, too?" she asks.

"Pancakes for everyone!" I announce, like it's my campaign promise.

She pours a second cup and says, "You seem lots better."

"I am! My brain feels so much less foggy."

"Tell me you're not working today. Can you hang out?"

"Actually," I say, "I'm going rock climbing with Charles at two." Her eyebrows go up.

"I know!" I say. "I want to talk to you about this development." As I feed her pancakes, I report everything I remember from Friday night—the veggie burger, the nice things he said, the way he asked to be friends and said all he knew about me is that I'm smart and wanted to have sex with him. "Actually, he said he figured the second part wasn't true anymore because he ruined my semester."

"I think this must mean he's over The Bread Fiasco," Margaret says as she cuts a stack of pancakes into squares. This is what we're calling it: The Bread Fiasco. Putting myself on the table, like bread. For sharing. Seriously, how can I be so good at organic chemistry and so bad at hooking up?

Margaret's good at *both*.

She goes on, "That was pretty smooth, actually. He gave you a way out of The Awkward. You don't have to be like, 'I take it back,' or 'Hey, about that—no hard feelings, right?' He made it easy."

"I don't take it back, though! I really thought we had A Thing. When he said the thing about being impressed with me and the world being a better place, I was like, 'Dude, just kiss me.' Shit like that is why I'll never win a Nobel Prize. Nobel Prize winners don't glaze over watching a guy's Adam's apple move while he talks and think, *All I want to do is lick his throat*."

"You don't know that!" Margaret says. "Anyway, it doesn't

matter that you don't take it back. He built a wall, and he did it while sparing you both The Awkward. He's a really good guy. Don't try to make anything happen. Be his friend. His friendship you can take with you when you leave IU. His sexy, sinewy throat you cannot."

"Truer words were never spoken," I say. "I will be his friend and leave his throat alone."

"Good," she says. "Now: what are you going to wear?"

Chapter 4

Brace Yourself, Bridget

"No. What do you say before you touch the wall?" Charles says.

For the first time, I've just put my hands on the rough holds that are bolted to the climbing gym wall. I've spent the last forty-five minutes renting equipment, putting on gear, and getting the climbing gym's official orientation and belay training, followed by Didactic Dr. Douglas's additional Scout Safety lesson. There was a slight risk of me getting bored, and then I realized Mr. SafetyPants's lecture was the only thing standing between me and the terrifying prospect of actually climbing up this wall.

But now I'm tied in and ready to go. *Tied in* means there is a rope that goes from a knot in my harness, forty feet up to the ceiling, where it loops over a pulley system, and comes back down forty feet to Charles's hands. This rope and those hands are supposed to stop me if I fall off the wall. Otherwise, I plummet to my death. So that's nice.

But right now I have two feet on the ground, and I'm being scolded by Charles. "Annie, what do you say?"

"Sorry. On belay?"

"Belay on."

"Okay."

"No, you say, 'Climbing.'"

"Right. Um. Climbing."

"Climb on."

So I start to climb.

It is much. Much. Harder than it looks. I move like a vertical tortoise, everything in slow motion as I search for holds that look remotely big enough. And then every time I move my feet, I have to look down and search for a foothold within reach before I can move. I'm making progress though. I feel like I'm maybe ten feet off the ground when Charles calls, "Annie, I want you to let go, keep your feet on the wall, and sit down in the harness. When you let go, say, 'falling.'"

I turn and look down—and I'm mortified to see that my feet are maybe three feet off the floor. "Why?"

"So you can learn to trust the gear. It's much easier to do by choice the first time than because you fall."

"Um. Okay." But my fingers don't want to let go of the holds I've been clinging to all this time. They really just don't want to.

Charles is patient. "In your own time. Fear is perfectly rational until your body learns to trust the gear and your partner."

I try letting go with one hand. That's fine. I try letting go with the other. That is also fine. It's letting go with both hands that's difficult, and my arms are starting to burn with the effort of clinging like a brontosaurus to the wall. "Okay, I'm letting go," I say.

"Say, 'falling.'"

"Okay." My arms are trembling now. "Okay." I take a deep breath. This is not a big deal. Even if I actually do fall, it's literally, like, four feet. "Okay. Falling." And I let go of the wall, grab on to the rope, and sit like I'm sitting in a chair, my feet still on the wall. The rope stretches and swings a little. My ass is, like, three feet off the ground.

This is nothing! It was easy! I throw Charles an ecstatic smile. He smiles back and says, "You don't have to hold the rope. Let your hands relax."

"Oh!" I let go of the rope and drop my hands to my sides. I

bounce my toes against the wall, swinging in the harness. "This is fun!"

"It is fun. Care to go higher?"

"Right on!" I reach forward and can't grab any holds. "How do I get back on?"

I'm looking at the wall as he answers, but I can hear the smirk in his voice. "From where you are now, you can put your feet on the floor and start over."

"Arrite, smartypants." I follow his instruction and start over. It's easier on my second try; I don't have to spend as much time searching for big handholds, and I don't have to look down at my feet as much.

But gravity, man. Not just a good idea; it's the law. It seems to me that the higher I get, the more the Earth is pulling me back down. My muscles move as if through sludge. My brain is slow and my body unresponsive, my arms trembling, my fingers unsteady. Nothing seems to work up here; it's just too high. Humans are not meant to function this way.

I call down to Charles, "Ummmm, I think this is high enough."

"You're only halfway up," he calls back.

"Yeah. Well. Halfway is pretty high. So. I think I want to come down now." There is a thin trembliness in my voice that I attribute to the extreme altitude. I'm about a hundred feet off the ground.

"I think you can do one more. See that big red hold about three feet from your right hand? You can get that one."

"Uhhhh . . ." I don't think I can get that one. Not because my arm is too short to reach it, but because my right hand seems to be Velcroed to the big blue one it's currently on.

"You can come down if you like, but I think you can get that red one. It's a bucket, you could fit your whole hand in it."

"Okay," I say. And I stop thinking and just reach for the red bucket. My fingers sink deeply and solidly into it and I pull myself a few more feet up the wall. My pulse is pounding in my throat, and I'm breathing like I just sprinted a mile. I press my body against the wall. I had initially been concerned about Charles watching me be a beginner at this, but that tiny worry has been completely subsumed by primal, life-threat fear.

"How about the green one on your left?" Charles calls. "The green one just below the blue crater. See it?"

"No. Where would my feet go?"

"Just stand up on your left leg. Straighten that knee and reach for the green one."

I turn my face to the left and see the green one. I don't think, I just reach and grab. And somehow my knee is straight, and my hand is on the green one. "Oh my god," I whimper. "This is really high." I close my eyes to stop myself from looking down.

"Two more, then you're there," Charles calls from about seven hundred feet below me. "See that big one on your right? That's got a big concave surface on the far side. Put your fingers in that pocket."

I see the hold he means. It doesn't look promising, just a bump on the wall, but fine. Whatever. If I'm going to die up here, let it be because I tried and failed, not because I gave up.

"Okay," I pant to myself. "Okay." I reach. My fingers touch the hold, but I can't get to the far edge of it. I have never worked so hard physically in my life—not so much because it's physically demanding, though it is, but that it's demanding and also ten thousand feet off the ground.

"Um," I call to Charles.

"If you step up and get your weight off your left foot, you can reach it," he instructs.

If I take my weight off my left foot, then only my left hand and my right foot are on the wall. Two points of contact are not enough. I am not going to do that.

But I can stand *en pointe* in my rented climbing shoes. I tried it when I first put them on. The rubber sole is so stiff, I can stand on the very tips. So I relevé to the point of the shoe, gain the necessary two inches, and reach the pocket behind the hold and pull my weight up with an unattractive grunt. The air must be thin this high off the ground. That would explain why it's so hard to breathe.

"Nice," Charles calls. "You've got this. See the giant one right at the top? That's it. That's the goal. Go get it."

Easy. I straighten my knees, reach up, sink my left hand into the topmost hold, and go, "*WOO-HOO!*" I'm smiling uncontrollably, even as my lungs are laboring to keep my muscles oxygenated.

"Nice job," Charles calls up. "Now say, 'Take,' and sit down in the harness."

"Take," I say, and I bend my knees into the harness without letting go of the wall. I hear Charles's laugh drifting up from the canyon far below. I stand back up and call, "It's not funny!"

"You haven't got my view," he calls back. "Try again. Say 'Take,' *let go,* and sit down in the harness."

The trick is not to think about it. You just do it. You do the irrational, stupid, ridiculous thing of letting go of the wall you're clinging to thirty-five thousand feet above the ground, and sit back into empty space.

I do it.

And it's easy. The rope stretches a little, but I'm totally secure.

"Let go of the rope, Coffey."

Woops. I let my hands dangle at my sides. My palms are burning and my forearms are trembling.

"Now keep your feet on the wall and walk yourself down as I lower you. When you're ready, say, 'Lower.'"

"Go slow, please?"

"Yep."

"Okay, lower."

"Lowering."

He does. I descend only slightly faster than I went up in the first place. It's bizarre to drift downward this way, my feet guiding me along. When I reach the ground, I hold the rope again as I put my feet on the floor—and then realize what I've done and let go.

Then I look up at the wall, all the way to the ceiling.

I climbed that.

My muscles are shaky, my blood is tanged with adrenaline, my lungs are still working like bellows, and I feel alarmingly close to tears. I did it!

"You did it," Charles says.

I turn to him with wild delight. "I did it!" I cry, throwing my arms around his neck. I'm rewarded with a bear hug, the rope sandwiched between us.

When he lets me go, I bounce on my toes and say, "I wanna do it again!"

"You will," he says. "But take a break, and then we'll switch. You belay me."

My smile vanishes. "I belay you?"

He nods. He's still smiling, and he's undoing the figure-eight knot that's holding the rope to my harness. "You belay me."

He lets me rest for a few minutes—I have some water, I waggle my forearms and try to move more blood to them—and then he ties me in to the belay end of the rope, saying things like, "Never let the lines cross," and I laugh, but apparently he's never seen *Ghostbusters*. Then he also ties me to a rope that's bolted to the floor.

"What's the anchor rope for, young Coffey?" he asks. It's a pop quiz.

"Uhh . . ." I look at the system of ropes. Floor, to me, to pulley on the ceiling, to . . . Charles. Probably twice my mass in meat and bone on the far end of this rope I'm tied to. "Oh. Gravity. If you fall suddenly, I'm in the air."

He nods approvingly. "So where should you stand relative to the anchor?"

I think through what would happen if he fell. . . . "I should be right under the top rope, with the anchor rope already taut, so there's no slack there."

He nods again and says, "They don't give these honors degrees to just anybody."

Then he pulls slack into the top rope, which is looped through a belay device, which is clipped to a carabiner on my harness. The whole system seems insane to me, but clearly, it works. "Show me how you take up slack," he says.

I show him, pulling the rope through the device and locking it down. And again. And again.

"Good," he nods. "Let's do it! On belay?"

"Belay on," I say with an intrepid smile.

He puts his hands on the wall and says, "Climbing."

"Climb on."

He's fast. Shit. I take up slack as fast as I can, but I'm behind. "Wait!" I call, "I can't keep up."

He pauses and looks down at me. "You're doing fine."

I do not, I do not, I do not want to be responsible for the tragic death of Charles Douglas. I pull the rest of the slack out and say, "Okay."

"Climbing," he says.

And he waits.

"Annie. Climbing."

"Oh! Climb on. Sorry."

He begins to climb again, a little more slowly, I think, and I keep up, taking up slack as he goes.

It's an odd sight to stand below a climber. Mostly what you see is their butt. Charles has an amazing butt. He's wearing out-doorsy hiker pants with legs that zip off to convert to shorts, and a T-shirt that looks approximately as old as I am. The harness makes his pants bunch in unflattering ways as he climbs. And yet he's a beautiful sight, fluid and balanced. He moves like he's floating up the wall. His forearms and hands are perfectly steady, so unlike the way mine felt as I climbed—they're also massive and powerful, unlike mine, so that might explain at least some of the difference.

He calls down, "Little slack."

"What?"

"Slack. The rope doesn't have to be taut."

"Oh."

I loosen the rope, and he says, "Thanks. Climbing."

I catch it this time. "Climb on!"

He gets to the top in no time and has barely broken a sweat.

"It's your big moment!" he calls then, standing confidently on two invisible chips on the wall, fifty thousand feet above me. "I'm going to say, 'Take,' and let go, and you're going to lower me, just as I did you."

"Okay," I announce. "I'm ready." I'm locking the rope down ferociously, my feet spread wide. I keep my eyes on him.

"Take."

He lets go—and I fly off my feet with a *"Waugh!"* until I'm tethered between the top rope and the anchor rope. Now we're both dangling from opposite ends of the rope, which I'm still holding locked down with both hands. He's laughing. I am not. If I let go of the rope, I fall about two feet, and he falls more than twenty.

"Sorry!" I call.

"No problem," he says, smiling down at me. "Next time, brace yourself, Bridget."

"Who's Bridget?"

"I'll explain later. Just, when I say, 'Take,' next time, sit down in your harness the way you sit down up here. Got it?"

"Got it." I'm still dangling between the two ropes, holding on for dear life—my own and his.

"Okay, let's try again," he says, and he gets back on the wall— *how did he do that?*—and climbs enough to let me down to the floor and put a little slack in the top rope.

"Right. Ready?" he says. "Sit down in the harness."

I do, and the top rope tightens between us, almost pulling him off the wall. "Shit," he calls. "Not yet."

"Oh my god, sorry!" If I had a hand that wasn't occupied with preventing Charles from a thirty-foot free fall, I would facepalm.

"My fault, I was unclear." (It *so* wasn't his fault.) "When I say, 'Take,' keep the rope locked down and sit down in the harness."

"Okay. Ready when you are." Rope locked. Knees bent. Anchor rope as taut as I can get it.

"Okay. Take."

As he lets go, I sit, and he only goes down a couple of feet before the rope catches him. And both my feet are still on the floor. My heart is beating just as fast as when I was at the top.

"Well done," he says. "Now when I say, 'Lower,' you say, 'Lowering,' and just gradually let out the rope. Ready?"

"Yes."

"Lower."

"Lowering." I feed the rope out, keeping the pressure as steady as I can, though the nylon is burning against my already sensitive palms. It's a little jerky, and I slip once, but he makes it down in one piece. When his feet touch the ground, I am elated. Dr. Charles Douglas put his life in my hands, and I did not kill him.

"This is fun," I say.

"It is fun. Want to climb another wall?"

We each go about five times. By the end of that, my palms are red and throbbing, and my arms feel like they've been turned to rubber and then set on fire. I think this might also describe the smell emanating from my sweaty, disgusting armpits. About midway through, I took off my T-shirt—a pink one that reads NICE WORLD—LET'S MAKE IT WEIRDER that my mom got me when I graduated from high school—because it was literally soaked through, like somebody threw a bucket of warm water at my back.

So I'm there in yoga pants, a sports bra, and a climbing harness, looking . . . well. I want to tell you I look powerful and sexy, like those women in commercials for exercise equipment, where sweat beads on their toned, tanned abs as if they've just been Rain-Xed, but actually I look and feel like cooked spaghetti, pale and soggy.

I'm lying on my back on the thick mats that cover the entire floor of the climbing gym, trying to persuade more blood to flow into my throbbing arms. I tell Charles, "I had this gym teacher in middle school—"

"Middle school is how old?"

"I was, like, twelve?"

"Ah. Okay."

"This guy was a meathead. And one day we're all trying to do pull-ups, right, and a buncha twelve-year-old girls, we're not going to be able to do many. But I couldn't do *any*, not even one. And this meathead gets right in my face"—I put a hand over my face, to show where he stood—"and he yells, '*Upper-body strength, Coffey!*' And all I remember is this huge, red, bulging face. It was like my lack of ability to do a pull-up actually made him *angry*. Why would it make him angry?"

Charles hands me a paper cup of water from the fountain and sits down next to me on the mat. He says, "I don't know."

"I can do the biceps kind of pull-ups now, but I still can't do the front ones. And it's those front ones you need for this, huh?" I lean on my elbow and sip the water.

"You don't need them, but they help," he says. "The biceps kind is a chin-up."

"Oh. Those are the ones I can do. Chin-ups. I can't do any pull-ups." I turn my face to him. "Can you do any pull-ups?"

"I can," he says, and I don't think I'm imagining the smugness.

So I say, "How many?"

He gets up and walks over to the emergency exit door, over which is mounted a horizontal slab with a variety of grips molded into it. Charles jumps up and grabs it, and he starts doing pull-ups. Oh, this is hilarious and adorable. He's showing off. When he gets to ten, I start counting out loud. At fifteen, he's slowing down. He drags himself painfully through the twentieth, and then lets himself drop down to the floor. He walks back over the mats and sinks down next to me, breathing heavily and grinning. He lies back with his arms over his head, hands curled. There are

veins standing out on his forearms. Dude. I know he was showing off, but it fucking worked.

"That'll make the rest of today a challenge," he says through
his panting breath. He looks up at the ceiling and then puts his
hands over his face and says, "God, what an idiot I am."

"Who's Bridget?" I say.

"Hm?" he says, dropping his hands to the mat again.

"Who's Bridget? 'Next time, brace yourself, Bridget.'"

"I ought not to have said that. It's a stupid, rather mean joke."
He pauses for a minute and then says to the ceiling, "What's
foreplay to an Irishman?"

"Oh, I see. 'Brace yourself, Bridget,'" I finish. "That's pretty
funny."

We lie there, staring at the ceiling for a few more minutes,
until Charles says, "Right, young Coffey," as he drags himself up
from the floor. "Let's get out of here."

He holds out a hand to me. I take it, very aware of his cal-
loused fingers against my swollen, red palm, and between us we
manage to get me to my feet. In the lobby, I return the rented
harness and shoes while Charles packs up his stuff—he has his
own shoes and harness and a chalk bag and all kinds of stuff.

I pull off my soggy socks, look at my mangled feet, and say,
"Ah, memories."

"Hm?"

"The bleeding blisters take me back to my innocent youth," I
tell him. "Pointe shoes."

"You dance?" he asks.

I'm surprised by the question. "Wow, you really do know nothing about me."

"That's what I was saying. Well, that explains why you climb
so well for a novice. I'd have thought you were having me on, if
you hadn't been so nervous about the height."

"I climb well?" I can't help it. It's always exciting to hear I
don't suck.

"Balance, flexibility, strength, coordination—yes, you climb very well for a beginner. Practice would allow you to build the motor patterns so you can climb efficiently, and you'd construct decision maps for choosing moves, which would make you faster."

"And I can stand on my toes!" I add as I slide into the flip-flops I wore to the gym.

He smiles at me. "Yes. I can't do that."

"But you can do pull-ups, which I'm sure more than makes up for it. Also, even without that you've got"—I stand on tiptoe in front of him and measure flat across the top of my head—"three inches on me."

"But I can't put my knee in my ear. A skill worth coveting. Ready?"

We walk out to his car and head home.

"Well, young Coffey, what shall we do next? Coffee on Thursday?"

"I can't Thursday, I teach at the community center that night."

"What do you teach?"

"Dance, dummy."

"How should I know? You might have taught biology or maths or, for all I know, painting or poetry or Polish."

"Just dance," I say. "Ballet on Tuesdays, jazz on Thursdays, and this semester I rehearse on my own on Wednesdays too."

"What are you rehearsing for?"

"Just the end-of-year recital. All the teachers do solos. It's no big deal, but, ya know, you can't just throw something together."

"No," he says. "*You* can't just throw something together. Well. What time are you finished Thursday?"

"Seven thirty."

"How about I meet you there—on Grant Street, right?—and we can get some food and work for a couple of hours. You'd be working anyway, right? Me too. Might as well work together."

"Sure." I smile. In my head I'm already texting Margaret: *"WE MIGHT AS WELL WORK TOGETHER!!!" :-D*

And when I get home, of course I dissect the whole adventure with Margaret.

"So he showed off," she summarizes. "But mostly he was teachery."

"Yes."

"And on Friday he brought you food and said you were 'his sort.'"

"Yes."

"And you're having a study table on Thursday."

"Yes."

"Dude, he *likes* you."

"I think so too! But there isn't anything. . . . Like you said, he built a wall."

"Yeah, I don't mean he *likes you* likes you, I think he wants to, like, mentor you as you launch into the world." She makes a launching gesture that looks to me kind of a lot like masturbation, and we both laugh.

"There was totally mentoring happening on his side, at the rock wall," I say to my bowl of tuna and greens. "And on my side, it was mostly, 'I want to bite into your ropy forearms and run my fingernails down your treasure trail.'"

"He has a treasure trail?"

"I don't know, that was just my imagination. He kept his shirt on the whole time."

"Ah. That's a shame. But it reinforces the 'mentor not fuck-buddy' hypothesis. I bet he's got amazing abs, and he totally could have taken off his shirt and shown them to you."

"Well, I'll take what I can get."

Chapter 5

Burritos and Trauma

For the uninitiated, here's how a ninety-minute community center jazz class goes during the spring: thirty minutes of warm-ups, twenty minutes of floor work, and then forty minutes on the routine for the recital. I'm choreographing it to "Happy." They love the song and their dance, but I'm pushing them hard. By seven thirty, my eighteen tweens are sweating heavily, their heads down, their hands on their hips as they gasp for air.

"If it feels hard, you're doing it right," I tell them. "Get the heck outta here, and I'll see you all next week—Paul and Amy, see me please!" The students applaud dutifully, if desultorily, and limp, groaning, out of the classroom. Paul and Amy approach me.

Paul and Amy are twins. They're in both my jazz class and my ballet class, and they're helping me out with my solo in the recital. They're going to sing live, their mom accompanying on the piano. Their mom (a professor in the IU School of Music, so, ya know, no slouch) is arranging "No One Is Alone" from *Into the Woods* as a duet for her two children, special for this performance. It's a cheat on my part—I don't love putting on a show, and I'd rather share the stage with my students, plus who doesn't love a brother and sister singing together, right? And yesterday—two weeks after I chose the song—it was on that TV show *Glee*.

We'll be a hit.

I've been choreographing to a click track and the sheet music since I chose the song, and Professor Paul and Amy's Mom promised me a MIDI this week so I'd have something like music to rehearse with.

"Amy and Paul," I say to them very seriously. "Do you have the MIDI file from your mother?"

"Oh! I forgot!" says Amy. "It's in my bag."

"Run and get it, and you can watch my dance. Want to do that?"

They both nod ecstatically and run off together.

And then I notice Charles hovering at the studio door, looking uncomfortable. "Hey," he says.

"Hey," I say, "be just a minute. The kids are bringing me a thing, and I told them I would—"

Amy and Paul race back in, barging past Charles. "Here you go, Miss Annie," Amy pants. She holds her Android up to mine and transfers the file onto my phone. Kids these days.

"Cool! Let's see what we've got here." I plug my phone into the speaker jack and hit play.

The MIDI is not the most musical thing you've ever heard; it's basically the worst karaoke track in the history of the universe, but it's way better than a click track and my imagination. I start marking steps, and then I notice my students starting to gather at the door—Amy and Paul clearly told them I was going to run through my solo, and they all want to see.

I pause the music. "Ladies, if you want to watch, come in and sit cross-legged in front of the mirror and be very quiet. Understood?"

They nod silently and shuffle in.

There are parents in the doorway now too. And Charles. Well, no pressure. "The whole thing isn't even choreographed yet," I announce to the room generally, "but let's see what we've got so far. Call out when you see a step you recognize."

I run through what I've got, walking through the parts I haven't figured out yet, while students call "Ballonné!" and "Pas de chat!" There are gasps and whispers of "Four!" when I get to the pirouette at the end, which I finish in arabesque—barely. I stick out my tongue and wrinkle my nose as I wobble on my left foot, trying to salvage the finish. I could also just make it a triple, or finish on both feet like any normal person would. But it's a song about balance, so.

When the song ends, I curtsey ironically, all the way to the floor, as the students give a polite smattering of applause, and then I shoo them out. "Amy and Paul, thank your mother for me!" I call after the twins. Finally I turn to Charles and say, "Welcome! This'll just take a sec." And I start putting my stuff away. It's hot in here, with a little bit of sweaty tween stank.

"How long have you been dancing?" Charles asks.

I pull on sweat pants and a T-shirt—this one has a cherry drawn into a grid of the value of pi to the twenty-five-hundredth decimal (another one from my mom)—over my leotard and tights and say, "Since I was three." I shove my feet into my Chacos. "I kinda went the professional training route for a couple of years, but it wasn't for me." I pull the bandana off my hair and allow the sweaty, curling mop to make its own decisions about how to behave. I look at him and smile. "Okay, ready."

He's looking at me with his mouth open. "I had no idea."

"It's not that related to school, I guess. That's sort of why I changed direction." With my backpack on one shoulder, I lead him out of the studio. I wave and call bye to students, parents, and other teachers as I go. Once we're out, I turn to him and say, "Where to?"

"Do they know?" he says.

"Does who know what?"

"The students. The other teachers. Know that you . . . 'kind of went the professional training route'?"

"Sure. Where're we going? I have a fuck ton of work *and* I'm starving."

"What made you quit?"

"I didn't quit," I say, my index finger in his face. "I changed direction."

And he laughs. He laughs and starts walking down Grant Street. "Of course, what was I thinking? How about Laughing Planet?"

"Great."

It's only a couple of blocks, but I walk as slowly as I can. Spring has finally come—late this year—and the air has that fresh, muddy smell from rain earlier today. I think the sun should never set before eight p.m. There should be a rule.

"Petrichor," Charles says, walking beside me, his hands in his pockets and his satchel over his shoulder.

"Huh?"

"The word for that smell you've been inhaling as if it'll get you high. It's called petrichor. The stones release oils when they get wet, and that's what the smell is."

I look at him, astonished. "That," I say, "is my favorite fact ever."

And then we eat burritos and work on our respective papers.

I don't want to bore you with the details of my research, but the ultra-short version is that I study arousal coherence in anger. There're three levels at which we experience emotions: physiology (like heart rate), involuntary behavior (like facial expressions), and experience (what you pay attention to when someone asks you how you're feeling). And sometimes they all line up (coherence), and sometimes they don't (noncoherence), and my project looks at how they do or don't line up when people experience anger.

To do this, we induce anger in research participants and then measure their heart rate, reflexes, pupil dilation, facial expressions, and we ask them how they feel. Got it so far?

And the thing Charles found in my data, which I failed to notice, is that there were some outliers that seemed to form a pattern of their own. And I've been spending all this time trying to figure out what the deal is with the outliers. My working hypothesis is that it has to do with our mood induction method. I think it might be producing inconsistent results.

And if you don't care about any of that, I won't be offended. There are days when I don't care either.

So while we're eating burritos and working, I'm running my hypothesis past Charles, and he nods eagerly. "I think you're on to something. May I suggest another approach that could dovetail well with that one?"

"Does it involve a lot more work? Because the clock is seriously ticking, dude."

"A bit more—for the purposes of your thesis, it's probably only necessary to be able to say you've considered it and it might prove a valuable avenue to explore in the future."

"Okay, what is it?"

"Trauma," he answers.

"Trauma?"

"Your outliers are all women. Women are disproportionately the targets of interpersonal violence, and this is not an otherwise at-risk group. I think a reasonable potential cause for the differences are different reptilian vagal responses that are characteristic of trauma survivors. You look troubled by this."

"Um, yes, because I don't know what you're talking about."

"Reptilian vagus. Trauma. Look it up."

I do. I go to class on Friday, and then I go to the library. I spend Saturday at the library too. Then I spend Sunday at the lab. So the next time Charles sees me, it's Monday morning. He finds me in the ducklings' office, fast asleep on the couch, with my face pasted to the pages of *The Polyvagal Theory*. He wakes me with a hand on my shoulder and a soft, "Annie."

As I rise to consciousness and he hands me a mug of shitty lab coffee, I tell him, "Dude, I fucking hate you."

"Finding it hard going?" he says, sitting at the far end of the couch. He takes a sip of his coffee.

"It's not just that it's hard to understand—which it is! It's *hard*, man. I'm not dumb, and this is *hard*. But the part that really sucks is—" I'm suddenly choked by the tears that have been chasing me through the weekend, that forced me out of the library, out of the apartment, into the lab, where I could be alone.

Charles sits calmly and blows on his coffee, waiting.

I start again. "The part that really sucks is reading the stories from the women, you know?" I sniff and gasp through my tears. "And I don't have a clue what my research subjects brought into the room with them in their central nervous systems; we didn't even *ask*. For all I know they could have been hit by cars or sexually assaulted or experienced birth trauma or been targets of violence— I mean, is this what the world is like? Are people walking around with these scars on their nervous systems, and we can't even see them?"

"Yes," he says.

"I mean, have you read this?!" I brandish my book at him.

"Yes," he says.

"I mean, listen to this." I flip the book to the page that knocked me out of the library on Saturday, and hold up one finger while I read. " 'For example, following the rape, sexual encounters, even with a desired partner, may elicit a vagal syncope. Or the raped women may become anxious about sexual encounters and physiologically mobilized via sympathetic excitation to escape.' I mean . . . both of those are *terrible*." I look up and stare at him, my jaw dangling in horror.

He nods, and a corner of his bottom lip tugs downward, like an apology. "I know."

"You know what I loved?" I yell, like it's his fault, though I know it isn't. "I *loved* my cadaver dissection lab! I loved seeing how all the parts of the machine work, what they look like on the inside! It *never* bothered me—it's how I knew for sure I should be a doctor! But you know what grosses me out? Nauseates me? The way living humans treat each other!"

I'm choked again, and I just sit there and let myself cry.

We sit together, silent apart from my tears, which fade at last into a couple of noisy sighs.

Then Charles gets up and walks to the door. He stands there, his hand on the doorknob.

"Going to med school then, young Coffey?" he asks gently.

I nod and sniff.

"Good," he says. "Want the door open or closed?"

"Closed," I say.

And he closes it behind him as he goes.

As I sit, staring at the closed door, I remember that for the whole first year, I could hardly make eye contact with him, much less cry in front of him. I couldn't even say his name. I called him Dr. Douglas. In return, he called me Miss Coffey. Until one day, I was in a shitty mood because it was raining—I love the rain, honestly I do, but there's just some days, you know? Anyway, I was all grumpy, and I complained, "Can't you just call me Annie like everyone else does?"

And he said, very calmly, "Can't you just call me Charles?"

Which is when it all changed between us—I thought, anyway. That was when I was like, Charles and I have A Thing.

I practiced saying his name on my walk to campus each morning. "Charles," I'd mutter. "Charles. Charles." It sounds nice in his accent—"Chahls"—but it's awkward in mine. And then I'd get to the lab and say, "Good morning, Charles," and he'd look up from whatever he was doing and say, "Good morning, Annie," and I'd feel totally sure we had A Thing. And then he'd ignore me for the rest of the day. But it was like . . . "ignoring me" ignoring me. Ignoring me because he knew I was there.

I don't even know anymore if we have A Thing—if we ever had A Thing, or if it was always in my head. But the last few weeks, ever since Veggie Burger Friends Night . . . I don't know. I feel like he really is my friend. It's like the wall he built dammed off a lot of awkward stuff that made me feel anxious, leaving only the friends we could have been all along if I hadn't been distracted by my crush. I can't even tell now if I still have that crush. I only know that the closer I get to the end of thesis writing, the more I feel like he's the person I want to celebrate that with, more even than with Margaret.

It doesn't feel the same. I don't feel giddy or nervous; I just feel happier when he's in the room. He understands something about what I'm going through that Margaret can't. He's the person I feel comfortable around. First I made a fool of myself in front of him, then he corrected a mistake I made, then I was terrified on the rock wall, then he saw me dance, then I bawled all over the place in front of him. And now I feel like I could do anything, and he'd just sit calmly beside me, drinking his coffee.

Margaret was right. I can't take his sexy throat with me. But I have a feeling medical school will be a lot better if I can take his understanding and patience with me.

I spend the next week incorporating the literature on trauma and stress response into my thesis. Never have I been so grateful for my dance classes. It has always been true for me that in the studio, everything else disappears. As a teacher, I find it easy to let go of my academic work and focus on my students. I know I'm doing a good job when the tension in their shoulders and faces eases, when their bodies are resonating, freed, at least for now, from whatever troubles them outside their time in the studio with me, and they're completely focused.

And I've learned that the best way to make that happen in a ballet class is to kick. Their. Asses.

On Tuesday we do *grands battements* at the barre to Lady Gaga's "Born This Way" ("Hips square, my friends!") and then do *échappés* in the center to Katy Perry's "Roar," with me clapping on the downbeat and shouting at the top of my lungs, "SPRINGS! IN-YOURHEELS! SPINE! STRAIGHT! THEFLOOR! ISON-FIRE!" I correct a couple of students, sticking one of my fingers in their belly buttons and another at the base of their spines while they bounce in front of me and I mouth the lyrics.

It's one of the most beautiful sounds on Earth, the rasping, desperate gasps of a dozen tweens, their sweaty palms on their knees as they pant for air in the silence after I turn the music off after *échappés*.

"Feels good, huh?" I say with a grin.

They groan.

I laugh evilly and then begin, "Adagio, fifth position . . . and prepare."

There is no ass-kicking like an adagio ass-kicking. I walk out that Tuesday night feeling like I've burned away a demon.

I haven't hung out with Charles since Burritos and Trauma Night, as Margaret is calling it. Mostly I've been in the lab or at the library. When he sees me in the lab, he says hi, but it feels a little like he's keeping his distance.

But by Friday my thesis is done.

It's done! . . . At least, this draft is done.

I e-mail it to Dr. Smith, and then I text Charles:

Hey, it's Annie. I just turned in a draft of my thesis!!!
Do you have time to go climbing again this weekend?
It's cool if you don't, I just thought I'd ask.

Well done you. Saturday at 3?

Sure, that would be great!
Do you want to meet there or go over together or what?
Is there a bus, do you know?

I'll pick you up.

Charles Douglas: not a loquacious texter.

"I wanted to say," I begin on the car ride to the rock gym, "that I don't fucking hate you."

"Hm? Oh, that. No, I didn't think you did," he says, eyes on the road.

"And I wanted to say," I continue, "that I'm really grateful for all your help."

"All part of the service," he says.

"Rock climbing isn't part of the service," I say. "Sitting with me until I'm done crying definitely isn't part of the service."

He's silent until we park in the gravel lot at the gym. He looks at his hands on the steering wheel and says, "My last year as an undergraduate was hard. It's rewarding for me to offer you the kind of support I would have liked for myself."

"What made your senior year hard?" It's impossible not to ask.

"Oh, the usual storm and strife," he sighs, dismissing the question. "Come on, we'll climb some rocks."

We go in and gear up and start to climb. We don't talk much, except about climbing. He teaches me some techniques, shows me how routes are mapped with colored tape on the wall, explains how they're rated for difficulty. I don't feel ready to start measuring my ability on rated routes, and he doesn't push me today. He teaches me to "hang from my bones." He says, "Let your skeleton do the work, Coffey. Your muscles will last longer." My muscles, in fact, crap out much sooner this time than they did last time, and I barely get through four climbs before I collapse onto the mats in gasping agony.

"You're trying to climb with your arms and hands. Climb with your feet and legs, and you'll last all day," he tells me.

"Dude, I don't know what that means," I say through heaving breaths.

"Never mind," he says. "We'll work on it next time."

Next time.

When he drives me home, he parks in a spot near my door, turns off the engine, and sits back in his seat.

And we just sit there.

And it's awesome.

It's awesome to be physically exhausted while you sit in silence with someone who gets it, and you don't have to explain that all you want and need is to be quiet and still together. To smell the faint warmth and spice of his skin, to hear him breathing, to watch his chest move lightly with each breath. To imagine—it can only be imagination—that the tension in his forearm has nothing to do with climbing, and everything to do with him wanting to reach out and hold your hand. To be enclosed in a warm dry car as the rain begins to fall, first in scattered specks on the windshield, and then more steadily.

"Starting to rain," he says. "Better get inside."

I nod and put my hand on the door.

He stops me. "Tuesday? We'll practice your defense?"

"Yup," I say, my hand still on the door.

"Are you ready for it?"

"Not yet. I've got time this weekend."

He nods. "Better get inside," he says again, but again as I turn to open the door, he stops me. "Annie."

I turn my face toward him but don't look up.

He says, "Er."

And then I raise my eyes to his. And it's right there between us, as tangible as the gearshift. The Thing. The rain is growing louder around us, outside the car, and it feels like I'm nearer to him than I have ever been in my life, cloistered together in here. Charles swallows, and I want to put my lips on his throat. I want it so badly, I can barely remember to breathe.

He breaks the moment, tearing his gaze from me and staring instead at the steering wheel. "See you Tuesday," he says.

I get out of the car and run inside before I get soaked.

Chapter 6

I'm Not Wrong

It's been raining for three days.

I walk the two miles to the lab under the giant, cheerful umbrella my parents sent me last year after I called them in tears to explain my certainty that I would never graduate from college because there was no way the precarious balance of events required to make that happen would ever actually work out; it was all going to fall to pieces and I would die alone.

And yes, I know that's irrational. But sometimes—I don't know if it has to do with the phase of the moon or what—sometimes the rain has a strange effect on my mood. It makes me worry that with each step, the earth might crumble under my feet and I'll fall into a cavernous abyss, or that the tumbling cascade of events that make up my life will misfire in some small but momentous way, which sets off a chain of ruinous explosions around me, leaving me alone forever in a barren and desolate landscape.

I live at the edge of my abilities; I know that. I push hard against my own limits. And I've got a safety net as big as my parents' hearts in case I fall, so I can take any risk, knowing that the worst possible consequence is a bruised ego. Most of the time, I trust the infrastructure of my life; I trust the universe to be a safe and loving place.

But what if it all . . . just . . . breaks into pieces?

My parents tell me it started when I was ten. I think I had just seen the movie *Annie*, and the combination of the name with the song "Tomorrow" . . . Apparently, I just have the kind of brain that wonders, *How do you* know *the sun will come out tomorrow?*

So I was worrying about this one rainy afternoon, crying at the apartment window—we had just moved to the Upper East Side, and I was watching the damp pedestrians in the park—and my mom came over and asked what was wrong.

I said, "Will the sun come back?"

"Of course it will," she said.

"How do you know?" I asked.

She said, "Because it always comes back. That's what the sun does."

So I said, "But how do you know it will come back *this* time? How do you *know?*"

And then my dad came over and asked what was wrong, and Mom explained, and Dad said, "I really believe it will, but you know what I think? I think we should make a plan in case the sun doesn't come out. How about that?"

So we sat in the apartment on that rainy afternoon, writing out a list of things we would do if it were never sunny again.

It turned out we would be okay.

However. I don't know if you've ever walked in the rain in Indiana, but it is not like the rain in New York. In Indiana the rain pours down like someone is dumping out a bucket of mop water on you. It's heavy and constant, and no umbrella on Earth can stand up to it. It is the perfect rain to make you wonder if the universe isn't, in fact, a malignant and deliberately cruel place.

And it's been raining like this for three days straight. It's the fucking Apocalypse.

The umbrella my parents sent me makes a bubble over me, of

alternating clear vinyl and pretty multicolor stripes. So I'm walking through the rain, looking at the wet springtime through rainbow stripes and worrying about the unstable chain of events that are about to unfold.

I'm rehearsing my thesis defense today, so that I can present my thesis defense next week, so that I can graduate the following week, so that I can start medical school, so that I can be a doctor, so that I can change the world.

Unless some tiny thing goes wrong and everything falls to pieces.

I mean, no fucking pressure, right?

By the time I get to the lab, I resemble nothing so much as a grumpy sewer rat. I'm wet and unhappy. I go into Charles's office and say, "Hey, Charles," and dump myself into the chair by his desk.

"Ah, young Coffey," he says, not looking at me—he's still finishing whatever he's typing. And then when he does look my way, saying, "Thesis defense," he stops, looking aghast at my state. "Do you not own an umbrella, Annie? Ought the lab to consider buying you one as a graduation present?"

"Dude, I had an umbrella! This is the level of wet I get *with* an umbrella in this godforsaken state."

"Is there a towel somewhere you could use?"

"I'm fine. I'll dry out in a few minutes."

"You'll catch your death, young lady."

I give him a dirty look. "Dude, you're a fucking *doctor*. You know that's a myth."

"One worries, nonetheless. Remember the world can't be a better place because you're in it unless—"

"Unless I am still actually in it. Yeah, thanks. That's very nice of you. Can we get on with the whatsit, please?"

He looks at me for a moment and then takes a deep breath and says, "Sure. Go for it."

I pull out my laptop and load my slides and get started.

It goes very badly. From typos in the slides to leaving out an entire section of the literature review to not being able to answer even the fairly simple questions Charles asks, my presentation is one big fail after another.

Finally I throw myself backward in my chair and sigh. "Today is not my day."

Charles leans back too and says, "You are not usually so under-prepared." Which is probably a more productive account of my difficulties. "But you know how to fix it."

"Yes," I say in disgust. "It's all just stupid mistakes."

"Not stupid," he says. "Careless. It's a crucial difference. You are never stupid, and you are rarely careless. What is wrong?"

I shift around uncomfortably in my chair. "It's the rain," I mutter.

"The rain?"

"Yes, the *rain*," I repeat, as if he's deaf. "It's been fucking rain-ing for three fucking days, and I can't fucking take it!"

"The rain prevented you from—"

"I know, I'm nuts!" I interrupt him. I sullenly tell him the story of the rain, leaving out the part about *Annie*, and adding, "Of course, when I finally took a philosophy class, I realized it was a matter of induction versus deduction. But it's not really about 'how do you know?'; it's about 'what will we do if it doesn't?' What will we do, how will we live, if the rain never stops falling?" I pause, my frowning eyes on Charles's little office window. Then I look at my hands and say, "Now that I'm a grown-up, ob-viously, I don't literally worry that the sun won't ever come out, but some days . . . I suppose I'm saying I'm underprepared be-cause my thesis defense felt pretty unimportant in the face of the fundamental unreliability of the universe."

"The fundamental unreliability of the universe," Charles re-peats as I glance up at him. He scratches his head and looks at me. "Annie, there are days when I do not know what to do with you."

All I want him to do with me is kiss me. He's looking at me with a warm, open expression, and the collar of his shirt is lop-sided. But I am a grumpy sewer rat who doesn't trust the uni-verse to catch her if she falls.

He oscillates a little in his desk chair, his hand in his hair, just looking at me in that warm way for a minute. Then he says, "I read your thesis this weekend. Diana forwarded it to me. It's . . ." He pauses. "I was very proud. I hope that doesn't sound condescending; I don't mean it that way. I mean it's work I'm proud to have been a part of, however small a part. Your defense will be a walkover—as long as you don't let the unreliability of the universe interfere with your slides."

He's proud of me. I sigh, and my body relaxes. I hadn't been aware of the tension until it left me.

"I'm gonna go home, take a nap, and start over," I say.

"Good plan," he says as I rise and move toward the door. He follows me. We stand in an awkward silence for a moment. His hands are in his pockets. He still has that warm, open look on his face.

"Sorry to waste your time," I tell him and, impulsively, I straighten his collar.

"You never waste my time," he says. He's looking at me.

No, he's *gazing* at me as I am gazing at him.

I am not a person with good sexual intuitions, but this is unmistakable. I have experienced what it's like to gaze at him while he looks back at me in a completely neutral way. I have had the experience of seeing someone else gaze at me while I look away so they don't get the wrong idea. This is neither of those. This is definitely him gazing at me while I gaze back at him. This is him definitely not looking away.

Our faces are less than a foot apart.

He's going to kiss me. Oh god.

Kiss me. Please, oh god, kiss me.

Kiss me!

WadderyouwaitingforKISSME!!

Fine. You know what? Sometimes a girl has to take things into her own hands. There's less than ten inches between our mouths. I can cross ten inches.

I do it. I lean forward and rise up on my toes. I put my mouth on his.

It is not a world changer of a kiss. In about three seconds he pulls away.

"Annie," he says, and it's a warning.

"Sorry," I say.

But no, wait. This was unmistakable. I look up at him, my eyebrows knit. "Can I just . . . I know today is not my day and the universe is an unreliable place, but can I get a reality check? I really could have sworn you wanted that too."

He takes another step back and says, very quietly and carefully, "It is genuinely, seriously, unambiguously inappropriate for us to have any kind of physical relationship, Annie."

"I know, but—"

"I could lose my job."

Well, fuck me. I am the selfish bitch who never even considered what the consequences might be for him. I lower my chin guiltily, still looking at him, and say, "I'm sorry."

He sighs, closes his eyes, and runs a hand through his hair.

"Look, you're not wrong," he says. He goes back to his desk then and sits down and gestures for me to sit down too—on the opposite side of the desk. "I'm saying this so you know it's not your fault and you're not imagining things. I did want to. And I'm your boss. Which makes it both not okay and my fault if anything happens. Does that make the remotest sense to you?"

"Not really," I admit.

"Okay," he says patiently, in teacher mode now. "Would you agree there is a power differential between us, that I control administrative access to something in which you have a vested interest?"

"I guess, *technically*, you could interfere with my thesis."

"And your work hours and your publications. I manage all that stuff. And what if I made sex a condition for getting time sheets—"

"You would never do that."

"Of course I wouldn't. That's what I'm saying."

"But you're—"

"Look, separate the people from the principle. This isn't about my character or yours, it's about the dynamics of the system. *In principle*, can you see why it's important?"

I huff. "That any generic supervisor who controls access to degree—or money—related resources not have any sexual relationship with their supervisees?"

"Because there's too much potential for the supervisees not to have full choice."

"But I totally have full choice!"

"The principle, Annie."

I huff again and roll my eyes. "Yes, in principle I see it's important."

"*Why* is it important?"

"Because the subordinate person might feel like they have to do things in order not to piss off the boss person, who could retaliate."

"Thank you."

There's a pause while I struggle not to say what I'm about to say. But it has to come out.

"But I'm not wrong that there is totally A Thing here," I say. "Between us." I make a "between us" gesture with my index finger.

"You're not wrong," he concedes. "But we are going to ignore it, because there is nothing we *can* do that doesn't risk your well-being, in principle, and my job, in fact."

"What about after I graduate?" I don't even say it. It just comes out, entirely of its own volition.

"Annie—"

"In *principle*," I say, "once a supervisor no longer has any administrative power over the supervisee, isn't it okay for them to do whatever the hell they want?" And then I just sort of lose it. "How is it fair that just because we know each other through school, we should *never* get to do anything about The Thing? How is that right? That *can't* be right."

"How did we get to this from the fundamental unreliability of the universe?" he asks, rubbing his eyes under his glasses.

"We have A Thing!" I say. "We've had A Thing for ages! I thought I was wrong, but I'm not wrong."

"I give up," he groans. "Look, why don't we talk about it after you graduate?"

"You agree we have A Thing?"

"Yes. We have A Thing. Christ on a bike." With his elbows on his desk, he rakes his hands into his hair and stares at his blotter.

"And you'll talk about it after commencement, on the tenth?" As far as I'm concerned, he has opened a negotiation.

"Sure. Yes," he tells his blotter.

"Classes end May second and I've got no finals, so really I won't be a student after that. We could talk about it then, on the last day of classes, instead of waiting until after commencement."

He looks up at me and throws himself back in his chair. "Annie—"

"Why *not?*"

"Saints defend me. Christ and all the apostles fucked up the arse by Moses, *fine*. All right. We'll talk about it on the second. Now for the love of god, *please* get out of my office, you harpy." He shoos me with one hand, from his trench behind his desk.

I rise, but I don't leave. "What *time* on the second?"

He turns his eyes to the heavens and says, "What time do classes officially end?"

"I don't know."

"Well, go and look it up. That's what time we'll talk."

"Okay, then." I'm smiling now, and when I go outside, the rain has stopped.

That night I text him:

Classes end at 5. Where should we meet?

About ten minutes later he replies:

I will not discuss this until after your defense.

I answer:

Spoilsport.

Get back to work.

OoOOooH, I like it when you're dominant.

Stop it. I'm turning off my phone. You are a termagant and a shrew and, furthermore, you have a thesis defense to prepare.

I turn off my phone and plug it in for the night, and decide to go to bed early. I get myself off to sleep with a fantasy about what will happen at five o'clock, Friday, May 2.

Chapter 7

The Thing Is Super Sexy

My oral defense is not a formal part of my degree requirements. Professor Smith has her undergrad research assistants do it as practice for grad school defenses, but there's nothing really at stake. I mean, nothing apart from standing up in front of faculty and peers and talking about the project in which you've invested the last two years of your life. So. Nothing at stake but basic pride, I guess. And if there's anything I know for sure about myself at this point in my education, it's that I can withstand any injury to my pride.

For me, it's also practice presenting the talk I'm giving at the World Congress on Psychophysiology in Montreal at the end of May. Charles is going too, so I won't be completely on my own up there—Professor Smith can't go because she's Pregnant Like Whoa, but she's helping me be as prepared as I can be for my first academic conference presentation.

Charles is right. It's a walkover. I've thrown myself into fixing the problems with my presentation, and I've prepared for the most abstruse and picayune comments, criticisms, and questions. I can respond to everything they throw at me, even Charles's curveball of, "What methodological changes would you suggest to better control for individual differences in life histories of research subjects?" Why, I'd add the Adverse Childhood Experiences questionnaire, I tell him, as part of the standard protocol, the same way assessing for menstrual phase is becoming standard for all female subjects. Even when Professor Smith asks me about changing mood induction methods, and my real answer is, "Shit, I have no idea," I manage to say it in a way that sounds like I kind of know what I'm talking about.

After my defense, there's cake and pizza for the whole lab. Professor Smith gives me a giant hug full of baby belly and says, "You'll be great in Montreal." Margaret squeezes me around the shoulders and says, "Dude, you *totally* nailed that." The younger ducklings look at me with something like awe—I recognize it because it was how I looked at seniors defending their theses the prior three years. Charles stands five feet from me and says, "Well done, Annie," and then goes into his office and closes the door.

Well.

Margaret and I go out to dinner in preparation for the drinking that will be happening tonight. As we're getting ready to go out, I text Charles:

Hello. Where were we? Oh yes, 5pm on Friday. My place or yours?

I don't have any idea where he lives, but it's surely better than my undergrad shithole, so I'm hoping he says his. But he answers:

We're going to TALK. Soma?

Oh. He wants to talk over coffee. Sigh.

That's not super sexy.

Well spotted.

I'm not wrong that we have A Thing. The Thing is super sexy.

There is a long silence. I wait fifteen minutes for this next text:

You are not wrong. And The Thing will only be enhanced by the early addition of some rational decision making, for which I shall require a context that provides the necessary barriers. Tables. Strangers. Hot, spillable drinks.

Is it just me, or does this sound like he wants to fuck me *a lot?*

Are you saying what I think you're saying?

And rather a lot more, my termagant.

Okay THAT was super sexy.

Now fuck off. Go get drunk with the ducklings. Congrats on today. Be safe.

:-x

My friends get me drunk that night.
That's about all I can tell you.
When I wake up in the morning, I am in an unfamiliar bed, which is not something I have experienced before. I am, fortunately, alone, but that means I have no clue as to where I am. Also, my entire body hurts. There is no part of me that feels okay.
I blindly feel around me and find my phone, which I check for the time, and I find this enlightening series of texts from the night before, which I read through a haze.

I cn se your pantis poodlepie.

Annie?

What. What. What have I done? Oh, sweet motherfucking Jesus, I texted Charles Douglas that I could see his panties. I called him poodlepie.

I read on.

Sorry thoght you wre Magrt. Easy mitsak amirite.

Would I be wrong in supposing that you've had a drink or two?

No, sirreebob. No, you would not. Except yes. I had clearly had more than two. So that would, in fact, be wrong.

Anie is to drnk to text now ples leave a brief mesag after the beek. Beeeeeeeeeeeeeeeeeeeeeeeeeep.

Where are you?

divas where yo|?

The Lion. Have you got a lift home?

No.
Marbey drivig mr.

What?
Do you have a safe way to get home? YES OR NO

WY ARE YOU TELLING YEING YELLING

BECAUSE THE MUSIC IS VERY LOUD IN HERE. TURN ROUND.

Bits of memory assemble themselves in my brain as I read. Margaret on the dance floor, her underwear visible over the top of her jeans. Charles dropping into the chair beside mine. Dancing down Kirkwood Avenue, singing, possibly, "Let It Go," and possibly—no. Not possibly. Definitely taking off my clothes. I look under the covers at my body and find I'm in my camisole and underwear. Shit. Balls. Shit balls. Who was there? Who was there?! Whose bed am I in?! *Fuuuuuck!*

"Fuck," I say out loud. I close my eyes again and lie there with my hands over my face. I've had hangovers before, but this is an order of magnitude beyond anything I've experienced.

"Hello," a voice says. "You among the living?"

It's Charles. Does this make it easier or harder to cope with reality?

"I'm not really sure," I say through my hands.

There's noise, and then I feel movement on the bed—Charles sitting on the far side.

"Please don't move the bed," I beg quietly. I move my hands to my stomach. I haven't reopened my eyes yet. "I don't feel good."

"Ah, poor you," he says. It sounds kind, even though I think he might be being facetious. "Remember much?"

"Flashes. It'd be really interesting from a memory-consciousness point of view if it weren't so frickin' scary."

"You're all right. You just drank too fast."

"Am I at your place? How did I get here?"

"No one was in a state to take you home, so I walked you here as the safest place to sleep it off."

"Did I . . ." I lick my dry, sticky lips with my dry, sticky tongue. "Um. Was 'Let It Go' in any way involved?"

"Indeed it was," he answers softly but eagerly. "Never again will I hear that song without thinking of you." I can hear the smile in his voice.

"I'm going to open my eyes now," I say. "And then I'm going to sit up."

"Okay," he says.

"And then, depending how that goes, I might throw up, or I might pass out."

"There is a bin immediately to your right," he says, placid.

I tug my gummy eyelids open. That goes okay. The room is dark, sunlight coming in through breaks in the curtains. I tentatively lift myself to a sitting position, tucking the blankets under my armpits. That, too, goes okay.

"I think some water would be good," I say, not yet able to look at Charles.

"There's some on the nightstand there."

I reach over and find a Nalgene with a sipper in it. The bottle is sweaty and cool, like ice water that's been sitting for hours.

It tastes. Like. Nectar. It tastes like springtime. It tastes . . . a little minty, actually.

"Oh my god, that's good," I moan, still not looking at Charles. "What time is it?" I never did notice the time when I looked at my phone.

"Half eleven, nearly," he says.

An unpleasant spike of adrenaline hits me. "I have to be in class in two hours."

"You're going to class?"

"Of course I'm going to class! I'm hungover, not *immoral!*" I say. And then I put my hand on my forehead and add, "Ow."

"Why don't you try a shower first, see how that goes, and then decide about class?" He rises from the bed and clears his throat. "Your clothes are on the dresser."

"Okay," I say, still not looking at him.

And he walks out.

The shower helps a lot. Being clean is rarely a bad idea, but what I learn this morning is that when you're hungover, being clean can make the difference between wanting to die and being willing to live. It puts me in a stable enough state of mind that I can be curious about Charles's apartment. His bathroom is a dude's bathroom, basically. A tiny bit scuzzy, but not so bad, considering. It smells like him, which is nice, and it's totally mildew-free, which is more than I can say for my own shower.

I dress in my clothes from last night and shuffle from the bathroom into the living room, where I stand in a daze under my wet hair, regarding the bookshelf. It covers an entire wall, and the wall is not a small one. Charles is sitting on the couch, his ankles crossed on the coffee table. He's reading.

"Are my glasses anywhere?" I say. "And do you have painkillers of any kind? And can I use your toothbrush?"

"Nightstand for the first two, and there are spare heads in the cabinet over the sink," he says, looking up. "Feeling all right?"

"Better," I say, and I shuffle back to the bedroom for my glasses. I pick up the water and take four ibuprofen from the small bottle beside it. I detour to the bathroom and go back to the living room, where I stand in front of the shelves, reading titles and brushing my teeth using a fresh head on Charles's electric toothbrush. I wander back to the bathroom to spit and rinse. When I come back, I peruse the titles once more until I ask, "Was I . . . I mean, is there more to be embarrassed about than I already know of?" I finally turn and look at him.

He smiles at me—a different kind of smile, a new kind. Fond. "You were fine. I had been drinking myself, so I couldn't drive you home. I walked you back here—and yes, whatever you remember doing on Kirkwood, yes, you did those things. On the bright side, it saved me the effort of undressing you before putting you in bed." He raises his eyebrows at me significantly and adds, "You were hilarious, and I slept in the living room."

"You gave me your bed?"

"Yes. Coffee?"

"Hm?"

I think he's addressing me, but he says, "Do you want any coffee? And then I'll take you home."

"Oh. Yes, please."

He goes into the kitchen and returns with two cups. He hands me one and returns to his seat on the couch. I sit too, in the chair opposite him. We sit in silence, him reading, me just waiting for the painkillers to kick in.

I interrupt him to ask, "Why do hangovers feel so shitty?"

And he says, "Glutamate and GABA, apart from anything else. Surely, you've studied alcohol metabolism in the brain."

"Oh yeah," I say, remembering. "Fuckin' GABA."

He grins and goes back to his book.

There's more silence and then I ask, "Whatcha readin'?"

He holds his book up without speaking or looking at me.

Pleasures of the Brain says the cover, and there's a big picture of a brain. It's a book about the brain, I conclude.

"Is it good?"

"Yes."

"Can I read it when you're done?"

"Sure."

Another long silence, and then I ask, "How come you're not at work?"

"I had no patients and no subjects until the afternoon, so I told Diana I was working from home, to avoid distractions."

What he's saying is, *Annie, shut the hell up and let me read.*

Between the analgesics and the caffeine, my headache eases, and eventually I say, "I've never seen your apartment before. Is this where we're gonna . . . ?" I gesture to indicate fornication.

"We'll talk about it on Friday," he says, with a repressive eyebrow. "It isn't certain that we're 'gonna' anything, young Coffey, so don't start imagining it."

"Dude." I shake my head—then stop. I feel better, but not *that* much better. I drink more coffee and then start my sentence over. "Dude, I've been imagining 'gonna' for, like, two years almost. That ship has sailed."

"Annie," he says in his stern-teacher voice. "We will talk about it. On Friday." His expression is serious, but he's got that little bit of pink in his face again.

"What, we can't talk about 'gonna,' but it's okay for me to be here?"

"It's not okay for you to be here. You'll notice I'm trying to boot you out."

I give him a wink. "You kinda like it, though, really," I say, and I purse my lips provocatively.

"Annie!" he snaps, then he gets up and walks to the kitchen, muttering, "Mother of god. Oh help."

I follow him and find him, his hands braced on the edge of the counter, taking deep, slow breaths, and only now does it dawn on me that this really isn't fun for him at all. He looks like he's in physical pain. Oh. I was being mean. Shit.

"Charles, I'm sorry," I say, leaning against the counter next to him. "I won't do anything anymore. And if you don't even want to talk on Friday, I'll understand."

"Fucking ironic process," he mutters, and he moves—it takes so little, and now his hands are on the counter on either side of me. I'm pinned here.

"This is insane," he says mildly.

I nod seriously. "What's an ironic process?"

"I'll send you a reference," he says, and he relaxes a little, smiling into my eyes, but this close to him, I'm warm and pulsing and dissatisfied. I don't want to smile. I want him to kiss me.

"Look," he says, "I think it's pretty clear that your boss wants to fuck you, and not just in principle, so I'm going to ask for your help. Will you help me?"

I nod again, still watching his eyes.

"Nothing until Friday. No texting, no calling, no e-mail. I'm serious. Nothing more until you've turned in your last assignment and you're definitively off the payroll. No tormenting me. Is that understood, Miss Coffey?" Then his tone changes from stern to pleading. "It's only two bloody days."

I say, "You know, when you put it that way, you only make me *want* to torment you."

"And that, my siren, is the ironic process."

His eyes. Pale blue with gray around the iris. I've never looked at his eyes this closely before.

"Then I shouldn't kiss you right now?" I say.

He exhales slowly and puts his forehead against mine, eyes

closed. His nose bumps the side of my nose. Our glasses tap. "No, Annie," he whispers. "No."

And he kisses me. Full on. Lips, tongue. It's everything I wanted. I let out a noise, like a squeak or a whimper, and put my arms around his waist. I run my hands over his back, feel the muscles and warmth through his shirt. He grunts and moves his lips across my jaw to my ear and my throat, and now my knees are wobbly. I hold on to him, and his hands—oh, his hands move under the hem of my T-shirt, and as soon as his fingers touch my skin at my waist, we both shudder. My arms go around his neck, and my hands tangle in his hair as his mouth comes back to mine.

When he finally pulls away, he pulls all the way away, moving to the other side of the kitchen. He says, "That was disastrous. Get your things. I'll take you home." He runs a hand through his hair and starts looking around the kitchen.

I can't move.

He finds his keys on top of the fridge and turns to find me still standing there like I'm made of stone. Stone that is thrumming with blood.

"Annie," he commands in his teacher voice. "Get your stuff."

I obey.

He drives me home without looking at me.

"Friday at five," he says, eyes on his steering wheel. "Come over to mine?"

I turn my eyes to him with a half grin. "No tables and hot, spillable drinks?"

"Seems like we're past that now," he says, and he gives me the barest glance, a flash of a look that sets off a hot swell inside me and makes my lips part.

I hesitate, almost lean over to kiss him, then think better of it. He's staring at his gearbox now, one hand on the shifter, one on the wheel.

"Bye," I whisper.

He blinks and nods.

I get out of the car and notice once again that he doesn't drive away until my front door is open and I'm stepping inside.

"Annie's back!" Margaret calls in a pathetic voice when she hears me come in. "Did Charles drive you home?"

"Yup," I say, passing through the kitchen and into the living room. She and Reshma are curled up on the living room futon, watching a *Buffy the Vampire Slayer* DVD, still nursing hangovers.

"Did Momma Duck take good care of you?" she asks.

"Oh yes," I say, and I lift her feet and then sit under them on the futon. Then I say, "Yeah, he, uh . . . He, like, *really* kissed me this morning."

"*Really?*"

"Really."

"He . . . 'kissed' you?"

"No, no. He just kissed me, but it was . . ."

I catch them up on everything that happened, and Reshma says, "Dude, he wants you so bad."

"I think he kinda does!" I say. "We definitely have A Big Sexy Thing. Still! Even though, apparently, I acted like a fool on the way to his apartment."

"Apparently?"

"I don't remember much. Flashes of singing and dancing and"—I cover my face with my hand—"stripping."

"Oh man!" Margaret laughs. "It was so lucky he was there, though!"

"Uh," I tell her, "it wasn't luck." And I show her my texts. They both cackle with laughter, until Margaret's headache and nausea force her to be quiet.

And then I do go to class. Because I'm hungover and have A Big Sexy Thing with O Postdoc, My Postdoc, but I'm not immoral.

Chapter 8

Definitively Off the Payroll

I attend my last classes. I take my last exam. By Friday at two, I am off the payroll.

I spend the next two hours grooming, of course. I haven't shaved my legs for, like, a month, so it takes most of the two hours just to do that. Then I bike to his place and show up a little sweaty, but not too bad. I have removed all the books from my backpack and replaced them with a change of clothes, a bottle of lube, and a jumbo variety pack of condoms Margaret gave me. Ya know, the usual.

When Charles opens his apartment door, I'm standing there, heart thumping, fighting a nervous, dopey grin.

"Hey," I say, watching his face.

"Hey," he says, and his expression looks a lot like mine. His hair is damp. He's just shaved. He smells like soap.

He gestures me in, takes my bag, notes its lightness, and raises his eyebrows at me. "Symbolic," he says. And he sets it on the floor. Then he takes me by the shoulders and steers me backward into the living room, where he sits me down on the couch. He sits in the chair on the other side of the coffee table.

"Now," he says sternly. "You sit over there and I'll sit over here and we'll talk about this like civilized people."

This is not what I was expecting. I kind of expected he would grab me and carry me into the bedroom, throw me down, and ravish me. I was expecting a total lack of "civilized." My dopey grin slides into a pretty atrocious pout.

I say, "You do actually want to have sex with me, right? You're not just stalling because you don't want to hurt my feelings?" I can't help it. I have to ask. "Am I wrong about The Thing?"

He looks taken aback for a moment, and then a little embarrassed. Then he looks at me and says, "Look, before I answer that, I want to make sure it's perfectly clear and perfectly explicit between us that you are no longer a student and I am no longer your supervisor."

"Right," I agree, nodding seriously.

"I now hold no administrative power over you."

"Correct," I say.

"There is nothing to influence your decision making other than your own free choice."

"Correct," I repeat.

"All right. In that case," he says steadily, "you ask, are you wrong about The Thing? My dear girl. My sweet termagant, my dear little shrew, have you met you? You are the subject of my fantasies and the object of my most intense desires. Miss Annabelle Coffey, I have been imagining you naked since the day last summer when you came into the lab soaked through with rain. Your hair was plastered to your face and throat, and there was a dangerous moment when I almost licked the rain off your collarbone before I remembered where I was."

He says it calmly, looking right at me. His expression is mild, and he's just sitting there, knees crossed, in his chair.

As I'm sitting there with my jaw in my lap, he says, "Right. Let's do the practical stuff. Contraceptive?"

But I'm not over the rain thing yet. That was Call Me Charles Day. "That was almost a year ago," I say.

"It was," he says quietly. "I felt like a lecherous old man. I feel that way now, a bit, but I expect I'll get over it."

I say, "I want you too. All that stuff you said, the 'Have you met you?' That's how I feel about you."

And he smiles shyly and says, "I know."

He knows.

"Contraceptive?" he repeats gently.

I point at the implant in my upper arm. "All set," I say.

"Excellent. STD and HIV tests?"

"Oh, um. I've never actually been tested for anything."

"Never? For anything?"

"I've never had sex, so it didn't seem like a priority."

There is a pause.

He raises one eyebrow, his face tense. "What specifically does 'never had sex' mean? Never had oral sex? Anal sex? Penis-in-vagina sex?"

"All those things and a bunch of others. I guess I'm what would be called a 'virgin.'" I put it in quotes with my fingers and make a face.

"I beg your pardon?" he says.

"A virgin?" I say, like it's a question. "It's a medically mean-ingless idea, it's all just patriarchy and—"

"Yes"—he holds up a hand and closes his eyes—"I'm a feminist too, we needn't rehearse the arguments about purity as a virtue meaningful only in the context of male ownership of women."

(*You see why I like this guy?* He says it like it's just *understood* that any reasonable person would identify as a feminist. I didn't iden-tify that way until, like, two years ago, but with him, feminism is taken as read. Ah-mazing.)

And then he says, "Oh god," and he leans back in his chair and looks at the ceiling. "I had no idea I was so medieval." He's laughing now, a silent chuckle, both hands over his face.

"What?"

"Apparently, I'm a terrible human being," he says through his palms. Then he takes a great big sigh and straightens a little in his chair, gripping his hands together in his lap. "The idea of deflowering you has given me a raging hard-on and filled my brain with the most shamefully barbaric thoughts. There's a bit of self-knowledge I wouldn't have bet on." He's looking out the window, where the sun has just begun to set.

"Really?" I'm grinning, terribly pleased for no reason. It's not like I earned that hard-on, I mean, all I did was not have any sex yet, but still!

"All right, don't get too excited," he says with a grin of his own. "We're going to sit here—you, me, and my erection—until we talk all this through."

"Okay," I say. It occurs to me that I could go over there and *touch it*. I could put my hand on his crotch and feel what an erection is like. I can sort of see it bulging in his pants. I suck my lips between my teeth and stay put. But then I can't help saying, "First, maybe tell me just *one* of the barbaric thoughts."

"Annie, oh, Annie," he sighs, as he covers his eyes with one hand. "I . . . oh, I want to tie you spread eagle to my bed and make you come a hundred times with my hands and tongue before I finally fuck you when you're so exhausted from coming that you can barely move. I'm a Neanderthal."

"Okay," I say in a voice just above a whisper.

"Pardon?" he says, looking at me now.

"That. What you said. Tie me up. Make me come. Fuck me. That. Yes. Can we do that now? But then I wanna do stuff to you, too, okay?"

"God"—he wipes his hands down his face—"I am trying to be a responsible adult. I am trying, and you see what she does to me?"

I am both sorry and pleased by this.

"Where were we?" he continues. "Sexual histories. Right. Walk me through your sexual history, such as it is, if you would be so kind."

Reluctantly, I let go of the fantasy. "Well, I had a boyfriend in high school. We made out a bunch, and one time I had an orgasm while we were lying down together on the bed, kissing and sorta humping, you know, like teenagers do. We had all our clothes on and everything though. And pretty shortly after that I kinda got sick of him and dumped him."

"Mh-hm." Charles is looking a little strained.

"And then in my sophomore year here, I had this other boyfriend, and we got as far as taking off our shirts, and he touched my breasts. I liked that pretty well, but I had no interest in going any further, so he broke up with me. Which I thought was pretty lame of him, because he was smart and funny and I liked him, apart from that," I add, frowning.

"Right, I see. And then?"

And then Charles joined the lab, and I've been jilling off regularly to fantasies of him ever since. But I don't say that. I say, "And then you. Wednesday. And that's it."

"That's it," he repeats. "That's it?"

I nod and shrug. "I've been busy with other things. And you? What's your history?"

"Er," he says, "slightly . . . or, I should say *somewhat* more extensive than that."

"Okay. Go."

"Right. Er, I had a couple of nonpenetrative encounters with boys at school," he starts, "and rapidly realized this was really something I was more interested in doing with girls. I had my first girlfriend when I got to university, and we were together for something over two years before she left me for another fellow. She's married to him now, got two kids. After that, bit of a wild spell, I'm afraid. A number of partners whose names I either never knew or else quickly forgot. Went through *a lot* of condoms. Then, let's see . . . I got over that phase, got every test I could, turned out to be fine, had another girlfriend for about a year and a half, and that relationship ended when I came here."

"Did that relationship end . . . um . . . by mutual agreement?"

"No," he says. "No, Melissa wanted to stay together, even though I was going to be four thousand miles away. I couldn't face holding her hostage that way, and so I asked to end it. She acceded under protest."

I nod at this information, a little uncomfortable. If I had been with Charles for a year and a half, and he up and left for a residency in middle-of-nowhere, USA, I'd be pretty brokenhearted.

"And since you've been in Indiana?"

He shakes his head. "I'm only here for four years; it seemed unwise to get into anything that could only end badly."

I nod, pretending to be worldly, and say, "Can I ask about all those other things you mentioned? Oral sex . . . anal sex?"

"Ask away."

"Well, ya know. Have you done those things?"

"Oral sex, yes, giving and receiving. Anal sex, yes, giving only, but I'm open to suggestions." Then he grins at my widening eyes. "We can hold off on that, if you like."

"We should probably stick to the basics, at least to begin with," I agree, nodding. "My HPA axis already has enough to deal with."

He tilts his head, still grinning. "You are like a puppy, you know, sometimes—you know how a puppy's feet are massive compared to the rest of her body? And she's adorable that way, of course, but you know that when she grows into them, she'll be a dazzling beauty?"

"I have big feet?" What? I do, but what?

He shakes his head at me, and there's that new smile again, the fond one I like so much. "I'm saying you have a big brain. A big, knobby-kneed, coltish brain that you're just beginning to grow into. It makes me wish I could jump ahead five years and meet you then, instead." He bounces his fists on the arms of his chair and just looks at me for a second before he laces his fingers together in his lap and says, "Now then. Let's get a few things straight. You are leaving dear old Indiana . . . ?"

"June third, right after we get back from the conference."

"The nature of this liaison is therefore necessarily of a short-term nature. Are you completely sure you'd like your first venture out to be along the lines of a summer fling?"

Yes, if it's with you, Your Hotness. "Yes. A fling."

"Very well. And the parameters of the fling. Shall it include or exclude concurrent partners?"

"Uh . . ." The question had never crossed my mind. I've had no interest in sleeping with anyone else, basically ever. "Just from a risk reduction standpoint, it seems like excluding them is a better idea. Even if one of us suddenly gets the hots for someone else. I mean, it's only four weeks. Surely, those other hots can wait?"

"I agree. So then: no concurrent partners. You and I will be exclusive sex partners until the third of June, when you will ride off into the sunset—"

"Sunrise," I interrupt. "I have to drive, like, twelve hours that day."

"Into the sunrise," he says. "And I hope it goes without saying that I can scarcely imagine any possible future in which I would not be proud to get responsibly shit-faced with you at conferences or coauthor a chapter or attend your wedding. As far as I'm concerned, young Coffey, we are friends, we are colleagues, and only parenthetically are we lovers."

Lovers. I look down at my hands and squinch my mouth against a smile.

"Is that agreed?" he prompts.

"Friends, colleagues, and parenthetical lovers," I repeat. "Agreed."

"Now, with regard to tonight, my termagant." He comes over to the couch and sits down next to me and takes a deep breath, then sighs. He puts his hand on mine and says, "I suppose what I want to say is, there's a certain experience most people have before they get to the bit where one person puts their genitals inside the other person's genitals. There's deciding, moment by moment, whether you'd like to go further or simply stay where you are. There's all the bases to go round. I don't know much about baseball, but there are definitely four bases. And I have strong doubts about the wisdom of skipping over all that."

I shrug. I don't know. I don't even know how I'm supposed to know. All I know is that my body has wanted to be next to his body for a long time, and the heat of his shoulder next to mine and his hand on mine is making my heart pound. I want to touch his skin and put my tongue in his mouth and feel his hands on my skin, and I want those things right now. Not once in my fantasies have we sat together and calmly shared our sexual histories. Not once has he paid attention to the fact that he's my first. Always, his desire to touch and be touched is the same as mine, demanding, immediate.

"You're not saying no?" I say, my eyes desperately searching his.

"I'm saying yes, but I'm saying let's go *very slowly*. One base at a time, eh?"

Then he takes off my glasses and puts them, along with his own, on the coffee table. He looks at me again with an expression I can't interpret.

"I've never seen you without your glasses," I say in wonder. "You look younger."

He smiles, and I wait for him to kiss me. He doesn't. He says in a soft voice, "Well then, young Coffey, what next?"

So I put my hands on his neck and kiss him. I bite his lips. I press my chest against his and wrap my arms around his neck and in every way attempt to get my body as near to his as I can get it. I climb over him and straddle his lap, his arms going around me, his hands pressed flat against my back.

"This is not going slowly," he says, even as he kisses me just as hard as I'm kissing him.

"Don't care," I say.

And he lets me. He lets me push my pelvis against him, lets me lick and bite and kiss and suck to my heart's content. When I put my tongue in his ear, he makes a fantastic yelp, and when I bite his earlobe and tug, he gives a delicious groan. He likes it, the way I touch him.

Somehow he shifts so he's lying on his back and I'm lying on top of him. At last, I can lick his neck, suck hickeys into it, bite at his clavicles, all the things I've been imagining for so long. The texture of his skin, the smell of his body, the warmth and firmness of him under me, everything is beyond my imaginings. And the whole time, my hips are grinding against his.

Only when my hands stray under his shirt does he stop me—"Ah," he says, "first base."

"What?" I pant.

"Slow." He's panting too. "Let's stick with first base for now."

"When can we have second base?"

"Let's say . . . a base a day? And today is first base."

"So tomorrow will be second base, Sunday will be third base, and then Monday is all the way, right?"

"Er, sure."

"Okay," I say, and I put my tongue in his mouth again and scratch my fingers down his arm. I break the kiss and say, "Can I have orgasms?"

And he says, "I don't know, can you?" like it's a joke.

"I'm practically there already, I just want to know if it's against your rules."

He makes a strangled sound and says, "Your orgasms are never against the rules. Have all the orgasms you like."

So I do. I kiss him and touch him and press into him until the throbbing in my clit reaches a peak, and I come, sucking his tongue desperately into my mouth and rocking my body over his. He clasps his hands over the backs of my thighs and grunts his pleasure.

"That," he says as the throbs are fading into quietness, "was the most gorgeous thing I've ever experienced."

"Me too," I sigh into his throat.

We turn over, and he takes a different approach from my fairly rabid energy. While my heart is still pounding in recovery, he lies on his side and I lie on my back, and he kisses me softly, quietly. "Unless you've got other plans," he says, spreading kisses over my cheekbones, "we've got all night. No hurry."

"I have no other plans," I say. On the contrary, I told Margaret that if she heard from me before Monday, something had gone wrong.

He grips my hair and uses it to angle my head to the side, and he kisses and licks along the length of my neck with a methodical slowness I find meditative at first as I rebound from my orgasm, and then gradually crazy-making as I'm pulled toward another.

He experiments with all the parts of my ear.

And then he's quizzing me on anatomy.

"Miss Coffey," he says in a breathy version of his teacher voice, "can you name for me the morphological elements of the ear?"

"What?"

"I'll get you started," he says, and he tugs at my earlobe with his teeth. "Lobe," he says very, very quietly into my ear. "What else?"

"Are you kidding?"

"Do you or do you not want me to make slow love to your extremely attractive ear?" (My ears are proportionate to my feet.)

"Uh . . ." I start reciting everything I can remember from my anatomy class. "Lobe . . . helix, antihelix . . . tragus, antitragus . . . uh." Those are all the easy ones, and they're all I can recollect through the fuddle of his tongue and teeth on my helix, tragus . . . oh.

"Mh-hm," he hums into my ear, rewarding me with his hot breath and another tug on my earlobe with his teeth. "What else?" His tongue runs along the sensitive curve right under my lobe, but when I'm silent too long, he pulls away. "You can do better than that."

"I remember a symbol in a cave," I say desperately, thrusting my ear toward him.

"The cymba and cavum—I'll accept that," he says, and puts his tongue deep into the hollow spaces of my ear. I gasp. "And the incisura," he adds when he comes up for air.

"Fossa," he says, licking mine. "Scapha," he adds, breathing and then biting into mine. His hand is on my waist, light pressure tugging my shirt upward so I can feel the air of the room on my skin. His hand never touches my skin; always he touches me

through my shirt. Still, it occurs to me that this could be con-
strued as cheating. I find I don't care much. When his mouth returns to mine, I put my hand on his wrist and push downward,
prompting him to touch me directly.

He responds by taking my wrist instead, and putting my hand
on my own skin. He puts his hand over mine and guides it over
my lower ribs, over my abdomen, down to the top of my jeans,
making me feel my own body and the rapid rise and fall of my belly
with my breath as he's kissing me. This, too, I have never imagined. Of all the fantasies I've had, never have I thought he might
touch me without touching me, using my own hand to caress me,
even as he kisses my mouth, kisses my throat, kisses my clavicle,
bites at my trapezius muscle through my T-shirt. The heat of my
own hand, the pressure of his—they're making my belly shudder
with tension. The very fact that he is not touching my breasts
makes my breasts sensitive. I lift my chest off the couch to press
my breasts against his chest, but he takes his hand from mine to
press me back down, his hand over my heart.

"There's no hurry," he says against my lips. "You can be still."

I try. I do try. But he returns his hand to mine and continues
the warm caresses, until I pull my hand from his and wrap my
arms around his neck. I pull him over me, and he comes to me
easily, with a groan. I wrap my legs around his hips and run my
hands along his back and shoulders and arms as he kisses me and
kisses me. When my hips start pressing up from the cushion, he
pulls away a little and puts his hand on my face. He whispers,
"Slow."

"I've wanted you for so long," I say.

"And I've wanted you. Let's enjoy it while we've got it."

"Please," I whisper, my hips seeking more pressure. "Oh
please."

He acquiesces with a little noise in his throat, adjusts our bodies to slide a knee between my legs, and I press into it gratefully.
With his fingertips just touching my throat and his tongue just
touching my tongue in the warm, damp space between our mouths,

I come again, making faint noises and rubbing my clitoris on his hard thigh.

When I open my eyes, I find that his eyes are already on me. He's been watching me.

I smile with a tremble and whisper, "This is fun."

"This is fun," he answers seriously. And he kisses me again, one hand at the base of my throat, the other at the base of my skull.

I could kiss him for hours. I *do* kiss him for hours. We stop to eat, and we talk, too. But mostly we kiss. Lips, fingers, hands, arms, elbows, necks, ears, face. I discover the secret of the corner of his mouth—if you just touch it with the tip of your tongue, he will, quite reliably, make the most satisfying sound, a sort of half grunt/half sigh. I learned from him that the webbing between my fingers and the inside curve of my elbow are remarkably sensitive places.

Charles hasn't come once, and I'm a little worried about that, but I haven't yet figured out how to ask about it.

I am the one who notices it's past midnight. I get up to pee—peeing is difficult when you've been aroused for multiple hours, by the way—and when I check my phone, I see that it's 12:17 a.m.

Now, Charles could, I suppose, make a case that by "one base per day," he was not referring to midnight as the end of this particular day. I do not risk inquiring. When I return to the living room, I simply show him my phone, announce, "It's Saturday," and take off my shirt.

Chapter 9

Second Base

I'm not wearing a bra—bras are of no particular use to me—so I'm standing in front of him, naked from the waist up.

"Oh my god," he says, and in the darkness I can't see his face well enough to tell what he means. My breasts are never a worry to me when it's just me, but when it comes to public display, I get a little anxious about the notable lack of them.

"I don't know what to do now," I say, beginning to feel self-conscious. Beginning to wonder if this was a good idea.

Charles stands up too, his eyes roaming over my skin as he approaches me. He puts one hand at the back of my neck and the other on my chest, his fingertips brushing the curve of my clavicle while he meets my gaze. I've never seen this expression on his face before—almost like pain, almost like anger.

He says, "I was just thinking it was time to send you home."

"Oh." I frown, but then he kisses me, and I know he's not thinking about that anymore.

With his eyes on mine, he says, "You are—" He stops and blinks a few times, shaking his head minutely, and then he tries again. "You are unspeakably beautiful." His fingers trail downward from my clavicle bone to the faint little curve of my breast, down over the nipple and along the lower curve, continuing to my waist, and then around. He puts the full flat of his hand on my back, his warm hand directly on the skin, and kisses me again. I feel his blue Oxford shirt against the tips of my breasts. I'm trembling in his arms; my knees aren't steady. I put my arms around his neck to keep myself on my feet.

"Let's go to the bedroom," I say.

"Not a chance," he says. "I'll just fuck you if we go in there."

"I know!" I say.

He groans and kisses my throat, his hands traveling lightly over my back now. "At five o'clock I had very good reasons not to fuck you tonight. I can't currently remember what they were, but I'm sure they haven't changed."

"You wanted me to go around the bases," I say, knotting my fingers in his hair.

"Right. Right. The bases," he says, and steps away a little to look at my face. "Shall you stay tonight?"

"Unless you don't want me to."

"Oh, I definitely want you to," he avers, his hands still traveling over my skin. "I've got to go to work on Monday, unlike some people I could mention, but until then it seems to me the best possible use of every minute is finding new ways to give you pleasure."

"Yes, please," I say.

He smiles a little. "I like the way you say that." Then he takes me by the hand and leads me into the bedroom, saying, "The rules still stand, Miss Coffey. Is that clear? No hands or mouths below the waist. Until midnight tonight, that is." He pulls back the covers and gestures me in.

"Are we going to bed?" I ask.

"If you mean, are we getting in the bed," he says in a didactic tone, "yes. If you mean are we going past second base, no. And if you mean are we preparing for sleep . . . somehow I doubt it." His eyes slide over my body.

"Can I take off my pants?" I ask.

He answers by stepping toward me and unbuttoning my jeans, his hands lingering with rule-bending leisure over the task, while he kisses my shoulders and chest. He pushes my jeans down to my knees and I step out of them. I put my hand on the placket of his shirt and meet his gaze with a question.

"Go ahead," he says, and I start undoing the buttons of his shirt.

The ducklings were right. A Greek god. "Oh my god," I mutter as, with each button, I reveal more firmly muscled chest and abs, glowing in the streetlight through the window. When his shirt is open, I run my hands over his chest. I push the folds of his shirt apart and, wrapping my arm around his waist, I press my bare skin against his. We both gasp with it.

Before I can think, he lifts me off my feet and dumps me onto the bed. He follows me in, lying beside me, his chest pressed against mine. For a long time, we just kiss, our bodies pressed together this way.

Then I move my lips to his throat, then his shoulders. I press him onto his back and climb over him, to kiss and stroke across his chest and his ribs and down his belly. When I get to the tops of his khakis, I lick a trail slowly, tenderly, into the gap under his waistband. His belly contracts hard, involuntarily, and his hand grips onto my shoulder.

"Can I ask for something?" I say.

"Anything," he breathes.

"I want you to come," I plead into the dark. "I've had, like, five orgasms, and you haven't had any. That doesn't seem fair."

"You really want me to?"

"*Really*," I say. I crawl up and lie on him, brushing my breasts over his chest and watching the effect on his face.

"And how would you suggest that happen, given the rules of second base?" His hands are traveling all over my skin, my back, my arms, my shoulders.

My first three ideas are clear violations of the rules. I put them aside and say, "I could watch you?"

"Watch me . . . DIY it?" he says. Can you hear a person blush? I swear that's what's happening. "You'd like that?"

"Yeah," I say, and I slip off him to his side and kiss him. "Yeah, I'd like that. I want that."

He kisses me back, and my mouth explores his tongue. At last he makes an uncomfortable noise and says, "If you'll do it with me."

"Have another orgasm? That's the *opposite* of the point. I want to watch you."

There's a short silence, and then he mutters, "All right." I feel his hands go to his pants and undo them. He tucks me into the crook of his shoulder and whispers, "Tell me one of your fantasies."

No problem there. "Hm . . ." I say, trailing my hand over his chest and trying to select a fantasy I think he'll like—there're a lot to choose from. "There's the one where you turn up at a party and I'm all fancied up and it's like you're seeing me for the first time, realizing how irresistible I am."

"You *are* irresistible," he says. "What does 'fancied up' entail?" And I can feel that his hand is moving. I don't see anything in the dark, but I can feel the rhythm of it.

"A really, really short skirt and really, really high heels," I say.

He turns his face to mine and kisses me lightly. "Is that what makes you feel sexy?"

I shrug against him. "It's what I guess turns guys on."

"Mh-mh," he says, his lips still on my face. "Maybe some guys, but I like you barefoot. Barefoot and damp."

"Oh really?" There's a useful tidbit.

"Really," he says, gasping a little. His hand is moving faster, and I *so* want to put my hand over his, feel what he's doing. "Seeing you fresh out of the shower on Wednesday nearly killed me."

"Then you'll probably like the fantasy I had that night, where you didn't stop in the kitchen. You didn't call it a disaster. When you pulled away, it was to unbutton my jeans. You yanked them down to my knees and went down on me right there in the kitchen," I say.

"Oh god, I wanted to do that," he says. "What else?"

"Well." I lick my lips and say the rest quietly into his ear, feeling the vibration of his arm movements. "You go down on your knees in front of me and put your tongue on my clit and lick me until I'm desperate, then you pull my jeans off and fuck me on the kitchen counter."

"Tell me how you like to be licked," he breathes.

"I don't know," I tell him softly. "Nobody has ever done it before. I guess we'll find out in about twenty-three hours."

He makes an involuntary noise as his diaphragm contracts. I put my hand on his belly, and he puts his hand over mine, wrapping me more firmly in his arm. At first I think he's going to push my hand away, not let me touch him, but he grips my fingers between his, and his arm clamps around me, locking me close and tight against him. His other hand is moving faster now, and he breathes, "What else?"

"After you fuck me in the kitchen? You carry me over your shoulder into the bedroom and . . ." I stop, inexplicably shy.

"Yeah?" he prompts, squeezing me and pressing my fingers.

Blushing in the dark, I tell him in a small, uncertain voice, "I imagined you put me on my knees on the bed, and you put my hands on the wall, and fucked me that way, with your hands over mine."

"Oh god, Annie." He turns his face to mine again and kisses me fiercely as he comes, whimpering a little, pinching my fingers almost painfully between his.

When his muscles begin to relax and he's breathing hard but steadily, I say, "That was amazing."

"At midnight," he answers in a whisper between breaths, "I'm going to bury my face in your pussy and lick you until you come so many times, you can't move."

"Okay," I whisper back.

He laughs silently. "Oh, I like you," he says.

"I like you too."

"The tissues are on your side of the bed," he says, more pragmatically.

I roll over and grab the box and put the whole thing on his chest, telling him, "I don't know how many you need."

He laughs again. "A lot, I think."

As he puts the box on his bedside table and pulls a few to wipe himself off, I say through a yawn, "I'm gonna wake up early and take a shower so you can be tempted by my dampness."

"No arguments from me," he says, and I drift into unconsciousness, his lips on my forehead.

Of course he wakes up before I do. I emerge from sleep only when he puts a mug of coffee on the table by my side of the bed.

I have a side of the bed!

"What time is it?" I mumble, reaching for the cup.

"Just past ten."

"Oh my god," I say. "I usually wake up at, like, eight."

"You're on holiday." He kisses my cheek and joins me in bed. "What do you fancy?"

"What do I huh?" I drink my coffee.

"What would you like for breakfast?"

"Oh. Usually I just have coffee."

He shakes his head sadly. "That will never do, not for the day I have in mind for you."

"Does it involve a lot of exercise while naked?" I ask hopefully.

He takes the mug from my hand, and I almost protest, but then he kisses me. He tastes like coffee and toothpaste, but I taste like coffee and morning breath, so I pull away. "I'm yucky," I say.

"You're yummy," he says, and grips my jaw in one hand and kisses me harder. Who am I to argue? I move my hands to his back, noticing, now that I'm awake, that he's mostly naked, dressed only in his boxers. But he pulls away and says, "We need a plan that involves leaving the flat so I don't fuck you silly today."

"Or: you could fuck me silly today," I suggest.

"No. Behave," he says. "No fucking until Monday at the very soonest."

"But touching now," I say, and I guide his hand to my breast.

I have successfully distracted him. His eyes move to my chest, watching his own hand move over my skin in full daylight, and then his lips are on my nipples, first one, then the other. I lie back, relaxed and reveling in his touch.

"Can you come this way?" he murmurs against my skin. "Just from this?"

"I dunno. I never tried," I say.

"Let's try now," he says.

It's easy for his tongue and mouth on my breasts to turn me on— turn me on a lot. Turn me on wildly. With his hands and mouth on my breasts and my ribs and my waist and my belly and my throat and in my hair, within ten minutes I'm panting and writhing. My clit is throbbing for more direct contact, begging to be touched. I knot my fingers in his hair and try spreading my legs wide and rotating my pelvis. I try crossing my ankles to lock my legs together. Still I'm hovering on that desperate, agonizing edge. If only he would touch even the inside of my thighs, I'd come instantly. But he won't. He won't even put his knee between mine and let me hump him like I did last night. He wants me to come just from this, but I can't. I'm in agony.

"This is gonna kill me, Charles," I whimper. "Please."

Without changing the soft caresses at my breasts, he takes my hand in his and pulls it down to my panties. He presses my fingers against my clit, through my underwear, in slow, soft circles. All the while his mouth is on me, sucking and licking my breasts. In a matter of seconds, I break apart joyously into a million splintery shards. I make a grotesque sound with it, a desperate, gruff noise that echoes off the walls.

He kisses me with urgent little bites and grunts. "We have *got* to get out of this flat." Giving me no time to recover—which would give me time to persuade him to stay in bed—Charles shoos me like a stray chicken into the shower. Once I'm clean and dressed, I find him in the kitchen, where he has made French toast and turkey bacon. He looks me up and down—I'm dressed in leggings and a tunic and Chacos—and says, "Can you go for a walk in the woods in that?"

"Sure," I shrug, piling food onto my plate. Have I ever been this hungry in my life? No. No, I have never been this hungry in my entire life. "Not, like, ten miles, but sure." I start shoveling food into my mouth.

"You're allowed to chew," he says with a grin.

In the end, he drives us out to Brown County State Park, and we hike maybe five miles. We take our time, pausing to look at views and eat the fruit he brought with him. ("You brought food? It's only a few miles." "After watching you eat breakfast, I didn't want to take any chances you might die of starvation on the trail.") And we talk. Or rather, I talk. Most of his talking happens right at the trailhead. He says, "So. Story of your life. Go."

I begin with the usual, "Not much to tell," and then ask for more guidance. "The story of what aspect of my life? There're a few different stories."

"What about the dancing? How did that start?"

"Oh! How that started is simple. When I learned to walk, I would always walk on my toes, which my parents decided meant I should take dance lessons, so when I was three, they signed me up for Baby Ballerina lessons at Joffrey, which is—"

"What? You were training with the Joffrey Ballet when you were three?"

"No no, not 'training with,'" I say. "I took lessons, like lots of little girls do. And I liked it, so I kept taking lessons, and by the time I was ten, I started in the young dancers program, and then by the time I was twelve, I was dancing five days a week. I did the summer intensive when I was thirteen, and then I auditioned for the trainee program and got in, and then . . ." I pause and think.

"There was this moment when I was fifteen. I was in a guest instructor class taught by this really famous dancer, and she came over to me and gave me a correction—this really important correction, right? Like, I'm getting this life-changing correction from this amazing artist—and what she did was this." I hold the fingers of my right hand in the fingers of my left hand and adjust the angles of my thumb, index, and middle fingers. "And I was like, 'This is it. This is what it means to make art with your body.' And that was the moment when I knew . . . I didn't have the thing that dancers have. I could learn the technique, I could practice as hard as anyone, be as driven to be perfect as anyone, but it's not the way art expressed itself in me.

"I loved dancing, *loved* it. It was fascinating to me, and a glorious challenge. And I loved working hard. I loved being pushed and challenged and yelled at sometimes and hugged other times and told, 'Look, you can get there, you just need to work really hard on these three things, and you'll get there.' I loved it, the *toughness* of it. And there I was, dancing eight hours a day and doing my academics basically as a hobby, right, and I was—"

I stop, with sudden, senseless tears in my eyes, as I remember the intensity of my loneliness then, my sense of being torn away from a member of my family—a member of my own body. I swallow them back and continue, "I was really missing the math and science I'd been obsessed with in junior high. And what I realized is that it was *science* that made me feel like *me*." We've hiked up a big hill now, both of us a little out of breath. I pause and look at Charles. "Does that make any sense?"

Without answering, he waves us over to a fallen log, and we sit side by side at the top of the hill, overlooking the valley and the creek. "What then?"

"Well, I explained to my parents and then to my teachers, which was horrible, but they were all really understanding. Nobody was mean or judgmental—they actually helped me with transferring to Bronx Science. They understood. I mean, more than anything else to be a dancer, you have to *want* to be a dancer, it has to be your life, your identity, your art, your soul. And it wasn't my soul, it was only my body. My soul is science. My soul is . . . the biology of the brain."

We sit there for a few minutes. I close my eyes and let the sunlight warm my eyelids. I inhale the sweet May breeze and listen to it in the trees.

I put my head on Charles's shoulder and say, "There's this one student in the ballet class I teach—you'll see her if you go to the recital, she stands out a mile. She has it. She's eleven, and she's an artist. She doesn't even know that's not how everyone experiences dancing. She thinks it's automatic that your personhood just comes out when you move your body. I've been encouraging her to get preprofessional training, hooking her up with a school in Indy. They can give her a scholarship. I've had a couple of moments of envying her, when I see how her entire being shines when she dances."

I tilt my head up to face him. "But then I remember, I shine other ways."

"You do indeed," Charles says, and he puts his hand in my hair and pulls my face to his. He kisses me there at the top of the hill, in the sunshine and the breeze and the sweet smell of leaf litter. I fist my hands into his shirt and squeak with pleasure.

When he pulls away, I say, "I was afraid you would argue with me about when second base started."

"I probably would have, if you'd given me a chance."

"But then again, you proved this morning how little regard you have for the rules," I grin.

He grins back and stands up and says, "I never touched you. Come on."

We hike on, and he says, "So then, Indiana?"

"Yep, Indiana. I came here to work with Professor Smith, and I've been in her lab every semester but my very first one. And next, eight years of med school and research. It is weird as hell to think I'll be in school until I'm thirty. But that's what I get for being just ordinary smart and not a genius, like you."

"Am I a genius?" he says in surprise.

I stop and look at him. "Are you kidding?"

He just blinks at me.

I roll my eyes. "When we trade off and you tell me *your* life story, I'll be sure to point out all the things that prove you're a genius."

"Okay, Miss 'My Soul Is the Biology of the Brain.' " He leads me across the ridge for another half a mile, and then we begin the descent, which switchbacks sharply down the hill.

"Being a nerd is not the same as being a genius," I correct him.

"Is it the same as being a pedant?" he asks, turning his head to grin back at me.

Chapter 10

I'm Not Very Pretty

Back at his apartment, Charles's respect for his own rules is disintegrating.

"That's definitely third base," I pant.

"Your knickers are still on," he says, continuing to lick and suck at the cotton. I'm spread on his bed, and he's between my legs. He's shirtless, but I'm down to my underwear.

And soon he's nudging the fabric to one side with his nose, and his tongue is unambiguously touching my labia. I grip the mattress above my head as my knees lock and my abdomen convulses.

"Definitely, *definitely* third base," I say again.

"Tell me to stop then," he says, and with the very tips of his fingers he pulls the crotch of my panties entirely to the side. He puts his lips and tongue on my clit, and I clutch my legs around his head, lifting my pelvis to meet his touch. He moans against me and puts his hands at the tops of my thighs, his fingers gripping and pulling down my panties.

"Okay, we can make a deal," I say, having no interest in stopping him. "Whatever time you spend at third base today is time you aren't allowed third base tomorrow. How about that?"

"Deal," he says, muffled by my vulva. When I look down, I find his eyes on me.

He loses about forty minutes this way, in which time we discover that how I like to be licked is steady, hard flicks of his tongue right on my clit. He does lots of other things too, many of them extremely pleasant, but when he does the steady, hard flicking, my arousal spikes instantly. He does not use this information to make me come right away, though. Oh no. He starts and stops, taking me to the edge and back three times before he finally lets me come in sharp, jabbing contractions, my thighs clutching around his ears.

All of this has been his answer to my question, "Are you slowing us down because you're not that interested in sleeping with me but don't want to tell me that?" We got home from the hike, and I asked the question because I couldn't not ask. And so he took me to bed. And now I'm lying here, panting and glowing, still covered in mud to my knees from our hike, my underwear twisted and wet. He's dirty and sweaty and wearing way too many clothes.

"That is my very favorite thing in the world," he says, coming up to lie beside me afterward. He kisses me with a mouth that tastes like me, and I pull away, torn between pleasure and surprise.

"Really?" I ask. "That's okay?"

"Very okay," he says, and kisses me again, his tongue deep in my mouth. But then he stops and says, "Unless you don't want to."

"No, I like it. I just never thought, like . . ." I kiss him, sucking the taste of my own body from his lips, murmuring, "I like it."

He says into my ear, "Are you sufficiently reassured of my desire for you?"

I turn to my side and kiss him, my tongue in his mouth. He tastes like me, and I love it. He slides his palm up my naked back as I slide my palm up his. Then I mutter, "Third base," and start undoing his pants.

"Not until midnight," he says, grabbing my fingers. He pulls my arms over my head, rolls on top of me, and pins my wrists to the bed.

"That's so not fair! You just—"

"I cheated," he says as he kisses my throat. "I'm a cheat and a liar and a heartless bastard who'll make you come no matter what, even if it means double standards. What do you plan to do about it?"

What I do about it is say, "Ha!" and wrestle my wrist out of his grip and try to get my hands on his zipper again. He catches one hand again, and I rotate my wrists out of his fingers. I turn to my side and manage to pin one of his hands under my shoulder, so even when his free hand catches one of mine, I still have a hand free, and I undo his pants while he tugs at his arm, trying to get his hand back. We're laughing as we wrestle, but I'm serious, too: he started us at third base early, and now I want my turn. He pulls his arm out from under me, but not before I've got his pants open, so even when he rolls on top of me and traps both of my arms over my head again, I can wrap my legs around his hips and use my feet at his waistband to start pulling down his pants and his boxers.

He counters with an, "Oh, you sneaky," and rolling onto his back, me over top of him, and pinning my arms behind me, at my hips.

"Well then," he pants, smiling. "What's your plan now, Coffey?"

My own smile fades, and I kiss him, rolling my hips against his. All that's between our two bodies is the thin cotton of our underwear—and mine's still tangled and halfway off. Charles keeps my arms trapped behind me, but he lets me move against him, lets me rub myself along the length of his erection. I move my lips to his throat and determinedly suck bruises into his skin.

"Jesus," he breathes, and I laugh, even as I press my clitoris against him. He makes an *unghf* noise and grips my wrists behind my back with one hand while he uses his other hand to feel my ass moving over him. His fingers grip into my butt cheek, tugging me wide open. I struggle to pull my arms free so I can touch him, his face, his shoulders, his chest, but he keeps me trapped.

And somehow not being able to do what I want to do just arouses me more, as if the wanting is itself the most powerful pleasure.

"Charles," I whimper into his throat, still rocking my pelvis against his, still struggling with my arms. Would he let me go if I asked? I feel sure he would. So I don't ask. "Why do I want to come again so soon? How are you doing this to me?"

I feel the sound he makes in his throat, against my lips. The vibration travels all through me and I start to come, pressing my body hard against his. With my arms still pinned together, I rub myself against him, and he searches out my mouth and kisses me hard, pushing back against me, his cock throbbing noticeably. He comes, saturating both his boxers and my panties with semen.

"We've got to get out of the flat," he huffs, as I laugh in glorious self-satisfaction. And then, not pausing, he rolls me back to the mattress and puts his face between my legs, licking and sucking and even biting at the soaked cotton of my underwear. I'm still pulsing with residual throbs of orgasm, laughing with the quiet delight of making him come.

"Take them off," I whimper. "Just take them off." I push at them myself, but Charles comes up next to me and grips his hands into the fabric, tugging upward instead of downward.

"Why do you get to break the rules?" I complain as he pulls the fabric side to side against my vulva.

"Because I'm bigger than you," he says. "And I have better behavioral inhibition."

"But I don't even *want* to control myself!" And I'm not. I'm rolling my body against the pressure he has created with my panties.

"Which is why I can break the rules. You let me. I don't let you."

"But *why* don't you let me?"

"Because look at you. Just look at you. Why would I want anything but to make you come any way I can find?" He kisses and licks my breasts, still pulling and tugging the crotch of my panties. "Tell me what you want to do," he says through the kisses, "and I'll consider it."

"I want to go down on you," I squeak. "I want your cock in my mouth." I can say one sentence at a time, the tension in my body is growing. His mouth on my breasts, and the rhythmic pull on my panties are shortening my breath, filling me up. "I want you to lick me while I suck your cock. . . . I want to straddle you and . . . put your cock inside me and fuck you while you . . . while you spread my ass cheeks with your hands. I want . . . oh my god, Charles, I want . . . Oh god, I want . . . Please I want . . ." I come again, unable to tell him what I want, apart from the compulsive chanting of "Fuck. Fuck. Fuck. Fuck" with each throb as he bites my nipples.

When my body relaxes against him, he kisses me so, so, so, so sweetly and says, "You'll have all those things, my termagant. All you need do is wait."

"I don't want to wait, fuck me right now."

"No, sweetheart."

I groan and put my forehead on his chest. "Then we need to get out of here."

Instead of getting out of here, we shower—separately ("No, if I get in there with you, I'll just fuck you." "I *know!* Please?" "Behave")—I put on lots of clothes, and we have Chinese food delivered. The plan is to watch a movie, but I need us to have a reckoning first. Sitting at the opposite end of the couch from Charles, through a mouthful of crab Rangoon I say, "Tell me again why we're going around the bases."

"Is that your circumspect way of asking why I'm putting you off?"

"Yes."

He stabs his chopsticks into his food. "How do I explain it?" he says. He thinks as he chews his chicken and broccoli. When he swallows he says, "I did have every intention of shagging you blind last night. But then you told me how little experience you had, and I . . . I couldn't just toss you onto my bed and give you one. I . . . It's rather difficult to explain, I suppose."

"Well, I need you to explain it," I insist somewhat peevishly. "Because right now when you say no, when you put me off, it makes me worry you're not really interested in me."

He laughs a little and shakes his head at his chicken. "If my relentless pawing and my inveterate rule breaking are not enough to persuade you that I am, as you so delicately understate it, 'interested' in you, I hardly know what would be enough. Look . . ." But then he stops and pokes at his food again.

"What?" I prod.

He hesitates, but at last, his eyes still on his plate, he says, "Years from now—maybe months from now—after you have more experience, you'll look back on this with a different per-spective. And if you were just a girl I picked up somewhere, it wouldn't matter, I suppose. But you're you. I *like* you. I want us to be friends after you leave, and so I want you to feel, months from now, years from now, that I . . . well, to feel that I set a high standard."

He looks up at me, a crooked grin on his face, and adds, "If that sounds too condescending, let me admit that partly, too, it's simply ego. I want to compare favorably to your future partners."

"So"—I tilt my head, trying to understand—"we're going around the bases now because you think that in the future I'll be glad we did, even though right now I find it dissatisfying and anxiety-inducing?"

He frowns, looking back at his chicken. "Obviously, I'd rather you didn't find it dissatisfying and anxiety-inducing, and if there is something I can do about that, I shall do it gladly, but yes. That's the idea."

"Oh." I pause, thinking as I trade the tray of crab Rangoon for the carton of chicken mei fun. At last I say, "When you say I can't do things to you, and when you won't do things I ask for, then I think . . . you don't so much like me, like, in the sexy way."

"I see." He nods and chews. "So the problem seems to be that I'm slowing us down to protect my ego at the cost of yours."

"Is it my ego that your saying no to me makes me feel rejected?" I think I'm managing to keep my pouting on the inside, but I'm not sure.

"Is it mine that I want your good opinion in the future?" he challenges. "Think about it this way: I like you so much as a friend that I'm willing to delay slightly the glory of being with you 'in the sexy way' in order to make sure that when the sex ends, the friend is still there."

"But—"

"Repeat what I just said back to me," he says in his teacher voice.

"You're delaying because that's how you think we're most likely still to be friends after I leave Indiana."

"Yes."

"Oh." I pause and think. "So it has nothing to do with not being attracted to me?"

"On the contrary."

"And you do actually want to have sex with me?"

He raises an eyebrow and smiles in the direction of his plate. "Annie, the *only* thing I want more than your body is your friendship."

"I'm not very pretty," I say with sudden, stupid tears in my eyes.

Now he looks at me. "Are you joking?"

"No."

"You can't be serious." He looks genuinely puzzled.

"Of course I'm serious. I mean, it's fine, it's okay, I'm lucky in a lot of ways, and I'm not saying I'm, like, a hideous freak or anything. I'm just not what guys are attracted to. Like, no breasts and a weird face." I stop and battle valiantly against tears, but a few of them escape. "I'm not being self-critical. I'm going by the evidence. Not many guys have been attracted to me, so I can only conclude it's because I'm not actually all that attractive. I mean, it took you a year to notice me."

"You were a student in my lab; the fact that I *did* notice you is what's compelling in that story, not that it didn't happen the first year."

I wipe my eyes with the heels of my palms and say, "I'm being so stupid. It's just . . . I want to be liked in the sexy way, and hardly anyone ever has. I mean, there was that guy in my sophomore year, but he, like, *only* liked me in the sexy way. I guess you're the first guy who likes me both ways, maybe, and it's weird. I don't know how to . . . It's just a lot of feelings all at the same time."

Charles puts his food on the coffee table. "When I was a student, I would have avoided you like the plague."

"That's great, Charles, thanks. I feel better." I sniff and laugh.

He moves closer to me on the couch, puts a hand on my foot, and looks at me. "Because you'd have been wildly out of my league. Brilliant, funny, gorgeous, sweet as hell, so completely sane, emotionally generous. You'd have terrified me."

"I'm terrifying?"

He withdraws a little. "To the unworthy."

"I don't want to be terrifying."

"Then only spend time with those who are worthy of you."

"I think you might be trying to give me a compliment, but it's a pretty conditional one."

"I'm saying you're a powerhouse, and not everyone is comfortable around that. Look, if you actually believe, against all evidence, that there's anything about you that falls short of perfect desirability, there's nothing I can do that will convince you otherwise."

"You could fuck me tonight."

His eyes search mine. "Would that work? Would having intercourse now instead of thirty hours from now convince you that you are what I see when I look at you? Stunning? Warmhearted? Disturbingly intelligent? Is that all it would take? If I put my penis in your vagina now, rather than waiting another day, you'd feel certain, from tonight on, for the rest of your life, that any man who doesn't fall to his knees before you is a fool and a criminal? Because if it will, I'll do it. Frankly, I had no idea my cock had magical powers, but if it does then, by god, I'll use it as a force for good."

I laugh a little then, as I know he wants me to.

"Is that all it would take?" he asks again. He's being Socrates, and I play along.

I shake my head. "I guess not."

He smiles, sympathetic. "Then what should we do?"

"Wait another night."

"I think so too." He lifts my foot with both hands and kisses the toe of my sock, then presses my foot to his chest.

"On one condition," I say.

"What's that?"

"Stop breaking the rules. It's not fair."

"Done," he says solemnly.

"And tonight I want—"

"You said one condition!" he growls with a grin, and then I barely have time to shriek, and he's on top of me and wrestling me to my stomach. He grabs my wrists and pins them behind my back. With his lips against my ear he whispers, "Now, what was your 'condition,' Miss Coffey?" But I'm giggling too much to answer, so he nips my earlobe and then kisses my ear until my giggles fade into sighs.

"It's not a condition," I finally manage.

"What's not? Oh right," he says.

"It's a request. Tonight I want to go down on you, without you going down on me."

"Well, that's asking a lot," he says, a crooked grin against my ear. "But I suppose I can sacrifice myself."

And then we watch the movie. We lie on opposite ends of the couch, our feet tangled together, not really paying attention to the screen, but taking turns rubbing our feet on each other's shins and up thighs and generally teasing each other. And when the movie is over, we go to bed. Charles detours to the bathroom, and when he returns, I'm naked, sprawled on the bed, my hands behind my head. He stops beside the bed and lets his eyes roam over my body.

I say, "Take 'em off."

"You can have no idea," he says, "what seeing you like this does to me."

"If you'd take off your pants, I'm pretty sure I'd get *some* idea," I say, raising an eyebrow.

He takes off his clothes like it's nothing. But it's not nothing. He is beautiful. He is golden and strong and firm everywhere. Everywhere. I bite my lips between my teeth as I watch him walk to the bed.

He turns off the light, lies down beside me, and pulls me into his arms. We're all the way naked together now, for the first time. I kiss him and rub my skin against his.

"How do people ever get enough of this?" I breathe as he moves his lips to my ear and jaw and neck. How can I have missed this, missed him, when it's only been a few hours since we were here? I run my hands down over his skin, down his back, over his ass, feeling the firm muscle under smooth, peach-fuzzy skin.

"Oh god, your body," I sigh.

"Your body," he says, and he kisses under the slight curve of my breast.

But I'm determined not to be distracted. "I want to go down on you now," I say. "Can I?"

He lies on his back beside me, not touching me, not making the "I don't know, can you?" joke. He says, "I'm all yours, termagant."

I move to the end of the bed and start at his feet. I suck his toes, swirling my tongue around each, and listening to his breath and the little noises he makes. I kiss and lick and bite his insteps. I scrape my fingernails from the middle of his thigh to his ankles, listening to the changes in his breathing, the little hitches, the deep exhalations and sudden inhalations. I make my slow way up his body, and then I use my hair to caress his hips and abdomen and chest. His breath is uneven.

I put my hands on his hipbones and barely touch my parted lips to the shaft of his penis—he makes a sound, and it twitches under my mouth. I inhale the scent of him, and I like it.

I turn my head and look up at him. "I can do anything I want, right?"

"Right," he says with some effort.

"And you'll tell me what you like or don't like?"

"Yes," he says.

"And you'll ask for what you want?"

"No," he says.

I lift my head up abruptly. "Why not?"

"Because this isn't about what I want," he says, a little breathless, but looking right at me, one hand delicately caressing my hair. "It's about what you want. I'm yours to do with as you please."

"Okay," I say, considering. I tilt my head and look at his face. "What pleases me is turning you on."

"And what turns me on is your pleasure. Do what you like."

So I do—or rather, I explore. I try things. Do I like pressing kisses up along his shaft? Why, yes I do. Do I like putting just the head in my mouth and sucking on it like it's a Popsicle? Yup. Do I like burying my face at the base of his shaft, inhaling the scent of his body, sucking on his skin, holding his scrotum hot in the palm of my hand, running my lips and tongue up and down the shaft? Yes. Yes, yes, yes, and yes. I love the taste of him and the smell of him and the feel of him in my hands and in my mouth. I love the way he twitches and gets harder, I love the way his breathing changes and the way his face, when I look up at him, is out of focus, his lips parted, his eyes on me. And I love the way his belly tightens when I use my mouth and my hand together, one rhythm, one movement.

"Jesus, fuck, Annie," he says.

I stop. "Would this make you come?"

"Do you want me to come?"

"Uh, yes!"

"Then keep going."

I keep going. The tension in his belly increases. His breathing changes. Somehow he gets even harder in my hand; his whole body is tensing like a stretched spring. Only his hand, stroking lightly over my hair, is relaxed, and eventually that, too, goes rigid as he gasps.

I pull my mouth away, leaving only my hand stroking steadily up and down on him. With my lips hovering near the head of his cock, I say, "What would you do if I stopped right now?"

"You *have* stopped!" he says in a tight, cracked voice, and his hands grip the sheets. "You vicious, wicked, heartless—"

I laugh out loud, amazed, delighted at the unexpected pleasure of giving pleasure. His abdomen contracts, and his eyes and mouth open. "Oh god," he says, and he pushes his hips to thrust in my hand. I see the spurt and pull my face away, out of sheer surprise, then watch the jet of fluid that shoots up his torso to his shoulder.

"Whoa!" I say, impressed. I'm grinning like a fool. I did that! I made that happen! "This is fun."

He laughs and says in an unsteady voice, "This *is* fun."

Chapter 11

My Skinned Knee

Sunday morning I learn how complicated it is to split my attention between the sensation of Charles's tongue and mouth on my genitals and the sensation of my mouth and tongue on his genitals. Charles wakes me up with his mouth on my clit, and rolls me on top of him. I kiss and suck and stroke his cock in a lazy, half-asleep way as he licks me and presses into my vagina with a fingertip. The harder he sucks on my clit, the more aroused I feel, and the more aroused I feel, the harder I suck on his cock. But by the time I come, it's all I can do to grip my fists around him and hold my open mouth, breath suspended, against him.

After I come, I try to suck him some more, but he moves out from under me and pulls me up until I'm straddling his face and he licks me again. I feel his hands gripping into my thighs as he sucks hard on my clit. When he sucks this way, directly, in a steady, pulsing rhythm, I escalate right to the brink. I press my forearms against the wall and shudder over him. My thighs shake, my belly flexes to concavity, and I come almost against my will while his fingers press into my thighs.

He tosses me down onto the bed, even as the pulsing is still fading. He moves over me and rubs his cock against my labia, up and down, as he mutters in a gravelly whisper in my ear, "Do you want me to fuck you?"

"Yes," I whisper.

"Right now? You want me to fuck you right now, now that you're wet from my mouth and hot with coming and—"

"Yes. Now. I want you."

He growls and bites my earlobe and, with three hard thrusts he comes on me, heat and wetness coating our pelvises.

"Tonight," he breathes, his voice dark and muffled against my throat.

"We have got to get out of this apartment," I moan.

We do. Sunday afternoon I learn that it is much easier to let go by choice than it is to fall. Falling off the rock wall is a messy, noisy, humiliating experience that for me involves skinning my knee and shrieking like a little girl. Charles has me, of course—I'm dangling morosely from the top rope, which he has locked off securely. There was never any danger. I just feel and look and am stupid. That's all.

This all started because I was ambitious/arrogant/dumb enough to agree with Charles that yes, it might be fun to try climbing some of the marked routes, to challenge myself. I start with one he says I should find "pretty easy." It's marked *5.3* on the red tape that indicates the holds, and now that I'm used to the height, I go right up it, no trouble.

Then he climbs one marked *5.10c,* and that's when the trouble starts, that's when I start getting competitive.

My next route is a *5.5*—again, pretty easy. When Charles lowers me to the ground, I say, "This is *awesome!*" It is. I'm gaining ground fast.

Then he climbs a *5.10b.* He struggles a bit with it. I feel myself inching up behind him.

My next route is a *5.7.* This is not easy. This is very, very hard. It doesn't help that I've started to get tired. But I do actually stick to the wall perfectly well. I just stop to rest a lot.

Charles calls, "Take a sit. You can let go and not burn your arms out."

"No, I'm good," I call.

I'm not good. I'm in pain and I'm panting like a dog in summer, but fuck you, wall. Fuck you.

Which brings us to the *5.8* route, on which I have left a not insignificant quantity of skin from my knee. I'm hanging in my harness, holding my knee and feeling sorry for myself. "Can I come down now, please?" I call to Charles.

"You don't want to finish the route?"

"Yes, I do, but I can't. This one is too hard."

"Bollocks. Try again."

"Dude, I fucking hate you," I say.

"Good," he answers calmly. "Use it."

I try again. And I finish it.

"Nice," he says.

And I bite my lips together to keep from smiling too stupidly.

"Pizza and beer?" he suggests when at last he allows me to surrender.

"Oh my god, yes," I moan.

We go to Upland and split a pitcher of beer, but we order a whole pizza each.

As we eat, I say, "I don't fucking hate you, by the way."

He smiles. "I know."

"Hey, so, your turn," I say, remembering. "Story of your life. Go."

"Er. All right, only fair I suppose. Born in '88, birthday March twelfth. Er, ordinary, ordinary, mostly the usual thing for the first decade or so. Went to a boarding school—Eton, if that means anything to you."

"Oh yeah, Bertie Wooster went to Eton!" I say.

He laughs. "Yes. I went to the same school as Bertie Wooster."

"I remember because there was that episode where they wanted to break into a safe, and the code was the year of the Battle of Naseby, and Bertie didn't know when that was, and the woman asked him, 'Where did you go to school?' and he was like, 'Eton.' So I asked my dad, 'What's Eton?' and he said, 'It's a very good school in England.' When *was* the Battle of Naseby?"

"1645. Next time look it up if you want to know. Hang on— *'that episode'?*"

"Yeah, the miniseries with Stephen Fry and Hugh Laurie? My parents have it on DVD."

"Oh, you appalling, appalling American. When we get back, I'll point you to the Wodehouse shelf. You shall not leave Indiana without reading at least three novels. Anyway," he says. "Where was I?"

"School. A boys' school?" I ask with a cringe.

"Yes. A load of spotty, insecure arseholes with a pathological need to prove themselves. Me included," he says. "I was small and swotty and basically a total wanker. I was younger than the other boys, too, because my father insisted I was a prodigy—"

"You *are* a prodigy," I interrupt. "You finished college at the age I *started!*"

"I'm really not." He drains his pint. "Anyway, once I was away from home, I'd get bored and want attention, and so I'd start trouble."

Well, that's irresistible. "What kind of trouble did you start?"

"Just ordinary things," he shrugs. "Practical jokes. Clever dick nonsense—in the end it protected me, I think, from some of the bullying I might have experienced, because boys would vie to take the blame—or the credit, I suppose—if a trick was clever enough. Everyone knew it was me, beaks all knew it was me, but when you've got five other boys all saying, 'I did it, sir; sorry, sir, it was me,' there's not much you can do. My tutor confronted me directly once. 'Douglas,' he said, 'for my own edification and entirely off the record, how, hypothetically, might one have managed to get a pie to fall from the rafters at precisely the moment the headmaster walked under it?'"

"And how did you?" I ask.

He only winks at me over his pizza and says, "Flying but-tresses, my girl, flying buttresses. Anyway," he continues, "apart from that, I climbed and played cricket, and that's about all. Then I went to Cambridge, and I more or less stayed there until I came here."

"Did you always want to be a scientist?"

"No, I always wanted to be a doctor. When I started as a re-search assistant at the BRC and developed—"

"BRC?"

"Stands for Brain Repair Centre, sort of."

"Seriously, it's called the *Brain Repair Centre*?"

"Well, no, mostly it's called the BRC," he grins. "Anyway, I was working on traumatic brain injury and got more and more in-terested in how nonbrain trauma affects brain functioning, and that really became my focus." He shrugs. "I met Diana at WCP about five years ago, and she suggested I come do the fellowship if I could get the residency in the School of Medicine. And here I am." He chews his pizza.

"And how about family? Are your parents together?"

"Yes," he says.

"And . . . any brothers or sisters?"

"Yes," he says, "Elizabeth is nineteen, and Simon is twenty-two. Your age." He says it as if he's just realizing.

"Do you get along?"

"Well enough. I haven't spent much time at home."

"You mean, since you came to Indiana?"

"Since I was ten," he says.

I don't want to say the only thing I can think to say—*Like Harry Potter?*—so I just sit there with my mouth hanging open.

"It's been my choice, for the most part," he says. "My father's fairly unpleasant, and I prefer not to live under his roof."

I want to ask about his dad, but I can tell he doesn't want me to—I'm getting a "police line, do not cross" vibe. So instead I say, "How about your mom?"

He refills both of our glasses from the pitcher of beer and says,

"Mum's all right. She comes to see me sometimes. She was here last summer. Brought me the Wodehouse collection, actually. I took her to the Lion and fed her coddle. She loved it."

"You didn't take her to the lab to meet people?"

"I did. It was in July. You were away. She would like you," he adds, smiling at the remains of his pizza. "She'd be intimidated by you though."

"Why would I intimidate her?" I'm worried about a meeting that's unlikely ever to happen.

"You're . . . very American, I suppose. Confident. Sure of yourself."

"Am I?"

He nods and sips his beer. "And she's very British. Terrified of accidentally saying the wrong thing. Certain that she already has." His face grows dark suddenly, and he says, "Let's talk about something else. What time is it?"

I pull out my phone. "About eight."

"Four hours, then," he says, lifting an eyebrow. "What shall we do with the time?"

We go back to his place.

In a stroke of genius, I ask to take a bath. "On your own," Charles says. "There's only so much of you naked and wet that I can stand." While the water's running, he hands me a P. G. Wodehouse novel to read while I soak, but when I crack a joke about dropping it in the tub, he takes it back from me, looking affronted.

"Go on." He waves me into the bathroom, following me like a sheepdog with a stray. "Get in," he says, and I undress and step into the hot water. As I settle in, he sits on the lidded toilet, his ankles crossed on the edge of the tub, and clears his throat and reads, "*Very Good, Jeeves!* by P. G. Wodehouse. Copyright 1930—a first edition, you'll notice, not to be dropped in the bath by any careless young harpy who happens along. Where were we? 'Jeeves and the Impending Doom. It was the morning of the day on which I was slated to pop down to my Aunt Agatha's place at Woollam Chersey. . . .'"

And he reads to me. He does different voices and everything—an exaggerated bass for Jeeves and a floaty, silly voice for Bertie. Aunt Agatha herself gets a wobbly falsetto that cracks me up so much, Charles has to stop and wait, smiling, for me to stop laughing. Eventually he gives up on me and gets on his knees by the tub and kisses me while we're both laughing, and then the kiss turns serious, deep. I put my wet hand on his face when he bites at my lips. When he pulls away, he says, "Christ, woman." I bite my lip and look up at him.

He goes back to his seat and opens the book again. "Where were we?" And he begins reading again.

"Eton!" I interrupt when the book mentions it. "You went to the same place as Bertie Wooster *and* Bingo Little!"

"And that is a source of great pride to my family, I can tell you," he answers with a grin.

He stops too when I interrupt him for translations—

Like, "A cabinet minister is a government thing?"

"Yes, a government thing."

Or, "What's a soup and fish?"

"Dinner jacket and black tie, referring to the first courses of dinner."

Or, "How much is a couple hundred quid?"

"Er . . ." He stops and scratches his head, counting. "Maybe . . . I dunno, ten thousand dollars? Twenty? The joke is, it's a lot."

"You know many things," I say in response to this last one.

" 'And to all this he must yet add something more substantial, in the improvement of his mind by extensive reading,' " he answers.

"I know that one—Colin Firth unites all women, everywhere."

He shakes his head sadly. "I quote Jane Austen, she names an actor. Honestly, what is the world coming to?"

I look at him from the tub, where I'm lying up to my chin in hot water. "I'm pretty sure it's coming to streaming video on the Internet."

He gives a dignified snort. "Right. That's enough of that, miss."

He closes the book and stands up. "I'm taking this out of harm's way, and you can get on with whatever it is women do in the bath."

He has his hand on the doorknob when I say, "Hey, Charles?"

He turns and looks at me, an eyebrow raised.

"Thanks for reading to me."

He smiles and leaves me to my bath. I run more hot water and let myself soak in the heat, relaxing my climbing-fatigued limbs. In the end, I feel too lazy to wash my hair, so I make do with a quick soapy wash, and then I pull the plug, get out, and dry myself off.

Wrapped in a towel, I make my way to the bedroom. I lie down to wait for Charles.

Chapter 12

Gurflugblurgh. And you?

The next thing I know, it's Monday morning.

I've been woken by the sound of the shower.

Ah shit.

On the bright side, I got, like, nine hours of sleep—but on the dark side, it's Monday morning, which means Charles has work, and I have to wait all day for home base.

I hear the shower turn off and realize belatedly that I could have snuck in there with him. Then I hear him move through the apartment, hear water run, hear the coffee grinder, and at last there's the smell of coffee, which pulls me from my bed like an invisible hand. I pull on my clothes—they're waiting for me on the dresser—and find Charles in the kitchen.

He is dressed in his usual blue Oxford and khaki pants. He looks exactly like Charles.

Charles, whom I've spent two days and nights touching in every—almost every—way I can imagine.

And Charles, the postdoc in my research lab, scruffy and bedraggled with his wet hair and button-down shirt.

I spent twenty-something months fantasizing about all the ways he might seduce me or that I might seduce him, planning all the things I might do, if only he would take me to bed, dreaming of what his skin would feel like and taste like. And he turned out to be so vastly much more than my imagination could capture. He is beautiful in ways I didn't anticipate, kind and funny and gentle and erotic and demanding and surprising.

And there he stands . . . making toast.

And I'm still a virgin. Mostly. Sort of.

"Hey," I say, and he turns.

"Hey," he says with a grin.

"I fell asleep," I say.

"You did," he says. "You snore charmingly." And he seems perfectly content.

"I don't snore!"

"No, you don't. You barely moved all night, and you didn't make a sound. But you were charming."

I say, "I'm sorry we missed out on home base."

He looks at me, surprised. "Did we miss it? Was that my only chance? If I had known that, I'd have woken you up, charming snore be damned."

I smile and look at the floor. "I just mean, I'm sorry I have to wait all day while you go to work. Unless"—I rub at a spot on the floor with my toe—"you wanna be late?"

"No, siren, back to your shoals," he says, and his toast dings. "What will you do today?"

"Clean our apartment, probably. My parents will be here Thursday, and our place is enough of a shithole without a semester's worth of scuzz all over it."

"You know just what to say to turn a man on, young Coffey. Your parents and scuzz in the same compound sentence. How are you getting home?" He sucks marmalade off his thumb.

"I rode my bike here," I say.

"Right. How about I text you around noon, and we can make a plan for tonight?"

"What's to plan?" I say. "I come over, you fuck me. *Finally.*"

"I thought you might like to do something . . . I don't know, special, I suppose? It's not nothing, letting someone put their body inside your body."

"You've already put your hands inside my body, and your tongue. Is it really such a big deal to put genitals in?"

He comes over to me and puts his hands on my neck. He kisses me—our glasses tap against each other. "Yes, it is really such a big deal," he says, and he wraps his arms around me. He says into my hair, "It's a big deal, Annie."

All morning I can feel that hug, feel his body on mine. I feel his lips and his hands, like a phantom limb. I clean my kitchen and vacuum the living room and remember his body and his voice and his heat.

Margaret isn't home—she's spent the weekend in Indy with Reshma. They're talking about moving in together after Margaret graduates, and I find myself wondering how that's going. She hasn't texted me at all—but then, I haven't texted her either. We're both having pretty important weekends. I send her one message—

Gurflugblurgh. And you?

And she answers:

Me too!!!! So much to tell you—but not yet. So excited to hear all about it!!! Talk to you tomorrow!!!!

So, she's pretty excited.

I take a long nap that afternoon—much longer than I intended when I "just put my head down for a second" after having lunch around eleven—and I wake up to a series of texts from Charles:

I'll be home around four. Have you considered what you'd like to do tonight?

And an hour later:

Or, if you've changed your mind, we can play Go Fish instead.

And an hour after that:

You okay?

And an hour after that:

May I call you?

And finally:

Whenever you like, give me a call. I'm home.

That last text was about fifteen minutes ago. I look at the time. It's four thirty.

I call him.

"Hey," he answers softly.

"Oh my god, I've been asleep for almost five hours. I'm so sorry," I begin. "I just woke up and saw your texts. You must think I'm a total crazy passive-aggressive bitch. I can't believe I fell asleep."

I hear him exhale into the phone. "Nothing of the kind. You're all right?"

"Yeah—I mean, I have a nap hangover and I'm totally embarrassed about the ways sleep is trying to prevent me from losing my virginity, but otherwise, I'm great."

He laughs, just a rhythmic breath into the phone. "Good."

"How about you?" I ask. "Everything good today?"

"Yep. Everything good."

"Good."

There's a silence. Then he says, "I got you something. A present, sort of."

"Ooh! What is it?"

"It's a surprise, you ninny," he says. "Come over and get it if you want to know." He's smiling; I can hear it. I'm smiling too. My heart's beating very fast, considering I'm just sitting here, smiling into my phone.

"I haven't even showered yet today," I say, "so it'll take me a minute to get ready. I'll be there in maybe an hour? Little less?"

"In your own time," he says. "Unless you'd prefer I come to you, instead."

"Oh hell no, I haven't cleaned my bedroom yet, and anyway, your bed is way bigger and more comfortable than mine."

"So . . . beds are definitely on the table?" he says. "Like bread, for sharing?"

I laugh, surprised and touched that he remembers, and I wonder if it's possible that Charles Douglas might feel now some of the trepidation I felt that day in March.

"Definitely on the table," I say, and then, my smile trembling and my hand shaking as I hold the phone, I add softly, "Charles."

"I was worried I'd hurt you," he says in a quiet rush. His voice sounds as unsteady as mine. "It's so important to me, Annie, that I not hurt you."

"You haven't hurt me."

"I'm glad," he says in that same unsteady voice. "I feel this compulsion to apologize to you anyway."

"What for?"

"I don't know. For . . . not deserving to be the person you share this with?"

"Don't I get to decide that?" I say.

"Yes."

"Well, I'm choosing you."

After the slightest pause he says, "You honor me." The formality of his words, the intensity of his voice, make me believe him.

"I'll be over in an hour," I say.

I shower. I repack my backpack with clean underwear and a change of clothes. I bike the few miles to Charles's apartment.

There's an elevator up to his floor. When I rode it on Friday, it felt fast. Today it feels slow.

I knock on his door, just like I did on Friday. He opens it. Last time we did this, we were both smiling goofily. Tonight I'm trembling, and his face is serious.

"Hey," I say.

"Hey." His face eases a little. Like last time, he lets me in and takes my bag from me, but then he puts his hands on either side of my jaw and kisses me hello. It's more than a kiss hello, though.

When he breaks away, he says, "Before we begin tonight's proceedings, I'd like to offer you . . ." He pulls a shiny key from his pocket. "It is a key to the flat. I offer it without expectation or demand, but with the hope that the next several weeks will bring us both a great deal of pleasure, and that your free access to my bed will facilitate that."

I take it, warm from his pocket, and put it in my own pocket, trying to smother my smile.

"Listen, if at any point, tonight or ever, you want to stop, you must just say so and we will. The *least* doubt or hesitation. I can think of nothing less desirable than taking to bed a woman who isn't quite sure she's having an excellent time."

I nod. "Okay."

He's looking at me seriously, uncertainly, his hands on my triceps. "Are you interested in dinner? Would you like . . . I don't know, anything at all?"

"Just you," I say.

"Well then," he says with a wry smile but in a serious voice. "Annabelle Coffey, it would be an honor and a privilege for me to sully your maiden virtue this fine evening."

I break into a maniacal grin. "When do you want to start?" I ask.

"No time like the present," he says, and leads me by the hand into the bedroom.

Chapter 13

An Honor and a Privilege

He leaves me standing next to the bed, to pull the curtains. Instantly the room is in almost total darkness, only cracks of late-afternoon sun sneaking through breaks in the curtains.

While my eyes are still adjusting to the dark, he stands before me and brushes my hair from my face. "I don't suppose this is how you imagined it at all."

I shake my head.

He begins to undress me and says, "How did you imagine it? Tell me."

I raise my eyes to the ceiling, feeling awkward, my cheeks flushing. "A lot of ways," I confess. "In the lab, on your desk, was one. I imagined you, like, couldn't control yourself around me. Um. On the edge of the sink in the Soma bathroom was another one. Again, you simply could not contain your lust. It turns out in reality you can control yourself pretty well."

"You'd like me to be out of control for you?" My shirt is gone, and he's kneeling in front of me to pull my shorts and panties down slowly over my legs.

I bunch my lips over to one side and shrug. "They're just fantasies." I step out of the clothes tangled at my ankles.

"And this is real." He stands and puts his hands on my face

and kisses me, and it is real. Charles is kissing me and I'm naked and this is happening.

"You're trembling," he whispers into the kiss, but I can't respond. I clench and unclench my hands helplessly, unable to do anything but receive his soft, slow kiss.

"I don't know what to do," I say at last.

"Anything you like," he answers.

"How am I supposed to know what I like?" I say desperately.

He seems to understand. "Pretend we're still on third base, and we'll see how we go."

That makes it easier, a little. I untuck his shirt and put my hands on his back. "I like your skin," I say.

"I like yours," he says.

I begin undressing him with the same industriousness with which he undressed me, and I say, "So, how have *you* imagined it?"

"A bit like this," he says softly, slowly. "Here, in the dark, two naked bodies. You, bewitched and joyful. Me, wise and skillful." He's making fun of himself.

"I think I am bewitched," I say, standing before him. We're both naked now, with nothing but a foot of empty air separating us. He reaches out, puts a hand on my waist.

"Are you cold? Unsure? You can change your mind."

"No, I'm just . . . I don't know why I'm shaking."

"Come to bed," he says.

We lie down together under the covers. He puts his arms around me, kisses me, but the shaking is getting worse. "Sweetheart," he says, and just takes over for me. He kisses me all over, touches me all over, and with his hands and his skin and his mouth and his hair, his eyelashes, he touches me softly. He takes his time, and every sensation feels amplified. When he touches my vulva, I'm still trembling, but I press my body up against his hand, press my own hand over his.

"Yes," I say.

He kisses my neck and breasts as he moves his palm over my clit. I run my hands over his skin. The more aroused I get, the more my body shakes—my legs and my abdomen and my fingers. "I can't stop it," I tell him.

"Don't try," he says.

So I don't. I just let it, I let my body be what it is and do what it's doing. My arousal grows, and the tension grows, and I grip the edge of the mattress over my head as my muscles shudder and vibrate. Charles's mouth on my breasts and rib cage is warm and soft, and his hand is warm and firm, with steady, circular pressure. I can feel the tip of his finger just entering me.

"Charles," I say, and I'm surprised I sound worried.

"Annie," he says. "It's so beautiful, what your body's doing."

"Is it?"

"You are astonishing. You are breathtaking."

His mouth is moving lower, down to my belly and my hips. I feel his lips on the trembling insides of my thighs, I feel his hands over my trembling stomach, I feel him licking me, licking my clit, and my body shudders and shakes. I widen my thighs, straighten my legs, point my toes, but my legs just keep shaking. I put my shaking hands in his hair. He's still moving slowly, taking his time as he licks me, and he doesn't make me come, only brings me near the edge, where the trembling escalates and escalates. It's not the quiet vibration it was when I walked in the door, but an uncontrollable, muscle-twitching shudder that wracks through me in waves like a fever.

"Charles." My voice is trembling as much as the rest of me now. He comes back up to me, lies beside me, and I wrap my shaking arms around his neck.

He kisses my mouth softly and murmurs, "Pretty girl. Beautiful girl."

"I don't know what to do," I whisper.

"Would you like to come, sweetheart?"

"Yes," I breathe through the shuddering.

With firmer pressure on my vulva and a wet slide of his finger deeper into me, Charles kisses me with his tongue in my mouth. My fingers, shaking, grip at his skin. His body is so quiet and strong beside mine, his touch so sure. He knows my body now; in three days he has learned me, and he gives me exactly what my body wants.

"Oh god," I say in a high, weak voice.

"Oh god," he answers, and his voice sounds like a prayer.

I can't breathe. In a series of cresting pulses that seem to calibrate all my shaking into one shared wavelength, my body pulls me up to a peak of tension, my whole body vibrating, my arms gripped around Charles's shoulders, my hands fisted, my eyes squeezed shut.

"Oh my god," I breathe.

"Oh my god, Annie," he says.

With a singing cry, I fall off the edge, my body rolling wildly against Charles's solid, still form, his hand still pressed firmly against my vulva, his mouth now pressed against my ear. He's saying things, I can't hear what, but he's whispering to me about beautiful and come and darling and yes and yes and yes, while I stretch and press and writhe against him.

And at the end of it, when I fall into release and land in the soft, warm bed with Charles warm next to me, at last all the tension is gone. My body relaxes, sunk into the bed, pliant, sure, still. I feel in love with my skin and my breath. I feel in love with the dark. I feel perfect. He's perfect. Tonight is perfect. I run my hands up and down his back and turn my face to his, whisper his name, kiss him.

As we kiss, I say, "I don't know how to say it. Do I tell you I want you? Should I say I'm ready? Should I try to make it sexy like, 'Give it to me, big boy?' What do I say?"

"That'll do for now," he says with a half grin I can hear, and he moves on top of me. He takes my hand and guides it down between our legs. "Show me where," he whispers, still with that half grin lingering in his voice.

"How should *I* know?" I ask, fumbling a bit with his penis in my hand. I try a few places and shift around, and his face is doing remarkable things, but at last I have him lined up where he goes . . . I think. I put both my hands on his shoulders, searching the dark for his eyes, and say, "Okay. Ready."

"Me too," he whispers. He kisses me so, so gently.

And he pushes just a little.

There's a little sting, but mostly, it's pressure.

He watches my face as I'm watching his, and says, "Okay so far?" and I nod.

He pushes a little more. It stings a little more, but overall, it's nice. I feel opened and slippery. He pulls out a bit then, and then pushes deeper. He does it again, his eyes on mine, and then again.

"What's it feel like?" he whispers.

"Like you put your penis in my vagina," I whisper back, and we both laugh, and I can feel it inside me, the way he moves as he laughs, and I'm sure he can feel me, too. He kisses me, his hand against my face, and pushes deeper still, then pulls out again, and deeper still . . . and again. And again, deeper.

"Whoa," I say.

He stops. "Hurt?"

"No, just . . . deep. Big. Just . . . lots," I murmur incoherently. "Is that all the way?"

He kisses my eyebrow. "Not yet. Do you want all the way?"

"Yeah," I whisper.

He makes an odd *hhunh* sound through his nose and then pushes deeper into me. He says, "Sweet holy fucking Jesus, Annie. You're so—" He doesn't tell me what I'm so. He's breathing hard, and his arms are trembling on either side of me.

"Icebergs and baseball," he mutters against my throat.

"What?"

"What you're supposed to think about to delay orgasm," he pants, and then he laughs, "I don't know anything about baseball."

"You know about the bases," I giggle—and I feel my pelvic floor muscle contract around Charles. He flinches and makes another *hhunh* noise, higher pitched this time, and then thrusts into me, three quick, deep, sharp movements, not painful, but not particularly pleasurable, either, then he strains and pushes inside me while he grunts and moans, his face squinched above me. Then all his muscles relax and he sinks, his face against my neck.

"Oh god. Well"—he pants—"you wanted me to be out of control with you. That, my dear girl, is what out of control is like. Fuck. God. I haven't done that in a decade. Oh Christ. I can only apologize. I will make it up to you, sweetheart, I promise."

"Wait, that was it? You came?"

"I came, but don't believe for a second that that is it." He lifts his head and looks at me. He's laughing and pink in the darkness, and he says, "God, how embarrassing! I'm supposed to be the experienced one who shows you how it's done."

"Is it weird if I take it as a compliment?" I ask.

"Oh, it is a compliment," he says vehemently. "Undeniably. You are without a doubt the sexiest woman I have ever met in my entire life. I had rather hoped, on that account, to make a better showing, you know, so you could look back on your first time with the kind of bone-melting fondness that makes all the other blokes perpetually jealous."

All the other blokes.

"And instead you'll just giggle and tell them, 'He tried.' I did try," he says, laughing and kissing my neck.

Then he kisses a path down my neck to my chest and my breasts, saying, "Oh, Annie, god, you feel so good. You feel so good. God, you just feel so amazing. Ugh, listen to what you've done to me! You reduce me to the most facile, imbecilic . . . That's all the adjectives I can remember. The rest of them are gone. Whoosh!" He laughs and gently, slowly pulls out of me. He leaves his hands to explore my breasts as he kisses down to my belly and my hips and then—I pull my knees in, feeling awkward as his lips approach my vulva.

"You can do that?" I say as he puts his lips on my clit. "Even though you already . . . I mean, it's, like, really goopy now, isn't it?"

"Oh yes," he says, and he pushes my knees apart with one hand. "It's really goopy." And he buries his face between my legs.

I feel the combined sensation of his soft, wet, warm tongue against my vulva and his slightly stubbly cheeks against the insides of my thighs. But before I fully register what's happening, he's coming up again and kissing me with a mouth covered in our combined fluids. And it is fucking *hot*. I put my hands on his neck and suck on his tongue, drawing the taste of him and me into my mouth. I'm full of want and pleasure and uncertainty.

His hand is on me now. I can feel the slickness of his palm against my vulva and just the tip of one finger at my entrance. He tugs circles against my pubic bone. He kisses behind my ear and wraps a hand around the back of my skull, pressing his lips to my ear, but even with his mouth so close, I have to listen hard to hear him. He's saying, "I love making you come. I've been imagining your face at orgasm for ages. When you came that first time Friday night, when you said you were nearly there and then you ground against me, I nearly came with you. I wanted to lay you on your stomach right then, pull your jeans down to your knees, pin you down by your hair, and fuck you."

"Yes," I pant.

"I wanted to tear off your clothes and bury my face in your pussy, make you come a thousand times."

"Yes. God." It's his voice as much as his words that's building the heat inside me. His voice, and his hand still tugging wide-open circles on my clit.

"I wanted to drag you to the bed and fuck you until you couldn't think, until you couldn't see straight or construct sentences or move."

"Yes," I breathe.

"You'd like that? You'd like me to fuck you all night?" Charles is saying. "Until you can't move or think or see, until all you know is my cock inside you and my body over you and my tongue in your mouth, my voice in your ear telling you to come?"

"Yes." My hips are starting to move in a rhythm to match his movements.

"I'd like to be inside you again," he says. "May I?"

"Yes, please," I whisper.

He's lying on his side and I'm on my back, and I'm expecting him to get on top of me again, but all he does is raise my knee and slip the head of his penis inside me with a dark groan, and now I have this leg in the air and I don't know what to do with it.

"Uh," I say.

"Feel all right?" he asks. "Pain?"

I shake my head, still uncertain.

"Put your hand on your clit, sweetheart," he says. I do, and turn my eyes to his to ask if I'm doing it right. He wraps one hand around the back of my head, his forearm a pillow for me, and presses the other hand under my jaw. He puts his forehead against mine, eyes open, and begins to fuck me, moving just a little, not coming all the way into me.

"All right?" he asks again, his eyes watching mine.

"Oh," I say, trying not to close my eyes, trying to focus on his blue ones when my whole brain wants to notice what it feels like to have him inside me. "Yes."

He's begun to go a little deeper now, sliding with longer strokes, and I feel his thigh move between mine, pinning down the one on the mattress. Still I have this leg in the air and no idea what to do with it, but I'm caring less and less.

"More?" he asks, his fingers tightening in my hair.

"Yeah," I whisper.

He slides deeper and my hand moves on my clit while his hand strays over my breasts and abdomen. I make a noise, and he kisses me. "All right?"

"Yeah."

"Annie," he says. "Oh, you feel amazing."

All I can say in response is, "Ah." There's so much sensation, from my hand on my clit and his hand moving over my torso and his eyes so close to mine, watching me, and, above all, the utterly unique sensation of him moving inside me. He's *inside* me.

"I really like that," I say finally.

"I like it too," he says seriously. He kisses my ear, my throat, my mouth. My pelvis rocks in rhythm with his movements, pressing from the sensation of him inside me to the sensation of my hand and back again.

"More," I say.

"More?"

"Yeah. Charles. Can you be all the way inside me?"

His answer is a snarl and a grunt. His hand moves to my shoulder, presses down on it to brace me, I realize, as he begins to fuck me fully. My breasts bounce with it, and I find my hand has begun pressing down on my clit without my ever deciding to. I can scarcely interpret all the sensations I'm experiencing, but the familiar rising tension in my lower abdomen finally forces my eyes closed. My attention collapses to a few hypersalient sensations. The subtle bounce of my breasts. The pressure on my clit. The wet, hot slide of Charles moving inside me.

"Oh my god."

"All right?" he asks again.

"Please don't stop."

"I won't stop," he grinds out. "I want you to come, Annie. I want to watch you come while I fuck you." He keeps talking even as he kisses me, kisses my face, the crests of my cheekbones, along my eyebrow, my temple. He's murmuring about sweet and fucking and come and so, so, so . . . And still the pressure on my clit, and the bounce of my breasts, and his thigh heavy and warm between mine, the slippery friction of him inside me, all pulling me toward orgasm. The movement of my hand on my clit seems out of my voluntary control, and I'm pressing harder, moving faster, building up layers of pleasure.

When I realize I'm holding my breath, I exhale in a gust but then inhale with a wild gasp and hold my breath again. When I can finally exhale, I breathe, "Charles," and then barely draw another breath before my diaphragm locks again and I'm caught between inhalation and exhalation, my mouth wide open.

"Not yet," he commands.

"What?" I'm breaths away from orgasm, and he's moving over

me, without withdrawing from me, and shifting between my legs. He leans over and takes my hand, grips it in his, pressing it into the mattress by my shoulder. His other hand is on my face. His eyes are on me. He's not moving inside me; he's just holding me here, his pelvis pressed against my clit and his cock buried deeply, fully inside me.

He kisses me briefly. "All right?"

I can't answer; I just blink at him and gasp for air. He grins.

He kisses me again and says softly into my ear, "You want to come, my Annie?"

"Yes," I can barely say. "I want—"

He interrupts me, kissing me, putting his tongue in my mouth and fucking me in a sudden storm of fast, deep thrusts. With every movement, his pubic bone rubs against my clit.

I open my eyes and meet his. His eyes are dark, his jaw tight as he kisses me. He holds me, fucks me, holds my gaze, grips my shoulder, grips my hand, still fucking me even as my hips lift and push and writhe against him. I pull my hand from his and wrap my arms and legs around him and lift my hips off the mattress, desperate to press him as deep into me as he can go.

With a groan, he wraps an arm around my waist and lifts me bodily from the bed, my arms and legs still wrapped around him. The movement makes me dizzy in my desire. He's fucking me, fucking me even deeper, on his knees, holding my entire weight upright in his lap, pressing my body against his while I grind my pelvis. Both of his arms braced tight around my rolling hips. His arms are shaking around me, and my legs are shaking around him, trembling at the precipice.

And then I break open. Without a sound beyond my disbelieving sigh, my body cracks and crumbles like an avalanche. I grip and flail and pant. I dig my fingernails into his shoulders, I bite him, I'm wild to keep him in me as I fall to pieces around him.

The writhing has not yet ended when I feel him cross a threshold. "You are . . ." he says through a tense jaw. "I can't . . ." He doesn't tell me what I am or what he can't. When he comes, he shouts hoarsely and then bites my lip so hard, I taste blood and I love it. He lifts up under me, rises up on his knees, kneeling as he would at an altar, fucking into me, his arms trembling around my hips and his forehead against my throat. He throws me back down on the bed in silence and, with three final thrusts, he kisses me, one hand pressed into my jaw, the other fisted in my hair.

"Jesus," he says into my ear, out of breath.

My limbs are melting around him. We're both breathing hard. When I open my eyes, I see that for once he's not watching me. His face is utterly peaceful, eyes closed, the faintest smile on his parted lips. I put my hand on his face, and he opens his eyes then, kisses me briefly, and rests his forehead against mine, eyes closed.

"Oh my god, Annie," he says.

We lie together like that, warm, limp, and breathing, for a long time. Somehow the silence and the tangling of our breaths feel as though they're tying me to him, linking us together in a way that our joined bodies alone never would. This *is* a big deal. In this moment I know tonight will link me to this man, to this breathing body over mine, forever. When at last he opens his eyes and, with one hand, brushes my hair away from my face and tucks it behind my ear, I ask him quietly, "Is it always like this?"

And then he smiles at me, a warm, affectionate smile that I will never, ever, in my whole life forget.

He says, "It's never like this."

Chapter 14

Gangnam Style

We do it again in the morning. Compared with last night, it's quiet, calm, simple. We wake up, and it's as if we're already in the middle of it. I turn and kiss him and pull him over me and open my legs, and he slides easily into me. It's so easy. It's so simple, the simplest thing in the world for him to angle his pelvis so he's pressing against my clit while he fucks me. I'm learning what the tension in his body means, and the more aroused he gets, the more aroused I get. He waits for me. I come easily, no hesitancy, no delay, just easy response to the pressure of his body against mine. And as I come, he accelerates his movement and comes too, and then he lies on top of me, kissing me and kissing me and kissing me.

At last he lifts his mouth from mine and says with a sigh, "I have to go to work."

"Well," I say. "I guess we couldn't actually have sex all day anyway."

"On another day I'll be happy to try," he grins, and he gently, slowly pulls out of me.

And from there, it turns into a morning. Like, a regular morning. As if I haven't just spent the night Losing My Virginity. I don't feel like I've lost anything at all, to be honest. I feel just a little bit more grown-up, I feel taller, I feel . . . mostly the same. Also: sore, just a little.

He takes a shower and I make the coffee and we make out in the kitchen while the toast toasts—he's clean and I'm gross, but he doesn't seem to mind at all. When he sits down to breakfast, he says, utterly practical, "You're teaching tonight?"

"Yup." I sip my coffee.

"And I've got my climbing group. May I see you tonight, afterward?"

"Um, of *course*."

He smiles. "Why don't I come over to yours tonight, if you like, for a change? Around eight?"

"Sure," I say. "As long as you're okay with Margaret being around."

"Fine by me if it's fine by her," he says easily. Then he adds, less comfortably, "She knows about . . ."

"Oh god, she knows," I say. "She's been hearing about me lusting after you for years."

His smile goes crooked at this, and he blushes. "I hope . . ." he says, and stops. Then he tries again. "I hope you'll be glad about this, years from now. I hope you'll remember this—remember *me*—with pleasure."

In answer, I do my best to distract him from leaving, but he peels me off him and ushers us out the door. Leaving the apartment together is easy. It feels natural, like we've always done it this way.

I ride home—an interesting experience, postcoital—and find Margaret in the living room.

"Holy crap," I announce.

"Me too!" she says. "Who should go first? Oh hell, I should! We're engaged!"

"Oh my god!" I squeal like a little girl and hug her, and we jump up and down while I say, "That's amazing! Oh my god, that's so great!"

She tells me all about Reshma's proposal, which happened in

front of Reshma's parents, who cried and hugged them both and called Margaret the Thai American queer femme daughter they never had. It's a really big deal that Reshma's parents—her lesbian moms—are so welcoming and accepting, because Margaret's own family hasn't gotten there yet.

"So?" she asks, once we've squeed enough over her news. "How was it? Did you have wild and crazy sexytimes all weekend?"

"He's been so amazing." I explain about the bases and the hiking and climbing and sleeping and finally . . . last night.

Her face is a mixture of curiosity, empathy, and a little bit of horror as I explain what it was like. She's a gold-star lesbian, and just the idea of a biological penis is a little gross to her. I can understand that, I guess.

She tilts her head to the side, thinks, and says, "Maybe I just have no idea how guys work, but it seems weird to me that you'd have such a different number of orgasms from him. Isn't that sort of unfair? Or is that just how it works: The girl has way more orgasms than the guy?"

I fret about that for a minute, my lip between my teeth. "I don't know. Do you think Google could tell us?"

We look it up, discover something called "the orgasm gap," and generally learn that it's way more typical for a guy to come more often than a girl.

"Oh," Margaret says.

"Huh," I say.

But the whole conversation has planted a niggling worry in my brain that no amount of googling can quiet.

That night my ballet class must have no idea what the hell is going on with their teacher. We *battement* to "Gangnam Style" while I prance around the studio like a K-pop superstar singing, "Heeeeey, sexy lady." It's our last class, so I allow them to chalk it up to me psyching them up for next week's rehearsals and performance. We spend most of the class running their piece—I'm not polishing their technique at this point; I'm focused on building their confidence and their artistry. Most of the students hug me at the end of the class, and so I'm feeling blissed out with affection and a sense of purpose when I get on my bike to go home.

By eight I'm showered and excited and waiting for the doorbell to ring.

He knocks instead.

I open the door, smiling like a goon, and he's standing there, gooning right back.

"Hey," he says.

"Hey," I say. "Come in."

He does, saying, "It's okay with Margaret that I'm here?"

"Totally okay. Oh—we ordered pizza, it's on its way. I hope that's okay." I close the door behind him.

"Sure."

"Good climb?" I say.

"Yes," he says.

"Good."

"Good class?"

"Yup."

"Good."

We're standing there, grinning at each other like dopes, when Margaret comes down the stairs.

"Hiya, Momma Duck," she says.

"Margaret." He nods, and I swear he looks just the slightest bit shy.

"Pizza'll be here soon," she says as she wanders into the kitchen. "You want a pop?"

"Sure," he says, his eyes on me. "Oh, I brought you . . ." He pulls the Wodehouse novel from his satchel.

"Hey!" I say in thanks, taking it. And then the doorbell rings—it's the pizza. I lead Charles back to the living room while Margaret talks to the pizza lady. I wave him to a seat on the futon and say, "I played 'Gangnam Style' in my class tonight."

"In a ballet class?" Charles asks.

"That song is important sociopolitical satire!" I say.

If Charles and I have A Song, it's this one. See, "Gangnam Style" was a giant thing at exactly the same time Charles joined the lab—and when I say *exactly* the same time, I mean that the day we met, at the very moment he walked into the lab for that first meeting in August, Margaret and I were showing everyone in the lab, Professor Smith included, the "Gangnam Style" dance. We had been playing the YouTube video over and over for a week in our apartment, learning it. There we were, dancing, and then there he was.

At the end of the song, Professor Smith introduced us this way:

"Charles! Welcome to the madhouse. This is Annie, Head Duckling, and Margaret, who's a hatchling, new to the lab this semester, like you."

And she introduced him to us, the ducklings and the grad students, this way:

"Ducklings, this is Dr. Charles Douglas, your new Patrice. You should probably wait a few weeks before you start addressing him as Momma Duck."

I never did call him Momma Duck. He stood there, looking beautiful and serious, and I felt foolish. All the grad students and most of the undergrads called him Charles right away, but to me he was Dr. Douglas. It took me a year to get over that.

And now here he is on our futon, waiting for pizza and saying, "I'm sure the sociopolitical satire is why you played it."

I walk over and straddle his lap. "You remember that first day?"

He nods and puts his hands in my hair and gives me that warm, fond look that seems to grab me by the heart and tug me closer to him. He says, "I thought, *They're going to think I am the world's biggest wanker.*"

"Nuh-uh."

"I thought, *What have I done?*"

"Did you regret it?"

"Not even for a second," he says, and then he adds, "I like you on top of me." He pulls me toward him and kisses me.

And just then Margaret clears her throat and says, "Pizza, you guys."

I don't really want pizza. I want to take off Charles's clothes and fuck him right here. I want my tongue thrusting into his mouth in the same rhythm that his cock thrusts inside me. But I crawl off his lap and sit beside him on the futon as Margaret pulls slices onto plates for us.

"I was just telling Charles I played 'Gangnam Style' in my class tonight. You remember when we did the thing?"

Margaret snorts through a mouthful of pizza. "Oh my god, I forgot all about that! That was hilarious."

It's easy, the three of us hanging out together. Margaret has always liked Charles, Charles has always liked Margaret, and she's so glowing from her engagement, pretty much nothing in the world could make her cranky. In fact, she spends less than half an hour downstairs with us, mostly talking about her weekend, and then she goes back to her room to call Reshma, whose semester isn't over yet. They'll be on the phone for hours.

And so Charles and I are alone.

In the living room.

On the futon.

I turn my eyes to him and find him watching me. Without a word, he pushes me onto my back, his hand on my throat, and kisses me lightly, tiny, soft, slow kisses on my mouth. For a moment I let him draw me under, but then I take a deep breath and struggle to introduce the niggling topic.

I say, "I have an unsexy question."

"Okay," he says, still kissing me.

I pull away enough to ask, "You wanna meet my parents when they're here? I'm not trying to make it all awkward, but, like, if you want to, they're pretty cool."

"Sure," he says, creating a little distance too. "Will they be at the department reception? I can meet them there."

"Yeah, perfect," I say. And then, "Um."

"Hm?"

"So, also? I was thinking about it and, uh, I think I'd rather we didn't do stuff while my parents are here. Is that okay?" I ask, cringing.

"No problem," he says easily.

I say, "And can I ask a beginner's question?"

"Of course."

"Am I having, like, a *really* lot of orgasms? Or is this typical?"

"You are having a genuinely spectacular number of orgasms, young Coffey. You are having orgasms by the barrel, by the hogshead."

I make a mental note to look up what a hogshead is and say, "And you are having . . . way fewer orgasms than that."

"I don't know what the actual ratio is, but it's a largish one, yes." He gives me a cockeyed grin and starts biting along my jaw.

"There are even times when I come multiple times, and you don't come even once."

"Not even once," he repeats, and kisses behind my ear.

"Is that . . . That feels lopsided to me, and maybe a little un-fair?"

"From each according to his ability, to each according to his need," he pronounces against my neck.

"Well, maybe that's what I mean. Are you coming less because I lack ability, or because you have less need?"

"Sweetheart, watching you orgasm is more pleasurable to me than having my own." He's running his lips and tongue over the notch under my earlobe.

"Really?"

"Oh yes," he says, and his voice is quiet but definite against my ear.

Still, I have this niggling dissatisfaction. I explore it in silence as he nuzzles and nibbles, and I finally wonder aloud, "Well. It's maybe unfair in the other direction then. You might not want to come more, but I think maybe I want you to come more. I feel like I'm handing over an awful lot, and you're maybe like . . . holding back?"

"This is the losing control thing?" He's kissing my throat now.

"It's, like . . . you take over my whole body and make me come over and over again, but you hold off and stay in control and *choose* when you come."

He stops kissing me. He pulls away, looks at me. "Yes. It doesn't come naturally to me the way it does to you." He brushes a hand over my hair and kisses my mouth. "You let go so easily. You hand your body over to me with such trust."

"What would it take for you to do the same thing?"

He's silent for a long time, a thinking silence, so I wait patiently . . . and I am rewarded. He says, "Do you remember when you asked me to tell you one of my barbaric thoughts?"

"Yeah."

He raises an eyebrow, and his hand wanders over my chest.

"You want to tie me up?" I say. "And . . . make me come, I think you said a hundred times, so that when you finally fuck me, I'm exhausted and limp?" I pause and then add, "You don't mean literally a hundred, right? Because even having just four makes me feel like a heap of mashed potatoes."

"Not literally a hundred, no," he says, and there's a tension in his voice that stirs me.

"I want to do that," I say. "Let's do that tomorrow."

He shakes his head. "Maybe we can try something like that later, maybe after you've had a bit more time to get to know what you like."

"Oh." I try to mask my disappointment, my frustration, but clearly, he sees it.

"I'm not putting you off," he says.

I huff at him. "Well, it definitely feels like you're putting me off. It definitely feels like this is another 'Annie's a beginner, she doesn't know what she wants, I have to keep the brakes on,' blah, blah, blah."

"You can't know what it entails."

"Have you done it before?"

He says, "No."

"Then you can't know what it entails either. I'm *ready*," I insist. "I want to try things. I want to do your fantasy. Are you gonna decide what we do the whole month?"

His eyes close briefly, and his jaw tightens.

"Careful what you wish for," he says, and I'm not sure if he's saying it to me or to himself.

We make love there on the futon, then. He pulls me over top of him, and we push aside the minimum amount of clothes to get him inside me, and when I try to find the rhythm, he shows me, guiding my hips until we're moving together and kissing and I come, panting, peripherally aware that the lights are on and we're in the living room.

"I want you to come," I whisper, my mouth against his lips.

"Let's go to bed," he answers.

We reassemble our clothes, and I lead him upstairs to my room, where he closes the door behind us. He undresses me fully, undresses himself, with a quiet, focused energy. Then, very gently, he takes my hand and looks into my eyes. I smile.

"We'll have to talk through a plan for tomorrow."

"We can do that in the morning," I say. And then I start to giggle. He smiles. My giggle turns into an all-out laugh, inexplicable, joyful, excited. His hand tightens on mine, and in a sudden rush he tugs me toward him and then pushes me backward, pinning me against the closed door and pressing his body against mine.

"You are unbelievable," he breathes against my neck, and he shoves into me, fucks me hard against the door. I wrap a leg around him, claw my hands into his shoulders to stay upright. The door thumps a little with each thrust, and I think vaguely of the noise and Margaret across the hall, and then his hands are on my ass and he's shifting the angle of his pelvis against my clit, and when I make a sharp grunt, he breathes, "Shhhh," into my ear, and fucks me harder, faster, which just makes the door thud harder and makes me grunt again, louder. He presses a hand flat over my mouth, and says, "Shhh," again, and bites my jaw.

I don't want to come again—I want our ratio to be equal tonight—but the more I try to hold off and let him come without me, the more my arousal grows, until I can't not come. And when I do finally, with piercing, wild throbs and a desperate moan, he comes with me, nearly silent, breathing through his nose, with the three hard thrusts I'm learning to recognize.

"You are unbelievable," he whispers again when we're lying together naked in my bed.

"We'll make a plan in the morning."

Chapter 15

The Mechanoreceptors

After Charles goes into the lab the next morning, I spend Wednesday checking things off the shopping list he and I made, half-serious, half-giggling, over breakfast, and then I take all the stuff to his apartment. I nap in his bed in the afternoon, and by the time he walks in the door, I'm well rested, freshly showered, and vibrating with anticipation.

He suggests we eat, but neither of us has any interest in food.

"Come and see the stuff," I say instead, and I lead him into the bedroom. "We've got"—I begin piling things on the dresser as I name each item—"black stockings, the garter kind not the stay-uppy kind; a blindfold—this is actually just a black scarf I had anyway; earplugs—not sure what those are for; some high-tech lube; and my one vibrator, yours for the asking." I show him the remote-control vibrating Ben Wa balls I bought on impulse, thinking to strengthen my pelvic floor muscle. "Sorry I don't have more to choose from."

"It's more than enough," he says, returning my smile. We lock eyes, and I find I can't smile anymore. My heart is thumping, and my knees are unsteady.

He says gently, "You sure about this?"

I nod mutely and kiss him on the lips.

He puts his hands on me—one on my face, one on my trapez-ius—and says, "The plan would be, I take off your clothes, I tie you to the bed, I do anything I like, for as long as I like. My in-tention . . ." He pauses, eyes still on mine. "I'll make you come until you tell me to stop, or until you can't move, whichever comes first. And then, when you're exhausted to immobility, I'll fuck you."

I nod and we stand, looking into each other's eyes for a mo-ment. Then he begins to undress me with quick fingers as he says, "What will you say if you want me to stop doing what I'm doing?"

"I don't want you to stop."

He pulls my shirt over my head. "I'm saying, all night—all month, if you like. If you want to stop for any reason at all, whether it's because you want a glass of water or want to go to sleep or just don't like what's happening, what will you say?"

"Uh . . . 'stop'?"

"That's fine." He undoes my shorts. "That means that if you say, 'That tickles' or 'Uh-oh' or 'No' or 'Are you sure?' or 'That's too much' or 'Don't' or 'I can't' or anything else, I *might* ignore you." He pushes my shorts and my panties in a bunch to the floor. I step out of them, and I'm naked in front of him, beginning to recognize I've taken on something that might be a little more than I bar-gained for.

I ask, "Um, can we have a 'slow down' one too, rather than a full stop? Like a yield sign?"

"Sure."

"Then that one's 'wait.'"

"Right. 'Wait' and 'stop.' Are you ready?"

I nod and bite my lips between my teeth, heart thumping.

He stops. "You're sure about this? You must be utterly clear with me."

I nod again and take a deep breath. "I'm totally sure."

"Then lie on the bed." Something in his voice is different. It sounds like his teachery voice, but . . . different. I lay myself on the bed. He starts ripping open packages of stockings. "Now, young Coffey, I want you to recall your neurophysiology for a moment."

"You want me to *what?*" I say, turning my face to him in disbelief.

"You'll recall that different types of receptors in your peripheral nervous system respond to different types of sensation. Please, Miss Coffey, recite for the class the common types of receptors."

And then he begins to tie my wrist to the bed, using a stocking. "What?"

"Shall I start? Thermoreception . . . There—is that comfortable? Too tight?"

"No, it's good. Uh, thermoreception . . . chemoreception, mechanoreception, uh, photoreception . . . Is that all of them?" I tick through the sensory modalities in my head. "No, wait! Proprioception? And nociception."

"Full marks, Miss Coffey. Well done." He's tying my ankle to the bed now. "And tell us, please—is this comfortable? Good— tell us, please, four kinds of sensation perceived by the mechanoreceptors."

"Light touch, deep touch, temperature, and vibration." That one's easy.

He moves on to my other ankle, and now my legs are far, far apart, my feet right at the edges of the mattress. "And, for a bonus, which of those sensations is pleasurable?"

"Well . . ." Hang on—it's a trick question. I feel inordinately proud of myself for catching it. "You jerk, all of them or none of them potentially, depending on stuff like the affective keyboard in the nucleus accumbens. Is this supposed to be turning me on?"

"No." He grins, focused on tying my ankle. "It's supposed to remind you, young Coffey, that any sensation, from vibration on your clitoris to a blade at your throat, can feel erotic in the right setting," he says, tying my remaining wrist to the bed.

"Okay, that turned me on," I say, utterly sincere.

He comes up to my head, puts a hand on top of my head, and kisses me briefly. "Good."

When I'm fully bound, spread eagle on the bed, he pauses, standing beside the bed, and looks me up and down. "I've never seen anything more erotic than this. Never. There can be nothing in the world sexier than you tied to my bed."

I feel aroused and sensitive just from the sensation of his eyes on me. "No blindfold?" I say.

"Not yet. You'll need the sensory deprivation later."

"Ohhhh," I say. "That's what the earplugs are for?"

"Clever girl. Ready?"

I nod. I'm pulsing with it, edgy and restless.

He lies beside me and kisses me simply, softly . . . slowly. With one hand tracing circles over my throat and my collarbone, he kisses my mouth comprehensively until I sigh and writhe, inviting his hand downward toward my breasts.

But he doesn't move to my breasts. He moves his mouth to the palm of my hand and then to each of my five fingers, kissing and sucking and licking. His movements are leisurely, unhurried, involving his mouth and his hands. Even the pressure of his body beside mine feels orchestrated, an orchestrated rallying of every inch of his body and mind to the stimulation of mine.

"Whoa," I say.

He's still kissing and licking his way down my upper arm to my shoulder. He puts his mouth on my armpit and kisses and licks, and I am astonished that an armpit can feel erotic. He kisses his way from there down along the outside edge of my breast, and farther down along my rib cage.

"I like that," I say. I'm flexing my spine restlessly.

"Good," he says quietly with that teachery-but-different tension in his voice.

And then he starts the whole thing again, this time from my foot up. Sucking my toes, licking and biting at the arch of my foot, running first his fingertips, then his palms, and then his fingernails over my calf, my knee, my spread thigh.

I had no idea that the sensation of a tongue rolling around and between my toes could feel instantly and immediately like heat and wetness against my clit, but that is absolutely what it feels like, and I roll my pelvis in response, breathing in struggling huffs.

"Holy crap, dude, how does that feel so fucking good?"

"Your homework for tomorrow will be to draw the somatosensory homunculus," he says with a wicked little chuckle.

"What?"

He doesn't answer. From my foot, his mouth travels up my calf, up my thigh—first along the outside of my thigh, up to my hip, then along the inside of my thigh, almost to my clit, almost. I want him to lick me. I push my hips down and whimper. He avoids me.

I try a direct approach: I say, "I want you to lick me."

"Good," he says.

And he stands up and moves away from the bed.

"Hey!"

I watch him walk leisurely around the foot of the bed to the other side. He sits beside my knee and leans over . . . and begins again with my other hand—each of my fingers, my wrist, the inside of my elbow, my armpit, down along the inside of my breast. He's still moving slowly, like he has nothing in the world to do but touch and taste my body. And I'm getting a little more impatient with every passing minute.

He turns to my foot and begins again there. He sucks and licks my toes. He runs his fingertips and palms and nails over my leg. He bites the arch of my foot.

"Fuck, dude, oh my god." I squirm on the bed and wish I could rub my own clit, rub my own breasts, but with my hands bound, all I can do is flex and arch my spine. His mouth makes its leisurely way up my calf, over my knee, and then up my thigh—first the outside again, up to my hip, and then at last, at last, up the inside, almost to my clit.

And then he stands up again.

And starts to walk away.

"Where are you going?" I call wildly.

He pauses, his hand on the doorframe. "To brush my teeth. I'm going to kiss you, and I haven't brushed my teeth since this morning."

"I don't care! You kissed me before!"

"I don't care that you don't care." He steps through the doorway, then looks back. "Don't go anywhere," he grins, and then he disappears.

And he literally does go brush his teeth, the motherfucker. I hear water running, hear his electric toothbrush. . . . I lie there, all my attention trained on the faint sounds of him. He strolls back in, bringing the buzz of his toothbrush with him, and stands at the corner of the bed, his eyes traveling over my body. I'm half-frustrated, ready to tell him I want to call it off, and half-wild with arousal. When his eyes meet mine, he raises his eyebrows and points—hilariously—to the erection in his pants. I laugh and roll my eyes. Then he strolls back out. The toothbrush turns off. I hear more water running. . . .

He comes back, toothbrush in hand. He leaves it on the bedside table and then kisses me thoroughly, his minty tongue in my mouth. I want to wrap my arms around his neck, but of course I can't.

His lips and the palms of his hands travel all over me then, making a gradual journey down my body. I make *mh* sounds and breathe into the sensations of his touch. The farther down my body he goes, the more I lift my pelvis up, calling for his attention. When at last he arrives at my mons . . . he stands up and walks away again!

"Hey, fuck you, buddy!" I call.

He laughs out loud. "Don't worry. I'm just getting the lube."

"Uh, pretty sure I don't need lube at this point."

He retrieves the lube and the vibrating Ben Wa balls from the dresser and begins brushing the lube onto my vulva with two slow, circling fingertips.

I shift my hips and groan. I raise my head to watch his face. "I get to come soon, right?"

He grins. "Maybe."

I give him a stern frown. "I hope you're enjoying this."

"I really, really am." He's brushed lube over every millimeter of my vulva and mons and inner thighs. "I want you to pay attention to how this feels," he says, and he's pressing the weighty little pair of Ben Wa balls gently against my vagina. He pushes and withdraws, pushes and withdraws, the way he did the first time we had sex.

"How is it?" he says quietly.

"Nice," I sigh.

"Do you want it inside you?"

"Yeah." I press my body downward, trying to push it in. The first bead goes in. And he turns on the vibration.

"Whoa," I say, and he tugs against the tensed muscle that holds the fat, heavy bead inside me. I squeeze against the pressure and draw the bead deeper. Through this delicate tug-of-war, he gradually lets both beads settle inside me, vibrating, pressing, slippery . . . and then, kneeling between my thighs, he slathers his hands with the lube and begins massaging my breasts, my ribs, my belly, with his slick, glossy hands while the toy buzzes deep in me.

I writhe, aware of a certain indignity and greed in trying, trying to get some direct clit stimulation when he's giving me gorgeous sensation everywhere else, everywhere but my clit.

"Charles, I want you to lick me."

"I know."

"Well, would you please?"

He laughs a little in response and then lies beside me, his whole length pressed against me, his clothes pressing against my skin, and he kisses my mouth. The beads buzz steadily inside me as his hand travels from my throat, over my breasts, down my belly, to between my legs, just the lightest touch of my labia, and my hips bolt up off the bed, my breath stopped as he kisses me some more.

Then his hand is gone, wandering with light fingertips over my body, over my armpit and arm, over my thigh, my hipbone.

My body softens gradually down into the mattress, beyond my volition. Every movement changes the vibration inside me, so tantalizingly close to where I want it, so achingly far.

"Charr-ulllles . . ." I groan.

He pulls away from me, sits up, and I arch again, harder, rising off the bed, and whimpering. Charles puts one warm palm low on my belly, just above my pubic bone, as my body lifts and falls.

"Tighten here," he says, and I do, my belly going almost concave in the pressure of my muscle contraction. Still I don't come, but I roll my body against the sensation and feel my arousal inch closer and closer to the peak. His hand travels over my moving body to my breasts, caressing them softly, a warm palm brushing over the desperately sensitive areolae, and then down, over my belly, over my hipbone, along the inside of my thigh, a light touch that jolts me, pushing me another level higher.

I gasp, and I open my eyes. I see Charles. It occurs to me in a flash that he's still fully dressed, while I'm not just naked, but naked, tied, and thrashing like a fish on his bed. He's sitting beside me, the remote in one hand, his hand on his knee. His posture is so casual and relaxed, his face so passive, almost sad, as he watches my eyes, and I'm lying here, writhing and berserk. I tug at my bonds. If I could move my legs more, press them together, I might be able to come.

He's still caressing me with one hand, his eyes on mine. "Okay?" he says.

I nod.

Without letting his hand leave my body, he moves to the end of the bed and puts his mouth on my foot, his tongue swirling along the arch.

I shout and I almost come; I feel my body at the edge. I announce this to Charles with a grunting chant of "Fuck. Fuck. Fuck" and with the rhythmic lifting of my pelvis from the bed.

With one hand playing softly over the inner curve of my thigh, and the vibrator still buzzing deep inside me, he wraps his hand, warm and rough, over my instep and bites gently at each of my toes.

I whimper. I writhe. I flex my toes, and he licks the tender undersides—and I come, blessed relief, the thing buzzing away inside me, Charles's hand gentle and warm on the inner curve of my thigh, and he bites the meat of my big toe, of the ball of my foot, of my arch. I cry out, a bouncing sob of noise. It's so big, it would hurt if I had any attention to spare for pain, but my body is all pleasure, all relief, and the sting of his teeth seems to mingle with and escalate the hard spasms of my orgasm.

It's an orgasm that just keeps coming at me, built up over all this time, all this indirect stimulation. It seems to take minutes to flow through me, and all I can do is surrender my body to it, let it have me. I don't try to control the noises coming from me. I don't try to control the reflexive way my head is thrown back, or the uncoordinated pushing of my pelvis and breasts toward Charles's hand and body and tongue, like water flooding over a dam.

At long, long last, he palms my clit, rubs circles directly over it, and the dam seems to break. I push and press and rub my body like a cat against his hand, moaning, "Yes, yes, yes, yes," with each movement.

Right as the pulsing begins to fade, as my muscles begin to ease a little and the flexing of my hips diminishes, he puts his mouth on my clit and sucks and licks in precisely the way I've been wanting him to. My hips rise off the bed as I shout with the sudden renewal of my orgasm. He props his hands under my buttocks and holds me, lifted off the bed, licking and sucking at the apex of my body, the two fat beads buzzing in me all the while. There's hoarse grunting coming from my throat, and I press my body against his mouth and rock my hips against his supporting hands.

My thrusting slows and the tension in my body eases and my voice goes quiet. His mouth changes to soft, open kisses on my vulva, on my thighs. He lowers me slowly to the bed and, still kissing lightly over my mons and thighs, he turns off the vibrator—though he leaves it in place.

At last he moves to sit beside me and he kisses me hard, and I kiss him back forcefully, lifting my body to press my breast into his palm.

"Jesus fucking Christ," I pant when he pulls away.

He doesn't say anything, but closes his teeth gently around my earlobe and lets his palm wander over my body, lets his rock-calloused fingertips scrape me.

"How are you?" he says into my ear, so softly that, even with his lips right against me, I have to focus to hear him.

"Awesome." I'm grinning, still breathing hard.

"Good," he says, and I can hear him grinning back at me.

"I've never had an orgasm remotely like that," I tell him. "That was . . . I mean . . . holy moly."

"Good," he says again, and I feel him laughing, his body against mine, his hand still wandering along the inner turn of my thighs. I feel faint stirrings of interest in my body, and I sigh into his touch.

When I masturbate, I almost never want to come more than once. But there is something about Charles that keeps the fire lit, even after I've come. And now, tonight, though my body has softened into relaxation, there's something warm still moving through me. Something curious and unsatisfied that feels his hand move and wants more of that. I'm astonished at how easily my arousal builds again as his hand begins to press and pull on my clit, as his lips move to my ear, and his teeth pull at my earlobe.

With his palm tugging upward on my clit and his fingers moving in fast, light circles, he whispers into my ear with hot breath and hot words. He's telling me to let it build, let it be slow, don't push, don't try to come, Annie, just let it grow inside you, and when you come, just say so, I want to hear you tell me you're coming, tell me I made you come.

I do as I'm told. My muscles begin to contract involuntarily, and I'm aware of the beads inside me. I clench around them as his palm moves on my clit. When my body convulses, I gasp, "I'm coming, Charles. I'm coming. I'm coming. You're making me come," until he kisses me.

He kisses me long past the end of the orgasm. I return the kiss lazily, a little worn already, though I like his kiss so much, I moan in pleasure as his tongue explores my mouth.

He brushes a hand over my hair, and then he kisses my forehead and gets up again. Rather than watch where he goes, I let my eyes drift closed. I hear him walk to the dresser and back, and when he sits on the edge of the bed, I turn my face to him and open my eyes. He has the blindfold in his hands.

Chapter 16

You Must Answer Me

"Eyes and ears," he says. He ties the black silk, folded in thirds to make a fully opaque covering over my eyes. No light comes in from anywhere. I feel him shift on the bed near my head, and there is stillness, silence.

"What are you doing?" I ask.

"Rolling up the earplugs," he says. And then the first one is thrust delicately into my ear, and I listen to the foam swell. Charles says, "Tell me when it's expanded all the way."

"It is," I tell him, and he puts the next one in. I feel his hand on my breastbone, resting warm on me, as I feel and hear the foam expanding. His hands roam over my breasts and throat. The darkness and silence have done their jobs—my skin feels hypersensitive.

Then Charles's mouth is right at my ear. He says through the muffle, "Can you hear me?"

"Yes."

"What will you say if you want me to stop?"

"Stop," I say. "But don't stop now."

"No. And if you want me to slow down?"

"Wait."

"Good," he says. And then his mouth is gone. It returns on my nipple, a surprising, warm, wet sensation out of nowhere. I groan and roll my shoulders, thrusting my breast up, deeper into his mouth.

"I like that so much," I say, my voice muffled to my own ears.

The sensation of his touch seems to change in the quiet, dark world I now inhabit. My own blood rushing in my ears, my own breath, uneven and heavy, these are all I hear. But I imagine I hear the slide of his hand on my skin. I imagine I hear the pop of his mouth as he sucks on my nipple, releasing it sharply. I imagine I can hear him groan with me when I groan, could swear I can *see* him watching me when he makes me come yet again, his mouth on my clit and his fingers tugging at the beads inside me.

He kisses me again after I come. I kiss him back, fighting the swamping fatigue. It's a losing battle. With his mouth against my earlobe, he says quietly, "Do you want to stop?"

"Do you?" I pant.

"That's not the question. Are you done? I need you to tell me. Shall I stop?"

"No," I say.

And he doesn't stop.

He seems to keep finding new ways to make me come. I lose count of the orgasms; they come more slowly, and they change. They get deeper, darker, not bright, pulsing star orgasms, but dark matter orgasms. I start crying after one of these big, dark things escapes me, and Charles holds me, though I'm still tied to the bed. He kisses the tears that leak from under the blindfold. He says into my ear, "I'm going to take this out," and then he does, gently easing the foam from my ear.

"What is it, sweetheart?" he says against my earlobe.

"I don't know. I'm just crying. It's weird."

"Want me to stop? Just tell me to stop."

I shake my head. "It's interesting. I like it."

He makes a harsh sound—it's the first evidence of the control he's kept on himself, and it shudders through me down to my clitoris. He says, "So do I." He kisses me, his hands in my hair, and I receive his kiss almost passively, too enervated to respond.

He breaks the kiss and mutters softly against my mouth, "Sweetheart, I'm going to make you come again, all right?"

I nod a little and make a noise of assent. "I'm not sure I can."

"You don't have to anything, my harpy. Just let me touch you."

"Okay. Um, wait. First can you—?"

"Yeah?"

"Can you take out the beads now?"

"Sure."

He does, gently, slowly. Then he replaces the earplug and moves away.

When he comes back, I feel his weight on the bed and then a vibration and cool, smooth plastic on my clit and realize suddenly it's his toothbrush. I laugh at this—and he kisses me. And then he's gone.

His hand is brushing, warm and light, over the insides of my thighs. Then his lips join his hand, his lips and his tongue. Tension builds in me again, almost against my will now, but I let it. I let him. I let him do what he likes, and I love what he does, I love handing my body over to him, just letting my body be open to him.

All the stimulation, all the sensations are focused intensely on about six square inches of my body, while so many of my senses and even my breath are muted and constrained. My attention closes in on the warmth and pressure of his hands, the intense vibration on my clit, the wetness of his mouth, and the fact of my surrender. I let everything else go. My body is finished, ready for a nap. If there weren't so much sensation, so concentrated, I might actually fall asleep. And yet I flex and arch on the bed, bowing my spine and pressing my body against his hands and face. I hear whimpering coming from somewhere, and I realize it's me. I don't even really want to come anymore, but I need to. My body can't resist moving toward orgasm again, like a mountain climber within sight of the peak, too exhausted to take another step, but too close not to march on. When I finally climax, it feels more of a relief than a pleasure.

And he doesn't stop. Though all my muscles are slack and I'm panting hard, he keeps up the direct stimulation. I don't try to make arousal happen, and it doesn't, not for a while, but I let him do what he likes—and I love what he does, and I love letting him. I love saying yes to him, love coming for him, love the sound he made when I said I liked it.

And the vibration is too persistent, too targeted, and the experience of having my senses removed, of having my body bound and fully available to Charles to do with as he likes, is too erotic, for me not to get aroused again. At last he pulls from me another orgasm, an isolated pulsing that drains the last of my energy.

I feel Charles's mouth travel gradually up my body, until he's lying over me, his weight supported above me. He puts his mouth against my ear. "Sweetheart, I'm going to untie you, okay?"

I make a small noise of assent, and he removes each earplug gently. He pulls off the blindfold. I don't open my eyes—it seems too effortful—but I let the light penetrate my lids, and I feel the air move over them.

Then he kisses me. This time I don't move my mouth; I just let him kiss me. With his thumb, he tugs my chin downward to open my mouth for me, and he kisses me that way. I receive his kiss willingly, but I really just can't kiss him back. I have drained myself dry—I have let myself be drained dry. I have given Charles everything I had. And I've never felt more completely satisfied with myself, with my body.

He's cutting the stockings with the scissors rather than undoing the knots. My limbs bend and soften as they're released, but I can't muster the energy to move them down.

And then he's over me again, naked now, and I can feel his bare skin along my whole body, feel his cock pressing lightly into me. I inhale deeply at the sensation of his skin against mine, and exhale on a hummed sigh.

He says, "Shall I stop?"

"Mh," I say, too lazy to open my mouth.

"Annie," he says in a sharper voice.

"Ngh."

"You must answer me. Shall I stop?"

"No," I whisper.

In an instant he's sliding into me, and I let him, my body softened and pliant under his. He tucks his hands under my shoulder blades, his hands on my trapezius muscles, so I'm braced against his thrusts as he begins to fuck me—hard. His face is against my neck, and he's making raw, rough noises. This is not my usual Charles. He's fucking me deep and fast, almost rudely, and I think, *I have made him desperate.* It is exactly what I wanted. I am elated. Exultant. And totally still.

"Annie." His voice is wild, broken. "Tell me to stop now. Do you want me to stop?"

"No," I say, managing a little voice in the whisper.

Another raw noise, and then he's kissing my face, kissing my eyelids, then kissing my mouth, his tongue thrusting around mine while he fucks me almost painfully deep.

When he comes, with the final three thrusts, he holds my jaw with one hand and kisses me wildly, hungrily, and I love it and I want to kiss him back, though still I can't muster the energy. And when his body collapses, he puts his forehead against mine, breathing hard over me, saying with each labored breath, "Oh my god. Oh my god. I can't believe . . . you let me do that. Oh, Annie. Oh my god."

He bites my lips and kisses me again, the palm of one hand on my forehead. I consider putting my arms around him, but all I manage is to draw my hands closer to my shoulders. He notices the movement and pulls away a little to say, "What do you need, sweetheart?"

"I'm a little cold," I whisper.

"Yes." Immediately he pulls gently, carefully out of me and away, leaving me bereft. I feel his hands take mine, one at a time, and lay them lightly over my belly. I feel his hands run down my thighs to my knees and push them together. First a sheet and then a blanket fold over me. His hands lift my head, and a pillow slides under it. Then he's lying beside me, on top of the blanket, smoothing my hair back with one hand. He kisses my forehead.

"All right?" he says. He's still breathing heavily.

I nod slightly but say, "My feet are cold."

I hear him laugh at this as he leaves the bed. My eyes are still closed, my lids far too heavy to lift, as I feel the covers move off my feet, and Charles puts socks—I think they must be his socks, giant and woolly—on my feet, one at a time, and then the covers fold over my feet again.

He lies back down by my side and, with his hand over my heart, warm and affectionate, he kisses the tip of my nose, then my eyebrow, then my temple.

"Time is it?" I mumble.

"A bit past nine," he says. "What else can I do for you?"

"Just stay here," I say as I slide into sleep.

I wake to kisses on my shoulder. When I open my eyes and meet his, he asks quietly, "Well, and how are you, my termagant?"

"Sleepy," I mutter, and I turn over.

I feel his wet hair against my temple, feel his breath on my ear when he says, "I have to go to work, sweetheart. Text me if you need anything, all right?"

"Mh," I say.

I wake again to find myself alone in the bed, the curtains pulled over the windows.

I check the time on my phone: 10:38. Jesus. I sit up and notice aches in unusual places. But I get out of bed, wander into the bathroom to pee, and then, led by the smell of coffee, make my way to the kitchen, where I find a note on the counter by the coffeepot. I stand there in Charles's hiking socks, reading:

Apologies for waking you. I had to run subjects this morning, and I didn't want to leave without telling

you. Text me whenever. Text me, call me, e-mail,
anything. There are no words, my darling termagant,
for last night. I am on my knees.

  C_{xx}

In a matter of days, Charles and I have traveled this far, I think to myself, from having A Thing to him on his knees and me utterly, totally surrendered to him.

And now we have to spend the next four days barely seeing each other.

Look, I love my parents. I do. But seriously. They're in the way.

I consider just telling them about it, being like, "Hey, listen, while you're here, I'll be spending my nights having brain-melting sex with this twenty-six-year-old English dude whom I'll probably never see again after June third, so you might just want to get used to that idea."

But no. I love my parents. We've been planning this weekend for a long time. It's going to be amazing. And part of what I've learned in the last few days is that waiting for something you want does not make it worse when you finally get it.

Before I leave, I write on the back of his note,

> *Hey,*
> *Woke up around 10:30. I feel GREAT. My parents*
> *will be here around four today, and they'll leave*
> *around noon Monday. Will I see you at*
> *commencement? Want to hang out Monday after*
> *they're gone?*
> *Me too,*
>
> *Annie*

Chapter 17

Charles Won't Let Me Fall

My graduation outfit is pretty sweet. In addition to the black gown, I've got cream and crimson fourragères on my left shoulder and a white tassel on my hat and a gold cord around my neck and a crimson Stole of Gratitude with the IU seal on it. Not bad for an undergrad degree, though it pales next to Professor Smith's regalia. She is a sea of black velvet bands and royal-blue velvet and pink and white satin and gold cording, and when I see her, I want a doctoral hood so much, I could die.

"Nice outfit!" I say. "Have you seen my parents anywhere?"

"No, not yet," she says, and we both look around, as if they might be hiding.

I told my parents I'd meet them here at the psych department reception right after the commencement ceremony, but they're late. They probably got lost. I'm turning my head to look for them when there's a tap on my shoulder. I turn and find Charles smiling at me.

"*Phwar*," he says with the same ridiculous grin I can feel on my own face. He touches the gold cord at my neck. "Get a load of this."

His regalia don't make any sense to me. They're scarlet and black, and there're a lot of them. The main thing I notice is that he's had his hair cut, so it's glittering at his neck, like gold, in the sunny, glass-walled foyer.

"No hat?" I ask, still smiling uncontrollably. I haven't seen him for three whole days, though he's been sending me torment-ing e-mails.

He holds up a flat, floppy velvety black disc and wrinkles his nose. "I don't like the hat."

I scan him, still trying to make sense of his regalia. His gown is open, and he's—good gravy, he's wearing a *suit!*

The ducklings always said it was a mercy to the world that Momma Duck never tried to look good. In his khakis and blue Oxford, even in his baby-puke-colored duffle coat, he's head-turningly good-looking. In a suit and academic regalia, he is jaw-droppingly, heart-stoppingly, panty-throbbingly beautiful. He is the golden image of ideal maleness.

"You clean up good," I tell him when my capacity to produce language returns.

"Not so bad yourself," he says. "I have a present for you, but I've had to send for it from home, and it's not here yet."

"You didn't have to do that!" I say. "What is it?"

"It's a surprise, ninny."

I stick out my tongue at him. He hesitates, glances at Professor Smith, and then—wonder of wonders—sticks out his tongue at me.

And just then my parents wander up.

"There you guys are!" I say, and Charles flushes pink. "Mom and Dad, this is Charles. He's the postdoc in our lab."

"Nice to meet you, Charles," says my dad, holding out a hand to shake. They do the whole manly-greeting-manly-men thing, Mom and Dad become Frances and George, and then Mom and Dad greet Professor Smith, who has met them lots of times al-ready.

"I was only waiting to say hi to your folks—I've got to get home and get off my feet," says Professor Smith.

"Oh, hey, can I steal you for a sec?" I say.

I abandon Charles to my parents and follow Professor Smith

out of the reception. I give her my stole. She hugs me and we both start to cry and she makes me promise to keep in touch.

"Thank you so much," I say weepily. And then I say it again. Twice. Because what else is there to say?

She says, "Annie . . . is there something going on between you and Charles? I don't mean to pry, but there seems to be . . . something going on."

"Yeah," I say lightly, and then I sniff. "It seems like we have kind of A Thing, but ya know." I shrug. "It's no big deal."

She nods and searches my face. "Okay," she says. "None of my business. Keep me posted on your travels, and let me know if I can help in any way. *Any way,*" she emphasizes.

"I will." I hug her again and say, "Thank you so much," again. Then I watch her waddle out of the building, and I sniff hard before going back to the reception and my parents and Charles.

Mom and Dad look at me affectionately when they see I've been crying. Dad gives me a giant hug and I say, "That was my first big good-bye," and I laugh and cry at the same time when Mom hugs me too, and I'm the cheese in the sandwich for the first time in almost four years, when they left here after helping me move into my dorm.

When I let go of Dad and pull my shit together, he says, "We were just telling Charles here that we're all having dinner together. I was asking if he'd like to join us."

Charles is looking at the three of us like we're aliens.

"It's just a cookout at Annie's, nothing formal," my mom says, as if too much formality might be what's holding Charles back from asking if he can bring the coleslaw.

"You're sure it wouldn't be inconvenient?" he says, glancing between us uncertainly.

"God no," I say. "It's us and Margaret's family too, including her girlfriend and the girlfriend's family, so there'll be a bunch of people." And then I add hurriedly, "But no pressure. If you've got other plans or whatever, don't worry about it."

"I'd be very glad to join you," he says, sounding sincere but not very glad.

"Great!" my dad exclaims. "We'll meet you there. Come on by just as soon as you like—we're all biking back to the condo now. Margaret's there with her family, starting the grill. I brought bikes with us cuz I bet Annie I can beat her in a race—"

"That's a bet you'll lose," Charles says easily.

"I dunno," I put in. "He's been spinning." Then I see the question in Charles's eyes and hold up a hand. "If you have to ask, you don't want to know."

He takes me at my word, nodding solemnly, with just the tiniest wink at me.

"So we'll see you there just as soon as you like," finishes my dad.

I win the race, spurred on by the nerdy pleasure of speeding across campus in my academic regalia, but it's close. Dad chases me the whole way—he's so close, I almost let him win, but I know he'd know, so I let him lose closely but honorably.

My mom trails behind and shows up at the apartment complex about ten minutes later, not even out of breath.

"It's such a beautiful evening," she says. "Why hurry?"

She helps me hang up my regalia, and then we join the party.

When Charles gets to the apartment, we're in the living room—Mom, Dad, me, Margaret, Reshma, and Reshma's moms—dancing and singing along to the Symphony of Science's "Ode to the Brain!" When neuroanatomist Jill Bolte Taylor sings, "We are perfect, we are whole, and we are beautiful," I actually get tears in my eyes.

"Yay for the brain!" cheers my mom the neurosurgeon when the song ends, and we all hug, all of us. Reshma's parents are both doctors too, and our families have bonded instantly.

Hashtag: nerdlove.

And then there's Charles, back in his blue shirt—the windowpane-checked one this time—a bottle of wine in each hand that he brandishes like a pair of nunchucks.

"Booze," he announces.

"Awesome!" I say. "Come this way!" I lead him back through the hallway to the kitchen, where I try to take the bottles from him to put them in the fridge. He'll only give me one of them.

"This one's red," he says, holding the other one delicately.

I roll my eyes and ask facetiously, "Does it need to *breathe?*"

"No, but it should be decanted," he says, suddenly awkward. "I . . . er, I brought a decanter with me, on the assumption you wouldn't have one." He gestures to the kitchen table, where a wide-bottomed glass carafe sits. Charles wrinkles his nose, looking abashed, and the bottom corner of his lip tugs downward. He says, "Am I a pretentious wanker?"

I retrieve a corkscrew from the drawer and say, "I think you can only call something pretentious if it's fake, and if there's anything I've learned about you in the last week"—god, has it really only been one week?—"it's that you aren't fake anything. You just legit *are.*"

"I just legit *am* a wanker. Thanks, Annie," he says with a grin, watching his own fingers twiddle with the decanter.

I want his eyes on me instead, so I move into his space and say, "What have you been doing for three days without me?"

His eyes meet mine, and he says, "Thinking of all the ways I haven't yet made you come." He looks at me in that way that makes my lips part.

"We could go upstairs," I say very quietly. I imagine it. I imagine leading him up to my bedroom, closing the door, and letting him do whatever he wants, letting him pull up my dress and use his hands and his mouth, anything he wants, all with my parents and my roommate and her girlfriend and her family in the living room, laughing and talking and playing more YouTube videos, while Charles makes me come, his hand pressed over my mouth to stop me from screaming my pleasure.

Charles takes one step toward me—

"They're about to put the burgers on the grill," says my dad, poking his head around the corner and into the kitchen. "You guys wanna place your orders?"

His eyes dart from me to Charles to me again.

"Yup," I say, turning to smile at my dad. "We'll be out in a minute."

"Okeydokey," he says with a cheerful wave. He leaves us alone again.

"Better not, after all," I say with a sigh.

"Do you think they know?"

"Thirty seconds ago I would have said no, but even my dad could probably tell what was going on when he walked in."

Charles nods and then wrinkles his nose to ask, "Do you think they mind?"

"Nah," I say, *thwapping* him on the arm. "They like you."

They do like him. Late in the evening, Mom, Dad, Charles, and I split the bottle of red wine between us. Margaret's and Reshma's families have gone home, and Margaret and Reshma themselves have gone out to Diva's. So it's just the four of us and this bottle of wine—which it took Charles about three hours to pour into the carafe while I complained, "See, this is why I drink wine out of a *box*."

Anyway, once we're all sitting around the kitchen table, Dad says playfully, "Thanks for letting us come to your party, Annie Bee. Does this mean you've forgiven us?"

"What's this?" Charles asks me.

"Oh, nothing, my parents just totally lied to me." I explain, "They said the way to choose a college was to look at the faculty and their research and choose someone I wanted to work with. Well, I wanted to work with Professor Smith—I saw these Web videos of her giving talks about neural plasticity, and I was *so* into it. It wasn't until I actually got here and talked to other students that I realized that's how you choose a *grad* school. Nobody chooses their undergrad that way!"

"We got our punishment for it," my dad says, "when you came all the way out here to Bloomington and we hardly saw you for four years."

"Do Americans usually stay close to home for university?"

"I don't know," I say, wondering. "I got accepted to a bunch of places nearer to home, but I really wanted to work with Dr. Smith. Mom and Dad had me totally brainwashed. And it worked out great because I've been in her lab almost the whole time."

"And the lab is better for it," Charles says, lifting his glass at me.

"So, Charles," my dad asks him in an "are your intentions honorable?" voice, "what brought you to Indiana?"

"The same thing that brought Annie, it seems," Charles answers. "Diana's collaboration with the School of Medicine allows me to do psychophys research with trauma patients most psych labs don't have the facilities to study. It was a great fit."

"Tell us a little about what you do," Dad says. Of course.

But then Charles starts talking about things I never knew about.

Now, he's in the third year of his residency, so he splits his time more or less evenly between whatever medical stuff he does and his work in our lab. Which I already knew. But I realize only now that I really know *nothing* about what he does when he's not reading my papers, writing his own, running subjects, running analyses, and organizing time sheets for us ducklings. When I've considered it at all, I've generally imagined him in a white coat, in a little room, feeling people's glands and writing prescriptions. That's kind of what doctors do when they're not surgeons. That's kind of what my dad does. And my mom is a surgeon.

But Charles is . . . like . . . a *therapist*.

I stare at him, slack-jawed, as he tells Dad about his clinical training in outpatient trauma therapy, and there isn't any medicine involved at all, it sounds like to me. Dad nods and asks questions in a foreign language—I catch *somatic*, but the rest is gibberish— and Charles answers like he's being interviewed for a job.

I turn to look at Mom, but she's looking at Charles, her chin in her hand. She blinks slowly, the way she does when she's half-asleep.

"Was it hard, moving so far from home?" she says suddenly, interrupting Dad. "We missed Annie terribly, and she's been only a thousand miles away. I can't imagine if she moved all the way to California or to Europe. Your parents must miss you."

"My mother comes to visit periodically," Charles says.

"That's nice." Mom blinks. "How 'bout your dad? You got a dad?"

"I do," Charles says gently. "He doesn't come to visit."

I jump in. "I bet it was weird moving to Indiana. I only moved from the East Coast, and it felt like I was in another universe. There were times when I'd go to Starbucks instead of Soma, just because it looked a lot like the Starbucks at home."

Dad follows my lead. "You did that, Anniebear? You shoulda said something, so your mom and dad could have mailed you some New York."

We talk for another half hour, until Dad notices Mom's slow blinking and drags her off to bed—well, to the futon in the living room—with a "Nice to meet you, Charles," and a kiss on the cheek for me.

Which leaves Charles and me at the kitchen table, alone together in the middle of the night.

"I'm afraid I've outstayed my welcome," he says quietly, with a soft smile. "They are *really* nice people, Annie."

"I know. Kiss me."

He does. And then he murmurs, his lips at my temple, "Wednesday night . . . was . . . beyond words. Incredible. Astonishing. The most erotic thing I have ever experienced in my life." He holds my face in his hands, his eyes on mine. He says in a voice so quiet, I have to listen hard to hear, "I'm not exaggerating, Annie. You wanted me to lose control, and I did. I've never known anything like it."

I grin. "So we can do it again sometime?"

He makes a sound, half laugh, half punched-in-the-gut. "Yeah, we can do it again."

I kiss him and smile. "Then I'll see you Monday."

And I send him home.

My parents leave Monday afternoon. I have brunch with them at the Uptown that morning, and for the first time they bring up the subject I've been waiting for.

"Charles is nice," my mom says over her eggs.

"He thinks you're nice too," I answer.

"Do you think he might come visit you in Boston?"

"What? No, I don't know. Why would he?"

"Oh. I thought you were . . . That you and he were . . ."

"Well, we kind of are, but it's not, like . . . I mean, we like each other. We have A Thing. We're kind of exploring The Thing while we've got the chance. But that's all."

"Oh," my mom says in the high little voice she uses when she's trying not to give me advice.

"Honey," Dad preempts. "She's a grown woman." He's been teaching her to hold back on the advice, and she's gotten good at not actually saying the things . . . but not at acting like she doesn't have a thing to say. Dad says, "Anniebellie, you should do whatever makes you happy as long as you're safe. Are you . . . safe?"

I snort with laughter. "Of course!"

"I'm sorry," Mom says. "I just remember how terrible I was at all the . . . social . . . things . . . when I was your age, and I get this feeling like I'm walking around under a tightrope, waiting with a net in case you fall."

"I won't fall—I'm not even on a tightrope. I'm totally on the ground." I check myself. "Well, maybe a balance beam. But I'm safe. Charles won't let me fall."

"He's so much older than you," my mother continues.

"Four years is hardly anything. It only seems like more because he's already done with school and I'm not."

"No, you're *not* done with school," my mother says seriously.

"Frannie, honey, let her be."

"But what if—"

"What if what? What if she doesn't become a doctor?" he says placidly.

"I'm definitely gonna be a doctor—" I try to interject, but it's really not about that.

My dad continues, "She'd still be our Annabelle and she'd still be our favorite person in the world and we'd still trust her to make the right choice for herself and her life. Isn't that right?"

I kiss him on the cheek and say, "Thanks, Dad. You guys are my favorite people in the world too."

He takes my hand and gets tears in his eyes. "Well, that sure is good to hear."

"How did we end up with a kid this great?" Mom asks.

"We earned her," Dad says with a sniff, and he returns to his eggs Benedict. "With every diaper and every dance lesson and every broken bone."

"I only broke three bones, and they were all in my feet!" I protest.

"Only three," my mother says, rolling her eyes.

We've already loaded up their rented car with about half my stuff, which they'll be storing for me for the next couple of months, so when we bike back from breakfast, all I have to do is wave them off from my front steps after lots of hugging and good-byes.

As soon as they're gone, I get my bag, I get on my bike, and I ride to Charles's.

Chapter 18

The Cranial Nerves

I wake to the sensation of his lips on the back of my hand.

I open my eyes to find him sitting on the floor next to the couch, where I'm lying with *Very Good, Jeeves!* on my sternum, my fingers wrapped around the spine. I had every intention of reading it when I lay down.

But now here he is and his eyes are smiling at me and I feel an arrhythmic pulse in my heartbeat that makes me take a breath.

"Hey," I say.

"Hey. Do you always sleep this much?" he says with a ridiculous grin.

"At the end of the semester, yeah. My body spends two weeks, making up for all the sleep I denied it for four months. Last December I flew back to New York, got right into bed, and slept for thirty-six hours."

"Thirty-six hours straight?"

"I woke up once to pee and drink some water, and then went right back to sleep. And I only know about that because my parents told me—I don't remember it."

"God."

"I know," I yawn. "But like you said, right? They don't give these honors degrees to just anyone." I turn onto my side to look directly at him. "I'm awake now. Is it okay that I just came over like this?"

"Oh yes," he says, and puts a hand on my shoulder to push me onto my back again. He presses one hand against the book, still resting on my sternum, and rests the other on the top of my head, and then he kisses me, our faces perpendicular. The kiss starts out soft and sweet, just a little more intimate than a hello kiss. But he lingers, his lips returning again and again to my mouth, like I'm the dessert he ordered that he's too full to eat but can't stop tasting.

"What are your plans for this evening?" he asks when he shifts to kissing my cheek and my ear and my neck.

"Well, I was kind of planning on having athletic sex with you for several hours, if that's okay."

He laughs.

Several hours later, naked and sticky in bed, Charles whispers against my mouth, "Four. There."

"There?" I ask with a lazy grin.

"One for each day it's been since you were here. I felt I'd been neglecting my duty."

He lies beside me, and I curl up in his arms, wrapping my leg around him too, limp and depleted and soggy with pleasure.

"Missed you," I say into his throat.

"Missed you, too," he says, and then he sighs into my hair. "Oh dear, oh dear."

"Huh?"

"Diana has given me a talking to."

"Oh yeah?"

"Oh yeah. She said you told her we have A Thing, but it's 'no big deal.' "

"Oh. Yeah. That happened." Then I flush, suddenly less sleepy. "God, she didn't think anything happened before . . . I mean, you're not in trouble. She knows you wouldn't . . ."

He shakes his head. "No, she was clear that she trusted me. It was more that she's worried I might be a miserable bastard who will break your heart."

"Really?"

"Really. So"—he shifts to look me in the eye—"let's get perfectly clear on some things, my harpy. I am your fucktoy for the month."

"Right now I feel like *your* fucktoy," I grin at him.

He raises an eyebrow at me. "Who's making whom come? I am at your service. I'll make you come, I'll give you any pleasure you like. I am entirely at your disposal to play with. And then we transition out of the parenthetical lover phase and into the permanent friend phase, yes?"

"Yes," I agree, tucking my head into the crook of his shoulder. "We worked all this out already. No miserable bastards, no broken hearts. Of course!"

"Right. And . . . while we're getting clear on things . . ."

"Uh-huh?"

"I'm . . . I have a confession to make. I should have said it sooner."

He stops.

I wait, but he says nothing.

I prompt, "Okay . . ."

"Er." He clears his throat and runs a hand through his hair. "That night when you passed out drunk here. Do you remember the lift?"

"Huh?" I say.

"I thought not. In the lift, you . . ." He pauses and gives an embarrassed half-laugh. "You were down to your knickers and that camisole thing, and you wrapped your arms round me and licked my neck and . . . I knew you were drunk, but . . ." He looks at me earnestly then. "I put my hands on the rail; I didn't touch you. But I didn't stop you, I knew I should stop you, but instead I kissed you back."

"You did?" I'm grinning apologetically at this, though he looks serious and stern.

"And then"—he rubs his forehead and looks at the ceiling—"after I put you in bed, I lay there on the couch and . . . oh god." He puts his palm over his whole face. "Christ, this is so embarrassing and awful. I imagined what it would have been like if I had fucked you in the lift."

"Uh-huh . . . ?" I'm expecting more. I'm wondering now if this is leading up to something bad, because he looks so guilty, so serious . . . but he stops there.

"What else?" I prompt.

"What do you mean, 'what else'? I'm saying I imagined . . . I lay on the couch, wanking to a fantasy of . . . to the thought of assaulting you. Isn't that enough?"

"I mean, did you, like, go into the bedroom and do anything to me while I was passed out?"

"God, Annie, no!"

"So that's it? Your big confession?"

He's still all wrapped up in his embarrassment. "I ought to have told you the next morning, but it was . . . You were—I just . . . Well, the right moment never appeared, and then . . ."

"And then we didn't talk to each other until—"

"Until the night you told me you were a virgin, and it just got lost in all the other . . . What are you smiling at? You don't seem to mind at all."

"Of course not. Why would I mind? I trust you. If our places were swapped, wouldn't you trust me to have been respectful?"

"It's hardly the same."

"Why not?"

I watch him struggle with himself until he finally stammers, "The fantasy—it doesn't . . . That's not . . ."

"Dude, I can't even describe all the crazy shit I've done to you in my imagination."

"Rrrrrright," he says, looking at me in fascination.

I say eagerly, "For a while there, my favorite fantasy was where I'd break into your apartment in the middle of the night and go down on you while you were asleep, and then when you were hard, I'd ride you, and you wouldn't wake up until I was already most of the way to orgasm."

"And what would I do when I woke up?" he asks with that same fascinated look.

"All kinds of things!" I enthuse. "Most often I'd imagine you had wanted me terribly—I mean, of course, right?—but couldn't bring yourself to approach me, so you were, like, *so* into it right away, and we just fucked each other's brains out."

"Okay," he says, and I laugh because it sounds like he's agreeing to a deal.

"Other times you'd be so devastatingly turned on by the surprise, by how sexy I was when you had never noticed before, that you'd just watch me and touch me and say my name until we both came."

"Mh." He half-grins at me. "Did you really think I hadn't noticed?"

"That was before we had The Thing," I dismiss. "Sometimes though—oh! Sometimes you'd be really mad at me, you know, like you'd want to *punish* me, and so you'd flip me onto my stomach and press me onto the bed with your hands on my shoulder blades, and fuck me really hard."

"I'd punish you with fucking?" He looks bewildered.

I shrug and grin at him a little shyly. "I dunno. It was hot."

"Right, okay. Punishment fuck. Noted."

"Anyway, other times you'd—" I stop, embarrassed now. I bite my lips between my teeth.

"What?" he nudges, grinning at my embarrassment.

"Well, there was this one time, anyway, when I imagined you weren't asleep at all, but you heard me come in and you pretended to be asleep so you could just see what I'd do. And I went down on you and rode you and came on you and you pretended to be asleep the whole time, and I slipped out, thinking you would never know what had happened. And then the next day at the lab you acted like you didn't remember anything and then—" I stop again and glance at him. "I can't say it."

He just raises his eyebrows.

So I wince against the awkward, take a deep breath, and confess: "And then that night, you came to our apartment while I was asleep and fucked me, I woke up with you inside me, and when I made a noise, you whispered that I had to stay asleep or else you'd tell someone what I did to you. And you'd come every night after that, and I'd pretend to sleep through it." I feel so ridiculous but also a little proud. "I told you I'd done crazy shit in my imagination."

He moves over me and pins me to the bed. With his lips against my ear, he says, "Miss Annabelle Coffey. I had no idea you had such a filthy imagination. You're a dirty-minded little girl and the sexiest thing I've ever seen in my entire life."

I squirm against him and bite his nipple, and he yelps delightfully.

We spend the evening in bed, not fucking, but playing—with mouths and tongues and palms and lightly scraping fingernails. He doesn't make me come again, I don't make him come again; we just share the raw pleasure of our skins. We talk about what we like, what we want to do in the next few weeks, what we're not interested in doing. I tell him things I like about his body, and he tells me things he likes about mine. We forget to eat until after midnight, when my stomach makes a noise so hilariously unerotic that Charles hauls me into the living room in my panties and his blue Oxford, and drops me on the couch, where I lie, listening to him make sandwiches in the kitchen.

He comes in with a tray, looking adorable in his stripy pajama pants, and he pauses when he sees me lying there. He blinks once, puts the tray down, and kneels on the couch, straddling my hips.

"Unbutton it," he says softly.

I do, slowly, grinning up at him.

"Show me how you touch yourself," he says.

I do. I tuck a hand under my panties and press the other against my lower abdomen. I keep my eyes on him, but he says, "Do you have your eyes open when you masturbate?"

"Not usually."

"Then close your eyes."

I do.

"Do you fantasize when you masturbate?"

"I do."

"Tell me your fantasy."

"Dude, *this* is my fantasy."

"Then tell me this."

"Um. I'm lying on your couch, and you're kneeling over me, watching me masturbate in your blue shirt. Hmmm, in my fantasy version you're naked and hard and masturbating with me—"

I feel him move off the couch, and I open my eyes to watch him pull off his clothes. He comes back, kneels over me, and starts stroking himself, his other hand gripping the back of the couch.

"What else?" he says.

I close my eyes again. "Um—" And I stop, my breath catching, because the actual fact of his watching me this way has pushed my arousal up, and my hips have started moving of their own volition.

"Tell me," he insists.

"Uh, you . . . mh. I don't know, basically this is the hottest thing I can imagine right now, you watching me this way. I want to watch you too. Can I watch you?"

"Yes."

I open my eyes to find his eyes focused intensely on my face, his hand on his cock.

He says, "Tell me what you see."

"God, you are fucking beautiful," I say. "You're—ungh—you're tall and strong and so much smarter than me and you're looking at me like you—ungh—like you want . . ." I close my eyes and throw my head back, mouth open.

"Don't try to come yet," he instructs. "Look at me. What else?"

I open my eyes—they only want to open halfway—and I tell him, "Your body is—you're so beautiful. I love how strong you are, the muscles in your forearms. I love how strong your hands are on my body. When you touch me, it's like, I don't know. It's like I lose all control over myself. I've wanted you for so long, and now you're here, I can't believe you're here, that you want me, that you're watching me this way, and all my body wants to do is come over and over. I'm ready to come, Charles."

"Not yet," he growls, and leans over me. He says fiercely into my ear, "Turn over."

I do, my hand still rubbing my clit.

He yanks my panties down around my thighs, pins me by my hair to the couch, and slides his cock into me with a satisfied little grunt. He rests his entire body over mine, sinking me into the cushions, and he starts to fuck me, so slowly, so slowly, the fingers of one hand tangled in my hair and the fingers of the other tucked under us, pressed against my hand on my clit.

"You wanted me to want you? I've wanted you," he says, his voice low, his breath on my ear. "I sat at your thesis defense, imagining you laid out on the table for me to lick and fuck. I imagined dragging you into my office and pinning you against the wall and fucking you without a word, without even kissing you." Though his voice is urgent, his words hurried and slurred, he's still moving slowly, desperately slowly, inside me. "The day you came to practice your defense and you kissed me. You remember that day?"

"Yes." I feel like he's drugging me. Still fucking me so slowly.

"I went home that night and fantasized about what would have happened if I hadn't stopped you. How I could have fucked you so quietly, Diana and everyone would never have known that's what we were doing. I could have laid you across my desk and had you right there. You would have done it."

"Yes."

"You would have loved it."

"Yes."

"You would have wrapped your legs around me and begged for more."

"Yes!"

He laughs quietly as he fucks me harder, just a little faster as he presses my fingers rhythmically over my clit, and I pant and huff and grunt. Gripping my hair, he puts his lips against my ear and says, "Do you want to come?"

"Oh god, yes."

"Not yet." And he pulls my hand away from my clit—I cry out in protest. He pins my wrists together above my head with one hand; the other returns to my clit.

"'Oh, oh, oh,'" he says into my ear, moving in me again in that leisurely way. "'To touch and feel very good velvet. Such heaven!' Miss Coffey, you will recite for me the twelve cranial nerves, in order, please."

"What?" I groan, and I press my hips back into him.

"I've just given you the entire mnemonic. Can't you remember?" And then he kisses me, deeply and slowly—and has to stop when he starts laughing. "Come on, I want to fuck you while you name the cranial nerves. Is that so much to ask?" He bites my earlobe and whispers, "Do it, or I won't let you come until tomorrow, and that's twenty-three hours away."

"Olfactory," I groan, and then add, "weirdo," with a grin, and he rewards me by pressing directly on my clit. "Oh, I like that a lot."

"Good. Keep going."

"Optic. Oculomotor. Um." I let the sensation of his cock moving inside me mingle with the sensation of his mouth near my ear and the hot, slick pressure of his fingers on my clit. When I hesitate too long, though, he shifts his hand away.

I whine in protest and move against him, inviting, but he laughs again, and prompts, "'To touch . . .'"

"Trochlear," I say, remembering suddenly, and his hand returns to my clit. "Trigeminal, abducens, facial . . . oh god." His hand is moving steadily now and firm over my clit. My breath catches.

But I've paused too long, and his hand disappears again.

I laugh at my own frustration and grumble, "Oh, fuck you! Shit. Very . . . Um, to touch and feel very . . . Oh. Charles, please." He's still fucking me slowly, the way you'd pet a cat that's asleep on your lap, and it's just enough to make me a little crazy, though it would never be enough to make me come on its own. And I really want to come now.

"Vestibulocochlear!" I enunciate.

His hand comes back, firm and steady.

Glossopharyngeal, vagus, spinal accessory, hypoglossal. He tortures me. He teases me. He wraps me in pleasure like a silk robe, and he ties it around me with his laughing exhortations, he binds me to him with the pure, easy joy of union. When I come, he goes still, lets me writhe and thrust against him, under him, and he bites into my shoulder.

He comes after I do, on my ass and all up the back of his shirt.

A shower and a snack later, he hauls me over his shoulder, carries me into the bedroom, and drops me onto the bed. When he gets in beside me and kisses me good night, I sigh, "Charles."

"Annie."

"I just want to say that right now, in this moment, I am *completely in love* with my own nervous system."

He kisses my temple. "Good."

"And you know what?"

"What?"

"I love science."

He laughs. "I love science too," he says.

Chapter 19

Hump the Rock

And then the next morning he tells me the most astonishing thing I've ever heard, in response to what I consider a perfectly reasonable question. I'm reading *Carry On, Jeeves* as I eat breakfast, and I ask, "Why are some of the Wodehouse novels notarized on the front page?"

Answer: that's not a notarization; that's the family crest, put there by—are you fucking kidding me?—the sixth viscount.

"What the hell is a viscount?" I say, aghast, pretty sure I know the answer.

"It's like a . . . It's between a baron and an earl, if that helps."

"Are you fucking kidding me? You're a *viscount?*"

"No no, my father is. It doesn't particularly mean anything much; it's essentially a bit of a family tradition, you know, like opening presents on Christmas Eve instead of Christmas Day."

"Dude, that is nuts," I tell him.

"Why? Lots of people do it."

"Not the presents, duh. The royalty whatever."

" 'I do not think it means what you think it means,' " he says in a fake Spanish accent, like Inigo Montoya.

"What, like, being rich and living in a huge house and having servants and basically wringing your bread from the sweat of other men's faces? I don't mean actual slavery, but, like, serfs and shit?"

"Exactly. That's what it doesn't mean. Certainly not anymore."

"So what does it mean, anymore? Did you grow up in, like, a castle and stuff?"

"No, no, nothing like that. Well"—he wrinkles his nose, and the left corner of his bottom lip tugs downward briefly—"a bit like that. But not much. There's nothing left at all of the estate, so there's really nothing but the title. But people treat it as if it means something, and thus, in effect, it does mean something. My father's an arsehole, and the title means he gets away with it. He uses it to bully people."

I am stunned. I stare at him and ask the first question that comes to mind. "Does Professor Smith know?"

He grins at me. "God no. Can you imagine what she'd say? Look, actually," he says, his voice more serious, "I haven't told anyone in the States, precisely because it's not something that really translates. I'd be obliged if you wouldn't mention it."

"Okeydokey, your lordship," I grin.

But he says, "I'd really rather you didn't do that. There are . . . awkwardnesses and embarrassments I can't joke myself out of. Can you understand that?"

"Can I understand?" I consider the question seriously. "Nope. No, I probably can't begin to imagine what it's like. But I won't tell."

"No," he says, and he gives me the fond, sweet smile I'm starting to get addicted to.

We sit in silence over breakfast, and then I ask, "So how come you told me, when you haven't told anyone else?"

He takes a sip of coffee and says, "These last four days while you were gone, I thought about what I wanted this experience we're having to mean to both of us. And I decided I'd . . . just . . .

let you have me, as it were. Give you everything you ask for that I was capable of giving."

I smile at this. "I'll let you have me, too. Anything you ask for."

"You've already done that." He smiles back and touches my hair. "Though of course if I resisted anything you wanted, you'd probably question and prod and push until I gave in anyway. If you look back on our recent history, you'll find I haven't been particularly successful at saying you nay."

"Me either."

His eyes go a little dark, and he raises one eyebrow. When he speaks, his voice has that teachery-but-different tone, and I'm left slightly breathless. "No. You are astonishingly generous with your body and your mind and your heart. I can't hope to match you. But I will try."

I kiss him lightly, then prop my elbow on the counter, my chin on my hand. "Is there a name that goes with it? Duke of Earl, Earl of Sandwich, Viscount of . . . ?"

"Not 'of' anything. Belhaven. He is the Viscount Belhaven."

"Dude," I say, and I bite into my toast. "That is fucking nuts."

"Yes," he agrees. "Totally fucking nuts."

I am not, by nature, a secret keeper. So when we climb that evening, and I meet his climbing group, I spend the first half hour stopping myself from saying, *Dude, you guys, Charles is, like, royalty and shit. Did you know?*

But one of the best things about rock climbing is that while you're doing it, you really can't think about anything else.

They're a cool group of people, Charles's climbing group, mostly grad students, all pretty experienced climbers. Some of them have only climbed indoors, but most of them tell me stories of climbing outside, on actual rocks. They clearly like Charles, though they don't seem to know him well, but then again did I, before all this started? I would have said I did, but I knew almost nothing. I didn't even know he was a psychiatrist. They don't either, apparently, though they know he's a resident in the medical school and so they talk to him about their muscles and joints, their injuries, their stretches, the biomechanics of climbing.

But they welcome me in an open, friendly way, and let me climb with them as if I've always been a part of the group. About half of them are women, and watching the women climb is a revelation. They don't climb at all the way Charles does, and finally I can see what he means when he says, "Climb with your skeleton." The women climb mostly with their legs, and use their arms for balance and leverage.

Even Tara, whom I belay on a *5.12a* route and who has shoulders like a gymnast and forearms like a bass player, gives this as her best advice: "Hump the rock." She has taken my T-shirt seriously—this one says, IT'S FUN TO USE LEARNING FOR EVIL—and is coaching me, on the understanding that I will use my new skills for world domination.

"Hump the rock," I repeat blankly.

She walks up to the wall, puts her hands on two holds above her head, and thrusts her pelvis forward against the wall. "Hump the rock," she says again.

"Well, okay then," I say, and she belays me on a *5.9* route. I hump the rock. It helps.

But I still can't make it through the whole thing.

When I get down, I thank her and hug her, and then I collapse on the mats next to Charles and take off my glasses. "'Upper-body strength, Coffey,'" I grumble, and I rub my hands fiercely over my sweaty face.

"Look, fuck that arsehole," Charles says. "It's not about having a particular kind of strength; it's about using the strength you have to get to the top any way you can. Everyone here climbs differently because everyone here has a different body that has different strengths and different limitations. Everyone's power, everyone's center, is somewhere different in their bodies. Yours is about here." He pokes a finger midway between my belly button and my pubic bone. "Tara's is here on her." He pokes his finger just below my belly button. "Mine is here." He pokes a finger right into my navel. "We all climb differently because of that element alone."

I'm pouting, I realize. But it's one of those times when I have to go with it. "I just hate falling so much."

"If you ain't flyin', you ain't tryin'," Tara says, joining us on the mats. "You don't want to fall? The trick to not fall is not to mind if you fall."

I frown at this, thinking. "So tip number one"—I count off on my fingers—"use the strength you have, and don't worry too much about the strength you don't have. Tip two, your center is your power, so know where your center is—that one I get. Tip three, don't mind falling."

"Tip four: hump the rock," says Tara.

"Right. Hump the rock. Tips two and four, I think I get. It's that third one that's tricky, though. Don't mind falling."

"Want to know the best way not to mind falling?" Tara says.

"Yes."

"Fall a lot," she announces.

And so that's what I do. I tie in to the 5.9 again, this time with Charles on belay, and I navigate the comparatively easy first moves. I've never struggled with these first four moves; I had them the very first time I tried this route. In a flash, it occurs to me that this is because they're close to the ground, and I know if I fall, I don't need the rope to keep me safe. I say this to Charles as I climb, and he says, "No shit, really?" which makes me laugh, but I don't fall.

The fifth move is where I start to struggle. The handhold is small, and my fingers just don't have the strength to pull me up on it. But I'm not supposed to worry about the strength I don't have; I'm just supposed to use the strength I have. So I pause on the wall, my pelvis pressed against it and my arms straight, and say, "I'm gonna try jumping for that foothold."

I try it. I miss. I fall.

"Nice," Charles says.

I try it again. I make it, but my foot slips, and I fall again.

"Nice," Charles says.

I try it again, I make it, my foot sticks, and I shift rapidly into the sixth move, practically pinning my pubic bone to the wall.

"*Nice,*" Charles says.

The seventh move is a motherfucker, and I fall four times before I get it.

When I do get it, Charles says, "Come back down a few moves and try the whole sequence."

I do, and then I finish the route.

"Nice," Charles says, and I'm so proud of myself and so tired and my arms burn so much, I halfway want to cry.

And I've forgotten all about the secret I'm keeping.

It's only on the drive home that I remember.

"None of them know about the prince thing?"

"The what? Oh, the, er . . ." He laughs. "No."

"Do you just get used to there being a thing you never say out loud?"

"Most of the time I don't remember there's anything not to say."

I look at him disbelievingly.

"Did you feel that by not telling them about your dancing you're keeping a secret?" he challenges.

"No, but that's not a secret—if they asked, I'd tell them."

"And if they asked me, 'Does your family have a hereditary title?' I'd tell them."

I blink and try to puzzle this out. "But no one would ever ask that, for the same reason that everyone would be, like, *so* interested in the answer."

Charles says, "Surely, there are parts of your life and your history you share only with certain people."

"No, pretty much I'd tell anyone anything." Then again, there's nothing much to tell.

"Well, you wouldn't let just anyone touch you, though, make love to you?"

"Of course not."

"Well, it's rather like that. Only certain people, people I trust, people I want in my life, get access to certain things."

"Hm." I think about this for a minute. "And I get access to everything?"

"If I have it to give, it is yours." He parks in the garage under his apartment building, turns off the engine, and faces me. "I want you never to feel I have denied you anything it was in my power to give you. What you—last week . . ." He looks down at the gearshift, searching for words, before he looks at me again and says, "You humbled me with your generosity and trust. I want you never to feel that I took anything I didn't return in kind."

"You mean Wednesday night?"

He nods solemnly.

"I don't understand," I say, tilting my head. "I didn't do anything. That was like . . . You're the one satisfying the other person as fully as they're physically capable of being satisfied, and only then do you pursue your own satisfaction."

"You don't think there might have been more to it than that?"

"Like what?"

"Like, maybe the most insidious way to control someone else is to give them everything they want, anything they want, until they can't stop you from taking what you want?"

I shrug. "Same difference."

"If you say so," he says, and I can tell he's humoring me.

We do it again that night, not as ritualistically as before, no stockings, no blindfold, just a silent agreement between us that I will come—he will make me come—until I physically can't come, can barely move. This time when he's inside me, he takes his time, pulling one last orgasm from me while he fucks me from behind, all four of our hands sandwiched together between my vulva and the bed as he whispers with hot breath on my ear, "One more. Just one more, sweetheart."

"You said that about the last one," I pant.

"I'm a cheat and a liar, my termagant, but you can do it. Don't you want to? Won't you come for me one more time? Just one more, sweetheart."

I do. I can, and I do, whimpering and thrusting against our hands, and then he fucks into me, those three wild thrusts, coming just after I do, pressing his lips against my hair.

Then he sorts me out—lays me gently on my back, pulls the covers over me, puts socks on my feet, and kisses my eyebrows. He whispers, "You are amazing, Annie. You are unbelievable."

Chapter 20

I Have Never Actually Read the Thing

For three days we each give 100 percent of ourselves.

We're not really spending that much time together. During the days, while Charles is at the lab or the hospital, I go back to my apartment to help Margaret pack and clean, or I read more P. G. Wodehouse. And Thursday and Friday evenings I have rehearsals for the students' dance recital on Saturday.

But at night, for those two or three hours, or in quick, urgent bursts in the morning, I simply turn my body over to him. I feel safe with him. I feel challenged. When I have the orgasm he wants me to have, while he pins me by my wrists to the bed and fucks me hard, his pubic bone pushing against my clit, I feel delighted with my body. When I masturbate while he watches me, or when I'm on top of him, when his eyes are on me with a look of leashed hunger, I feel beautiful. When I can be as still as he wants me to be, my hands on the wall and my knees spread on the mattress, while he rubs his hand on my clit and presses the head of his cock little by little into my lube-slick ass and he praises me, whispers into my ear that I'm amazing, that I'm the best he's ever had, that he wants me so much that he can't breathe, I come so hard, my vision goes dark and my head spins.

And I feel him trusting me with his history, feel him trusting

more and more of his weight to me. Before sex, after sex, sometimes during sex, he tells me about his life, his fantasies, his future. We talk about his research—which we've talked about
before, of course; I ran at least half the subjects for his last study.
But now we talk about *why*. It's partly because the science is so
cool, but partly because he witnessed the effects of trauma in his
own mother. His dad, the asshole viscount, was abusive to her.

And so for three days, he lets me have him. And I let him
have me.

And then Saturday afternoon: the recital. My ballet class struggles, my jazz class does great, and Amy, Paul, their mom, and I
nail our piece.

Nail. It.

The tech rehearsal Thursday night was the first time I danced
with the music—the kids singing and their mom on the piano—
and I knew for sure we'd be a hit. While I'm dancing, these two
cherubs are standing at the front of the stage, over to one side,
singing this beautiful sweet good-bye song. It starts with Paul
singing to his sister, "*Only me beside you, still you're not alone,*" and
becomes a duet, brother and sister singing in harmony.

Like I said, we nail it. Even if my technique is sloppy, I'm so
right there in the moment with them, celebrating my students,
celebrating my four years with them, saying good-bye, and all the
parents in the audience are totally there with me. They get it.
When these two kids sing, "*Hard to see the light now, just don't let it
go,*" they're right there with me. We're having this big Feelsies
moment, and I love it. There're four long seconds of total silence
when the song ends, then a thunder of applause, and I burst into
loving tears and grab up the kids in a giant twin hug. We curtsey
together—Paul bows—and then I hoist them off their feet again
and carry them, giggling, off the stage.

It takes me so long to say good-bye—this is my second big
good-bye, after Dr. Smith; I hug everyone, talk to every parent
and student—I'm not surprised to find that Charles hasn't waited.

It has started to rain, a light, cool sunshower, and I turn my face into it as I walk back to his apartment. I grin, knowing I'll be damp by the time I walk through his door, knowing how he'll feel about that. As I walk, I imagine all the things he might do to me, all the ways he might lick the rain off my skin.

But none of that is what happens. Not even close.

I let myself in with my key, and find Charles sitting on the kitchen floor, his hands raked through his hair. There's a rose wrapped in paper on the counter, beside a padded envelope covered in stamps. He looks up at me, his face bleak, when I come into the kitchen.

"Hey," I say. "Why are you on the floor?"

"Hey. Er. Your graduation present came," Charles says, indicating the package.

"Aw! You didn't have to get me anything." I pick up the package. It's obviously a book. I sit down next to him. "Is that why you're on the floor?"

"I didn't get you anything, really—it's just something I had that I thought you might like."

"Aw!" I say again. "That's even sweeter! Can I open it? Is it a tie? Is it a toaster?"

"Sure. Here, before you open it—" He hands me a dish towel to dry myself off.

I can't figure out what's wrong, so I just wipe off my face and hands and hair and then open the package. I pull out a book wrapped in brown paper. Under the paper I find a couple of layers of tissue paper and then the book itself. It is old and green. I read the spine—and drop it instantly on the floor and cover my mouth with my hands.

"Oh my god," I say through my fingers, eyes on the green cover.

"I considered *Sexual Selection and the Descent of Man* and decided it was too, oh, on the nose," he says. I look at him. He has half a sad, crooked grin on his face.

He's making a joke. I can hardly breathe, and he's cracking

wise with sex puns. I look up at him, my hands still clasped over my mouth.

"This is not a reproduction," I say. I sit there, stunned, not daring to touch the thing.

"No, it—"

I cut him off. "But it's, like, a third or fourth or fifth edition, right?" I look at him, desperate to hear him say it's not, not, not, not, not a first edition.

"It's a first edition," he says, and a corner of his lip tugs downward, the way it does when he's apologizing for being fancy.

"Oh my god." I'm hyperventilating now. I stand up. I can't even sit down in front of it. I press my back against the counter, my fingers pressing against my mouth, staring at the book, trying to breathe.

Charles looks a little worried. "Can I get you a glass of water or something?"

"*No!*" I yell. "God, don't put me and water in the same room with this thing, I'll just spill all over it and ruin it. I'll just ruin it!"

Are you religious? If you are, then you might have some understanding of how I feel about *On the Origin of Species*. It's a book that, like the Bible for many Christians, lays out a foundational system for understanding the nature of life itself. Unlike the Bible, it's amenable to the shibboleths of science, with elements being disproved, elaborated on, or otherwise made truer all the time. Evolution is, in my view, the most important scientific idea anyone has ever had, and this book right here, lying on the kitchen floor, is the book that first explained it.

And, like many Christians with the Bible, I have never actually read the thing.

I confess this to Charles, as I struggle for breath, my hands now on my cheeks, and he says, "Oh, you should. It's a blockbuster, a real page-turner. Though I would suggest not reading this particular one; this one's more for pretties than for smarts. Or go ahead—it's yours. Do as you like with it."

"How"—I gasp—"can I possibly accept this? What the *hell*, Charles? Wait, you said this is something you *just had?*"

"Yes, it's . . . It's from the family library. Sort of." After a pause, he explains in a rush, "The library was sold between the wars for tax, but the steward responsible was reluctant about it and so kept excellent records that have enabled me to track down and buy back a number of the more important . . . that is . . . And by 'I,' really I mean the agency. So you see, it's really just a book I had that I thought might give you pleasure. Look," he says. He takes up the book—in his bare hands! Like it's just a book!—and opens the cover. There's that large stamp, like a notarization, in the center of the blank page.

"Charles," I scold. "Don't be obtuse. A first edition *Origin of Species* isn't 'just a book' under any circumstances, and when it's part of your family's fucking . . . whatever . . . *ancestral* collection, that makes it an even *bigger* deal! And you're giving it to *me?* This girl you're fucking for a couple of weeks before I drive off into the sunrise?"

He scowls at me and says softly, "You are not 'this girl I'm fucking.' You're . . ." He hesitates and smiles a little. "You're *the* girl I'm fucking."

I give up trying to argue. I sit back down on the floor beside him, and I stare at the book. "It's the most beautiful thing I've ever seen in my life," I say. With my arms crossed over my knees and my chin on my arms, I gaze at the green-and-gilt cover and breathe, "Oh my god."

Charles watches my face. "I want you to remember," he says. "When all the other blokes come along, I want you to remember our time together, remember it fondly."

I turn my face to him. "You think I could forget? Have you forgotten *your* first person?"

"It was rather different," he says with a downward pull of his bottom lip. "It was years, we had. And it was the first for both of us. And we were younger and . . . I don't know. I have this dread that when you go away, you'll look back on this and wonder what on Earth you were thinking."

I don't know what to say.

"Please accept it, Annie. It would mean a great deal to me if you would accept the book and give it a good home."

"I don't deserve this," I say.

"Any less than I? What does it mean to deserve a beautiful thing? Annie, I don't hold on to things just for the sake of having them as my possession.

"Please," he says. "I want you to have it."

I shift on the floor and sit mirroring him. I say, "Ten years from now you'll be like, 'Why the hell did I give my *Origin* to that random girl?'"

He shakes his head, his eyes on mine. "Ten years from now I'll see you at a conference where you're accepting some award or giving the keynote and I'll think, 'That woman is a gift to the world. She is my friend, and for a very short time she was the most exciting and joyful lover I've ever had. How on Earth did I get this lucky?' And then you'll introduce me to your partner, and I'll think, 'Crikey, no wonder she tossed me over. Look at this chap!'"

He's teasing me now, but I can't smile. I scoot over to him and curl myself into his arms, hugging him around the waist. I put my head against his heart.

"Thank you," I say.

He wraps his arms around me and says into my hair, "This book is the scale of my appreciation and gratitude for what you've shared with me. It's . . . Well, it's rather selfish, in the end. I want it to be a thread that ties us together, even if it's just in memory."

"I'll keep it safe," I tell him. "I'll always keep it safe."

Chapter 21

It'll Be Like in *Frozen*

I look up at him. "Is the book why you were on the floor?"

"No," he says. "It was just in my mailbox when I got home."

"So why?"

He sighs and kisses my forehead, then disentangles himself from me and stands up. "Let's get off the floor."

I follow him to the living room with the book, which I place reverently on the coffee table, and sit at my end of the couch.

He sinks into his end of the couch with a vocalized sigh, and runs both hands through his hair. Then he takes off his glasses to rub his hands over his face. He puts his glasses back on and looks at me, smiling a lopsided, halfway version of that smile that melts me inside.

"You created a beautiful thing this afternoon," he begins.

"Thanks!" I smile. "My technique was pretty wobbly, but I feel like the kids and I really nailed the performance side."

He nods. "And that's why I was on the floor."

I nod, understanding. "Feels? All the Feels, right in the Feels?" I bump my fist against my chest.

"If that means moved beyond language, yes."

"Yay," I say. I clap my hands a few times and fold them over my heart. I snuggle into my end of the couch and tangle my legs with his.

"Nothing about it was an act," he says. "It was . . . really you, really saying good-bye, and those two siblings, really singing to each other."

I bite my lips between my teeth and smile. He got it, 100 percent. I knew he would.

He continues, and I listen. " 'Really you' is an extraordinary thing by itself. I think you're not aware of your transparency, of your . . . hm. The clarity and openness of your heart. That on its own was lovely and moving. But it was the mother at the piano, accompanying her children, that struck me particularly. The warmth and tenderness of her having arranged this music, practiced with her son and daughter, and then playing with them as they sang. It was an act of such obvious affection, such love."

He's silent for a long moment, so I say, "Yeah, their mom is totally great," to fill the silence, but it's a pretty banal comment in contrast with what he seems to be experiencing over there on his end of the couch.

"It—look, this is difficult for me to . . . I don't talk about these things, not with anyone, and I'm only saying it now because . . ."

"Because you're letting me have you," I say.

He meets my eyes. "Yes. So if you're not interested or don't particularly care, just say so and I'll shut up, okay?"

"Okay," I say, then add, "but I'm interested."

Haltingly, he says, "I found myself thinking about my mum and what it was like for her when I was that boy's age. I was off at school by then, of course. I left her with two young children and my father. You've probably put it together that my father was . . ." He stops and clears his throat against a constriction.

"You said he was an abusive asshole."

"Mh. He's quite cruel, in fact. And I left my mother alone with him, pretty much from the time I was nine or ten. I wanted my own escape more than I wanted to protect my mother. And so I abandoned her."

I tilt my head. "You feel like you should've protected her from him?"

He nods, his face tense against his grief.

"When you were, like, ten?"

"It's not rational, I know that. But the fact is, I left her there and forgot about home as much as I could for the next"—he pauses to clear his throat—"decade or so."

"Have you told her this?"

He shakes his head. "No point. She'd only feel guilty."

"Have you told *anyone?*"

He takes a deep breath before he says, "I've told you." He smiles at me fully then, the warm, open smile that melts me.

And this is the moment. This is when I recognize that this warm feeling of being at home, of being humble and proud at the same time, of opening my heart wide and letting this man in, of wanting to wrap him up inside me, of wanting to be wrapped up in him, this feeling has a name: love.

The recognition bubbles through me like champagne fizz, makes me buoyant with joy.

I'm in love!

I've never been in love before!

This is what being in love is like!

As I think this, he's saying, "Maybe the transparency I'm practicing with you left me vulnerable to this sort of, well, let's face it: self-indulgent self-pity. I'll be over it soon; I just need an hour or so to move through it. What do you want to do about dinner?"

I climb over to his side of the couch and straddle him, my hands on his shoulders. "Charles?"

"Mh."

"Can I tell you something?"

"Sure." He puts his hands on my wrists.

"You know this Thing we have? The Thing I wasn't wrong about?"

"Yes, I am quite familiar with The Thing." He's looking at me with a lazy half smile and hooded eyes still clouded with pain.

"Well, I've had an *amazing* insight regarding the nature of The Thing."

"Oh yes?"

"Oh yes! It turns out: it's not just A Sex Thing; it's actually A Love Thing. Somewhere in the middle of all this sex, I've fallen in love with you." I say it joyfully, with a wide grin.

But the grin doesn't last long.

I don't know what word would describe the expression on Charles's face. Shock? Sure. Appalled? Maybe. Horrified? Definitely nothing along the lines of joyful or loving. He takes his hands away from mine and looks from the door to the window, like he's looking for an escape route. Then he takes off his glasses and rubs his hand over his face again.

There's something cold doing somersaults in my stomach.

I climb off his lap and say, "Okay, wow, now it's awkward. I thought this was good news."

"Oh god, Annie."

" 'Oh god' what? What did I do? Did I screw up? What's wrong?"

"We agreed—no broken hearts."

"My heart isn't broken."

He just looks at me blankly.

But I'm not wrong: my heart isn't broken. It doesn't even hurt. It feels happier and healthier than ever before in my entire life.

I curl up at my end of the couch and say, "So I . . . I mean, no pressure or anything, I'm just asking for a clarification, but it's sounding like you definitely don't love me. Is that . . . Is that right? I mean, it's cool if it is. I just want to know."

"Jesus Christ, Annie," he groans.

"Because I have to say it does actually *seem* like you kind of love me. I'm not sure I'd feel like I loved you if I didn't also feel like you loved me."

"Are you going to stay in Indiana?" he asks, clearly trying to be patient. "Not go to Boston?"

"No," I say, crossing my arms.

"Do you expect *me* to leave and follow you?"

"No."

"Then what is it you have in mind, exactly, as a nonheartbreak ending to our little liaison, if it's 'A Love Thing'?"

"I don't know. I didn't think about that."

"You didn't think at all," he mumbles. Then he adds, "Sorry. Rude. Sorry."

"No, I *didn't* think—I felt. I said it because I felt it. Because it's true. Because I wanted to share it with you. I just . . . felt it and wanted to say it." I pause and frown at him. "Did I ruin everything?"

He sighs hugely. "No, you didn't ruin anything, Annie. It's my fault. I should have known this was . . . I should have been more . . . Ah, fuck." He wipes his hands down his face and up again, then grips his fists in his hair.

Well, fuck me. What did I think was going to happen? Did I expect him to say, "I love you too" and throw his arms around me and love me passionately for two weeks and then wave good-bye to me as I drove away? Did I think he'd decide he wanted the long-distance relationship with me that he didn't want with Melissa, whom he was with for more than a year?

I didn't think anything. I just felt it, so I put it on the fucking table.

Like bread.

Fuck.

"Everything *is* ruined, though. Is that what you're saying?"

"I don't know. It can't be just sex now, can it." A statement. Not a question. A shield.

"It was never just sex," I say, stung. "You said it yourself. We're friends, too."

Charles sighs again, and I watch him deflate. "Yes," he says. "Yes, Annie, we are friends. I hope we can stay friends after all this is over."

"Well, then what else is there?" I insist, leaning forward. "Friendship, great sex . . . What else is there to love?" I'm still arguing with him, even though I can feel he has given up arguing with me. It feels like punching a half-inflated Bobo doll.

"There's . . . Annie, there's how you feel about a person, and then there's the kind of relationship you can have with them. You don't know me very well, and you don't know anything at all about relationships—you've never had one. I have, and what I've learned is that I can't. It's not that I don't want to, and it's not that I wouldn't prefer it if I could. It's that I'm not built that way. Surely, that's been—no, I suppose not."

I feel arguments rise up inside me: I think you *are* built that way! How do you know if you don't try? What hasn't worked with other people could work with me, because I'm . . . But I stop. What am I? Am I magical? Am I the girl who opens men's hearts? No. I'm smart and I work hard, but are those the attributes of a woman men fall in love with? Hardly. I'm not pretty or alluring. I'm not a girl guys feel that way about.

I don't say any of this out loud, but I give up too. I stop arguing. He said no, and that's that. So I sink back on the sofa and say, "Okay."

"Fuck, Annie," he says, and he rakes his hands into his hair yet again, his eyes closed.

I bunch up my lips against the sting of tears, swallow, and when I get control of my voice, I say, "It's okay. I get it. It's no big deal."

"You will insist that these things are no big deal, these enormous gifts you give me that I can't possibly deserve. My inability to accept them graciously is proof only of my unworthiness, not of yours."

"It would help . . ." I begin. I battle the stinging in my nose and eyes, and then try again. "It might help if I understood *why*. Like, if it's about my lack of pretty or—"

"Sweetheart, it has nothing to do with you—"

I roll my eyes. "Oh god, seriously, you're going to say, 'It's not you, it's me'?"

"Annie," he spits. And then he seems to talk to himself more than to me: "Right. Let you have me." He sits, knees crossed, one elbow on the back of the couch and his palm over his eyes, as he says, "So, look. When I was six, I watched my father beat my mother with the butt of a rifle, while explaining to her why it was her fault he had to do it. And then later I listened to my mother repeat those reasons to me, explaining to me that it wasn't *my* fault; it was her fault. For a while I thought she was trying to protect me from the reality of it, but now I know she believed him. She *believes* him." He stops and looks out the window at the rain. "It's taken me rather a long time to forgive her for that—and to forgive myself for blaming her, when it was no one's fault but his.

"My father is a monster, as bad as men come," he says, looking directly at me now. "And I have that monster inside me. And part—"

"What? No, you don't. You would never do something like that."

"When I was eight, I beat the shit out of another boy—he was smaller than me and he had no friends and I decided I could make myself feel bigger if I picked on him. I had all this rage and I just . . . I split his lip and broke his nose. After I knocked him down, I told him—" Charles stops and grimaces. "I've never told anyone this. It's the worst thing I've ever done. Worse, maybe, than beating on him is what I said to him. I told him he wasn't allowed to tell anyone it was me because I was a peer of the realm. Oh god, what a horrible, entitled little shit I was." He rubs his palm against his forehead and adds, "Am."

And then he continues, "Of course he did tell, and when my mother heard about it, the way she looked at me . . . It was how I saw her look at my father. Cowed. Afraid."

"Afraid of a little boy?"

Charles nods. "So, in my eight-year-old wisdom, I shoved the monster into a deep well and locked him in, but I notice him quite regularly—he's beating on the door right now as a matter of fact." He stops, his jaw tight, and swallows twice. He says mildly, "I hate talking about it. I sound schizophrenic."

"Duh, it's a metaphor. I know you don't think there's a literal monster inside you."

He gives a tiny, embarrassed laugh, his face splotchy with emotion. "Thanks," he says.

"Well, I'm not afraid of your monster," I say.

"You should be," he says in a choked voice.

"Why? The monster is eight years old!"

And Charles laughs, surprise easing his tension. "I hadn't thought of it that way," he says. "That might be true."

"Only one way to find out," I declare.

I'm pretty sure what's going to happen next is he's going to free the monster, and therefore free himself from his fear of the monster, and it'll be like in *Frozen*, where the answer—spoiler—is love, and everything spontaneously turns into springtime.

That is not what happens.

He says, "Anyway, I'm telling you this because the consequence is a broken attachment system. You've learned about attachment?"

"Um, a little . . . Kids and parents, stability, love, that stuff?"

"Yes, that stuff," he says with a grim smile. "I can only go so far before the thing simply shuts down. I didn't notice until I was at university and in a relationship and I just . . . didn't fall in love with her. I had an idea how I was supposed to feel, and I acted as if I felt it—sometimes I even believed I felt it—but she could have walked away at any time in our two years together, and it would scarcely have bothered me."

"Huh," I say. "You preemptively broke your own heart."

He pauses and looks at me, wearing a sad, crooked grin. "I hadn't thought of it that way," he says for the second time, I note.

"But you don't—"

He shakes his head. "You can't understand—and I'm glad. Growing up with George and Frances, how could you?"

"I do understand. You're saying the only way for you to fall in love is to become friends with your monster."

He looks at me, looks at the floor, is silent for a full minute, and then he says, "Jesus, Annie."

"Is that a yes?" I am proud of myself for sitting there in silence for a whole minute while he thought about stuff, but I am getting impatient now. I feel like we're closing in on the answer, and I'm ready to wrap this up.

He doesn't answer; he just looks at me, a frown on his lips and a ghost of that heart-tugging smile in his eyes.

"Yes?" I prompt again, testy now.

"Yes," he whispers.

And so I pounce: "Well, then maybe this is the time to choose a different way of dealing with the monster."

"It's not about choosing, Annie," he sighs. "It just doesn't happen. The mechanism is broken and irreparable."

"There's no such thing as irreparable," I say.

Charles rolls his eyes with a smile. "Americans. Isn't their endless optimism charming."

"You can change anything you want to change," I say earnestly.

He looks at me blankly for a moment—and then laughs. A simple laugh of genuine amusement. He pinches the bridge of his nose, eyes closed, and laughs like I've just made a joke. Which pisses me off.

"What? What's so funny?"

"I'm sorry, Annie. I'm not laughing at you. It's just—do you suppose I've concluded that this is a perfectly satisfactory state of affairs and decided not to change? Or that it didn't occur to me? Or that I haven't tried?"

"Yes, I do!" I say, which isn't literally true, but I'm annoyed he's not taking me seriously when I'm working so hard to solve this. "I think you kind of like your little story about the poor little rich boy with a mean dad, who almost became an asshole, so he broke himself in half. It means now you get to be all distant and not risk anything."

"You don't mean that," he says quietly.

"I do!"

His jaw tightens. "Then grow up."

I feel like he's just slapped me.

He sees the look on my face and makes a noise, half growl, half shout, and puts his hands in his hair—which is sticking straight up from his head by now; he'd look adorable if he weren't acting like such a douche—and closes his eyes. "Sorry. That was a dickish thing to say."

"Are we done here?" I storm. "With this fight? I feel done."

"Sure."

I get to my feet. "I'm going home."

He leans back on the couch, sighing heavily, and says, "I don't blame you. Need a lift?"

"Why would I want you to give me a ride? We're *fighting*."

"What does one have to do with the other?" he asks.

I stare at him dumbly.

"You're a friend, no less because you're angry with me, and if you don't want to bike home in the rain, I'm not going to refuse to drive you just because we're in the middle of an argument. I'm fucked up, but I'm not a *complete* arsehole."

See, that's him. The man I love and the reason I love him. He's there with what I need. No matter what.

I throw myself back down on the couch, pouting, and say, "When I was walking back from the recital, I thought we were gonna have amazing, fun sexytimes because I was all wet, and instead there's this book"—I gesture at *Origin* on the coffee table—"and then there're my feelings"—I wave my hand up and down in the vicinity of my heart—"and there's your monster"—I gesture toward him—"and . . . what the *hell*, basically."

"What the hell, indeed." And he chuckles.

"I don't see how you can laugh!"

"Practice," he says gently from his end of the couch, and he gives me the soft, warm smile that strips me bare.

Chapter 22

Done with the Talking Part

It's still raining, so I accept the ride.

When he drops me at my front door, and before I get out of the car, I ask, "Did you pick a fight so I'd leave?"

He takes the question seriously, thinking before he says, "Not deliberately."

"Okay. I'll call you tomorrow."

"Okay."

I spend the night alone. I consider calling my parents, but then I remember that less than a week ago I said I was on a balance beam and Charles wouldn't let me fall, and I'm not yet ready to say I was wrong.

Margaret isn't home—she's in Indy with Reshma for the weekend, and when I text her, she doesn't text back. Anyway, she's not home, so I can sob as loud as I want.

It doesn't help that it rains all night.

In the morning, I check my phone—no new texts, no missed calls. I check my e-mail—ah. The subject heading is *mea maxima culpa*, and the full text of the e-mail is this:

doi: 10.1037/h0032843

I copy and paste the number into Google Scholar and get:

Suomi, S. J., & Harlow, H. F. (1972). Depressive behavior in young monkeys subjected to vertical chamber confinement. *Journal of comparative and physiological psychology*, 80(1), 11.

I read the article.

Then, over the next twenty-four hours, I read the twenty-five articles that this article cites, followed by the thirty articles that cite this one. In short, in one day I develop a minor level of expertise on the effects of long-term isolation on primate attachment.

It is so.

Much.

Worse than the trauma research Charles pointed me to back in April.

Imagine being trapped at the bottom of a metal-walled well and trying and trying to get out and never being able to get out and never seeing anyone, just having food and water delivered without ever having contact with anyone.

Just try to imagine the despair of being trapped forever, hopeless and abandoned.

That's what they did to the monkeys. They broke the monkeys—some of them permanently—for science. Harlow actually called the vertical chamber "the pit of despair."

I go for two long runs, just to burn off the horror. I run through parks and neighborhoods, splashing through puddles left by the rain, which has mercifully dried out into a hot, sunny day. I blast Sondheim in my headphones as I run.

On Monday, after the second run, I reply to his e-mail this way:

Suomi, S. J., Delizio, R., & Harlow, H. F. (1976). Social rehabilitation of separation-induced depressive disorders in monkeys. The American Journal of Psychiatry.

He answers immediately:

Would you like to talk, or would you rather I die in a fire?

I write back:

Can you come over?

Tonight after work? I'll text you when I'm on my way.

I'm standing at the open door when he arrives, and I watch him walk toward me, this beautiful man, this brilliant, tender-hearted person I've fallen in love with. It's the stripy blue shirt today, crumpled from a day's wear, the cuffs rolled halfway up his forearms.

The words are on my lips. *I love you.* But I hold on to them. That lesson I learned.

When he gets to my door, we look at each other, search each other's eyes—search for what, I don't know—and then simultaneously we open our arms and fold ourselves together. We stand there, holding each other, feeling each other breathe for I don't know how long.

Charles is the first to speak. I feel the preparatory inhale, and then, without moving, he says, "I'm sorry, Annie."

"Don't be sorry."

"I never wanted to hurt you."

"You didn't."

He shakes his head. I feel his lips against my scalp, feel his lungs expand and contract in an enormous sigh.

It's me who pulls away first. "Let's go in."

He follows me through the kitchen and into the living room as I explain what I've been doing for the last day and a half. I wave him to the futon as I conclude, "So I'm pretty much caught up on the theoretical side of things, I think. You're saying the eight-year-old monster's been trapped in a pit of despair all this time?"

"That's the short version."

"Well," I say when we're sitting on far ends of the futon, "now not only am I not afraid of him, I want to rescue him."

"That . . . Fuck." He sits back and shakes his head. "I should have anticipated that."

"What did you expect?"

He faces me, blinks. "I expected you to give up."

I make a scoffing noise through my teeth. "Yeah, that's something I'm good at."

He grins at me. "What was I thinking?"

"I don't know, but you weren't thinking about *me*."

"No," he says quietly. "I suppose I assumed *anyone* would see it my way. And of course you don't."

"Of course I don't," I agree. "I see it as changeable, and you see it as permanent. And now I have evidence that my hypothesis is plausible."

He rubs his fingertips against his eyebrow. "Suomi et al, 1976," he says. "Forty-year-old research against my two decades' experience living with it?"

"All that says is you've been doing it wrong."

He lets out a "Ha!" half laughing and half, I think, offended.

"I don't think you were doing it wrong on purpose, but you were a little kid, and no little kid in a fucked-up family is gonna fix their own broken heart! And by the time you got to be a grown-up and could really work on it, you were stuck in all these old patterns."

"Oh god, you want to 'fix' me," he says, sounding resigned. "Of course. What an idiot I am not to have seen that coming."

Well now, I know enough about relationships to recognize that you can't actually fix another person, and you should neither need nor want to, or else the relationship is just inherently dysfunctional.

I know that.

I do.

But Charles is so amazing. Have you noticed how amazing he

is? He's smarter than smart, he's kind and generous and thought-ful; he's so beautiful, in body and spirit. He deserves for this monster thing to be healed. Even more, he deserves not to have had it broken in the first place, but I can't go back and change that for him. All I can do is give him everything I have in the two weeks we have left. He has already given me so much. Surely, I can do something for him.

So I say, "I want to *try*, anyway."

With his elbow on the back of the couch and his fist propped against his temple, he looks at me and says, "My termagant, I'd rather you simply take me as I am. Can you do that?"

I'm not an idiot. I know I should accept people as they are. And I do accept Charles—no, I fucking *love* him—as he is.

But I feel like he could be so much happier if he—

Fuck. Shit. I'm a liar. I mean *I* could be so much happier if he—

I want to throw myself into his arms and kiss him and tell him how much I love him, and I want the dam to break and for him to say he loves me too, for him to feel about me what I feel about him. I want to be to him what he is to me.

But he doesn't love me. And he doesn't *want* to love me. He's asking me not to try to make him love me.

He doesn't love me, and he doesn't want to love me.

He said no. That's it.

Which is fine.

I clap my hands over my mouth as I start crying.

"Oh, Annie," Charles says. He moves closer to me, takes my free hand and holds it as I curl my knees up and press my fore-head against them. He's calm and still, full of compassion, as the grief moves through me.

The tide ebbs after a few painful minutes, and I sweep my heart clean with a few huge breaths. Then I get up and get a box of tissues. After I mop up my face and blow my nose, I sit close beside him. He puts his arm around me and pulls me closer, holds me against his chest, his knees crossed toward me, his lips on my hair.

"Ready to talk?" he says.

I nod.

"All right. Let's get clear on what it is we disagree about." His voice is soft and slow, like his teacher voice, but like a teacher reading a very serious bedtime story. "Your claim is that the monster can be safely freed from the pit of despair, thus healing my attachment mechanism. And you want me to do that."

I nod again. "I guess, technically, I want to be able to do it for you, but I already know that's impossible."

"Right," he says, nodding. "And my claim is that freeing the monster would result in very bad things and it wouldn't help anyway, because it's a permanent, irreparable break. And I want you to accept that."

Nod. Sniff. "I do, but—"

He squeezes me and interrupts, "But me no buts."

"But you what?"

"Acceptance means without condition."

I make a frustrated noise and grip my hand onto his shirt—then I notice what I've done and let go, smoothing the fabric under my palm.

He continues, "In short, we have gotten ourselves into a terrible mess. And now we're searching for a path through the next two weeks that involves the least possible suffering. So. What do we do, young Coffey? Should we simply not see each other?"

"No!" I say, horrified.

He kisses the top of my head. "I agree. That's not the least suffering for either of us. So. What else?"

"I don't know," I sigh. "If we each wanted things we could control ourselves, that would be okay, but we both want things that the other person controls."

"Mh-hm," he says.

"So we should each do something that we can control."

"Agreed."

"And we should also each do something that helps the other person feel less shitty. I feel shitty. Don't you feel shitty?"

"I do, yes."

"Well . . . how about . . . What if I try to accept your thing—which is what you want—while you simultaneously try to change it—which is what I want? For two weeks?"

He laughs quietly and squeezes me again and says, "That is brilliant and hilarious. Annie, that's—that is exactly the sort of—" He's still chuckling when he puts his hand on the side of my face and pulls back enough to kiss me once on the lips. "Exactly the sort of perverse thinking"—he kisses me again—"that I adore about you." And again, on the cheek. "Utterly logical." On my eyebrow. "Makes no human sense." On my temple. "But precise." On my earlobe. "Pristine reasoning." And then he scrapes his teeth on my earlobe and whispers to me, "You are astonishing, Miss Coffey."

I move my mouth to his and kiss him as if I haven't kissed him in years—wild, starving, desperate for more, now.

"Hang on, Annie," he says eventually, trying to extricate himself from my arms and legs, which are twining around him. "We have to talk about—"

"I'm done with the talking part for now," I say, my hands busy on his buckle.

"Okay," he says, and he surrenders himself to me.

I open his pants, pull off my sweat pants, and straddle him, letting him guide me down onto him. He kisses me while I move on him, and he runs his hands over my body.

"Annie," he grunts, and he turns us on the futon, lays me on my back without ever pulling out, and fucks me in the deep, steady rhythm, his pubic bone against my clit, that he knows will make me come.

And Margaret walks in.

I mean, of course she does, right?

She walks right back out again with a, "Whoa, sorry!" but we can hear her cackling laughter in the hallway.

We might as well also hear a cartoon brakes-squealing noise. And a sad trombone.

"Oh my god," Charles groans.

"Woops," I say, flushing with embarrassment, my arousal dissipating as fast as it came.

We separate. We reassemble our clothes, catching Margaret's contagious laugh, which has been joined by Reshma's. We hear them whooping in the kitchen.

"What do we do now?" Charles asks, pink and grinning against his will.

"We go in there and say hi," I say. I drag him by the hand into the kitchen.

Margaret and Reshma burst into fresh peals of laughter when they see us. Tears are running down Margaret's face. "Straight people sex is so *weird*," she says in a strained, high voice. She waves her hands at us. "I'm sorry, I'm sorry! It's just such a"—she gasps—"such a surprise . . . to see Momma Duck's ass." She breaks down into helpless giggles again, her hands folded over her mouth.

Poor Charles is the color of a strawberry now. He puts a hand over his eyes and mutters, "Oh god, save me."

I intervene. "Margaret, if you want Charles's help moving on Saturday, you have to get over it and apologize for laughing at his ass."

"Am I helping Margaret move on Saturday?"

I put a soothing hand on his arm. "Didn't I ask yet? Yes, I'd like you to help us move Margaret to Indy on Saturday." I turn and scowl at Margaret. "If she can get her shit together."

"I'm sorry, Charles. I really am." Margaret's losing her battle against her grin, but at least she's trying. "I didn't mean to walk in on you guys, and I didn't mean to laugh. It's just a shock. I'm sure you have a very nice ass."

This is not really helping.

"Okay, close enough," I sigh. "I'm taking him home. I'll see you guys later."

I shoo Charles to the front door, and we depart to the sounds of Reshma and Margaret making a genuine effort not to laugh anymore.

By the time we get back to his apartment . . . the mood is somehow broken.

So we make dinner—or Charles makes dinner, putting together some kind of tomato-y pasta thing and a salad, while I sit at the counter, watching him and drinking a glass of wine he's decanted for me.

When all the salad vegetables are chopped and the sauce is simmering and the noodles are boiling, he stands on his side of the kitchen and says, "How now, Ophelia, what's the matter?"

And so I sit back and say, "I have questions."

"Ask them."

"Well, first . . . you don't seem broken."

"No, I don't," he acknowledges. "The protective, deceptive gloss of privilege."

I nod as if I understand that, and I ask, "Isn't it bad for a psychiatrist to have avoidant attachment?"

"I find it's an advantage."

I nod as if I understand that, too. "Do your brother and sister have the same stuff? The same attachment stuff?"

"I don't know."

"Do you want to know?"

He pauses, his mouth slightly open, until at last he says, "I don't know."

I nod and take a sip of wine. I recall, idly, the total bafflement I experienced in the face of my first organic chemistry class. This feels like that.

I did eventually understand o-chem. It all just clicked one day.

Presumably, this will all click eventually too.

But for now, I give up, with a sigh and a shrug.

"Other questions?" Charles asks.

I tilt my head at him and ask shyly, "Did you miss me yesterday?"

He steps toward me, takes my face in his hands, and looks into my eyes for a moment with that sweet, heartrending smile, and then kisses the corner of my eyebrow. He kisses the crook of my jaw. The bottom edge of my lip.

When he starts to pull away, I stand up.

"Charles," I whisper, and I put my arms around his neck. I capture his mouth with mine and thrust my tongue into his mouth.

His hands go under my shirt, to my back. What we started on the futon ignites now inside me, and I clutch at him. He makes a deep, helpless sound and kisses me, hoisting me off my feet and pinning me against the wall with his hips. I wrap my legs around him and he grinds against me, right against my clitoris. My breath catches. He pushes himself against me harder and his tongue thrusts into my mouth and I rock my pelvis against him and my fingers are kneading the muscles of his back.

Right when his hands start pulling at my clothes, the noodles boil over.

He lets me slide, still panting, down the wall, and goes to rescue dinner.

So we eat on the couch, our plates in our laps, and I shovel food in huge mountains into my face. I'm actually starving—I barely ate for two days, went on two runs, and have had All The Feels. I hear Charles laugh quietly, and I look up to find him watching me.

"Watching you eat is almost as satisfying as watching you come," he says.

Eventually I lean back, giving a groan of overstuffed satisfaction. Charles takes the dishes into the kitchen and I sit there, eyes closed, digesting and listening to him putting things away. For the first time in two days, I've begun to feel satisfied and calm.

When he comes back, he has *Origin* in his hands.

He clears his throat and says, "Er, you left this." He sits, and he puts the book in the middle of the couch, between us.

I make a "get ye back" gesture at it. "Can we talk about it later?" I plead. "I've already had too many feelings today."

"Definitely," he says, and I hear relief in his voice. "What shall we do instead?"

I sit up on the couch and look at him. "I want to take a shower, go to bed, find you there, have simple, undemanding sex with you, and then sleep for, like, ten hours."

"Done," he says. "Go."

And that's what we do.

Because Charles is there with whatever I need, no matter what.

Almost whatever I need.

Whatever I need that he has to give.

We're lying together in the interval between sex and sleep. I'm watching the way the light of the streetlamp through the window shines and glints in the sparse, pale gold hair on his chest.

With my eyes on his chest, I say, "Do you still want me to have it? The book?"

"Yes. Annie, yes."

I blink, genuinely puzzled. "I can't figure out why. Is it a consolation prize?"

He says nothing until I look up at him. When I'm meeting his eyes, the inner corners of his eyebrows lift and he says, "It is an inadequate token of my appreciation for the generosity of your heart and mind," in a voice so sincere and warm, it pours through me like hot chocolate when you come in from the snow.

"That sounds to me like you'll miss me when I'm gone," I whisper, fighting off the tears at the backs of my eyes.

"How should I respond to that? Would you like me to play the doting partner or the dominant lover or the casual fuck-buddy or . . . whatever it is I am?"

"Just be honest. No"—I correct myself—"be honest, and also keep the lid off the monster. That's the deal."

Dully, he says, "In the name of honesty only then do I say: I'll be more relieved than I can express when you're gone."

I am breathless at this, like he punched me in the gut. "Ouch."

"Still want me to be honest?" The corner of his lower lip twitches downward.

"Dude."

It's good, though. This single sentence—*I'll be relieved when you're gone*—shifts the puzzle pieces into place, and I see a pattern at last: He will let me have him, he will try to face the monster . . . until I leave. And when I leave, he can close himself back up. He can shove the monster back into the pit.

And until then, that twitch of his lower lip tells me, he will torture himself.

For me.

I move a little away from him to put my head on the pillow next to his. Lying nose to nose with him, I ask, "You're gonna try the thing I want? The Monster Deal?"

He nods.

"Why?"

"Because you'd do it for me without thinking, without even trying. And because . . ." He pauses, twiddling the sheet over my shoulder. "I know you'll turn yourself inside out trying to practice the thing I want from you. The Acceptance Deal."

I nod.

"I think you don't know how hard it will be for you," he says, looking earnestly into my eyes.

I open my mouth to protest—but then I stop. How hard *do* I think it will be?

I think it will be easy. I've got the easy side of this deal. He's the one who has to face a monster. All I have to do is . . . accept him, whether or not he faces the monster.

Even though I really, really want him to face the monster.

Even though I really, really believe that if he does that, he'll love me.

And not only do I really, really want him to love me, I really, really want to be worth all that effort, to him.

So acceptance will be easy as long as he's facing the monster.

But acceptance means without condition, without any "as long as."

"I have no idea," I admit. "But there aren't many things I've tried to do, that I really wanted to do, that I couldn't do eventually." In fact, I can't think of even one thing I really wanted to do that I haven't succeeded at, eventually.

"Well." He kisses my forehead and gets out of bed. He pulls the curtains closed and then returns to the bed, sitting on the side and holding my hand. "I want you to have the book, either way, but you don't have to decide now."

"Okay."

"I have some work I need to finish tonight. Would you like me to stay here until you're asleep?"

"Oh," I say, only now realizing I had been assuming we'd be going to sleep together, realizing too how disappointed I am he hasn't assumed the same thing. "Um. I thought—"

He clears his throat. "Again, honesty: Most of the nights you've spent here, I've stayed until you've fallen asleep, and then I've gone into the living room to work for a few hours."

"Oh."

"I didn't mean not to tell you. It just didn't come up."

I pout. "Like the family title."

"And the elevator incident."

"And that your specialty is psychiatry."

"Psychosomatic medicine, if we're being precise about it."

"Shit, I don't even know what that is. Who the hell *are* you?" I say, rolling to my back and throwing my arms out to my sides.

He lies down beside me on top of the covers and tucks me up

next to him. He says, " 'I am large, I contain multitudes.' Same as you. Look, can I give you a hint?"

"A hint?"

"A hint about the Acceptance Deal."

"Okay."

"When you're finding it difficult, focus on the present. We have only these few days, only this one chance to share pleasure. Right now is what we have. Pay attention to what feels good right now, and let go of the past and the future."

"See, that sounds pretty easy," I sigh drowsily into his chest.

I feel his laugh more than I hear it. "I'm glad it sounds easy. I hope it is. Go to sleep, my harpy."

He wraps his arms around me, and I feel I know exactly who he is, no matter what else I might still learn about him.

Chapter 23

His Bloody Elbow

"Annie, try this."

"Try this" turns out to be a route marked *5.10a*, a far more difficult route than I've ever climbed before.

I just look at Charles.

"It's balance-y," he says." I think you'll like it."

I don't just like it; I flash it. I mean, I go right up it on the first try, without falling or having to take a sit even once. It's difficult, the handholds small and the footholds positively minute—in one place there isn't even a foothold; you just have to stand on the wall—but I do it. And the whole group—Tara, Charles, all of them, cheer for me as he lowers me back to the ground.

"You're getting stronger," Charles says as I undo the figure-eight knot.

I grin at him. "I'm getting better at using the strength I have."

"Six of one," he says. "Right, miss, tonight's the night for your ego. Watch this."

We swap ropes, I tie in to the anchor rope, and I belay him on the same route.

He struggles mightily.

"Balance-y," he calls down. "I'm better at the brute-force routes."

"You gotta get your feet up, man," Tara calls.

I turn to look at her. "What does 'get your feet up' mean?"

"Bugger!"

"GAHH!" While my eyes are turned away, Charles slips off the wall and I'm pulled off my feet.

"Sorry!" I call, dangling between the top rope and the anchor.

"No problem," he calls back, rubbing the elbow that got knocked in his fall.

I dropped him.

He has never dropped me. Not once. Not even close.

Instead he showed me a route I could do that he couldn't.

And I dropped him.

"I'm really sorry," I call again.

"No problem," he repeats.

"Sorry," I say again when we get home and he's cleaning off his bleeding, grimy elbow. "I shouldn't have taken my eyes off you."

"No problem. No harm done."

I wonder how a bloody elbow counts as "no harm," but I can't bring myself to ask out loud. Instead I say, more obliquely, "I don't think you're letting the monster out very much right now."

"Okay," he says, dabbing at his elbow. "Suppose I do that, and my hypothesis is the correct one? The monster's not a depressed eight-year-old but a vicious man, full-grown, who's been rock climbing for half his life and swinging a cricket bat for the other half?"

"Whatever. Fine. What's the worst that could happen?"

"The worst? I could kill you."

"You would never do that."

"Are we having an argument now? I only ask because I'd like to finish with this first." He gestures with his elbow, on which he's pressing a wet cloth.

"It's not an argument," I argue. "It's a discussion."

"Right. Well, toddle over to the sofa, and I'll join you for our discussion just as soon as I've put a bandage on this."

I do. And he does. Once he's done with his first aid, he sits at his end of the sofa and says, "You were saying I would never kill you. *I* never would, no. But my father would, and that's what we're talking about."

I roll my eyes. "You're exaggerating."

Charles scratches his nose and says lightly, "He put my mother in hospital for two weeks when she was pregnant. That was the first miscarriage. She thinks I don't know about it, but he told me."

I look at him, my mouth open, not believing him, not wanting to believe him. "Why would he tell you?"

"He was complaining about her inability to sustain a pregnancy. I was twelve."

"What?" I whisper, stunned.

"I'm sure he's raped her too, multiple times. And I'm sure she's not the only one."

I'm sitting there, the blood draining from my face. I feel cold and prickly, nauseated.

"I'm telling you this because you asked what was the worst that could happen if the monster got loose. This, by the way, this right now, is me genuinely trying the Monster Deal. I would never tell you these things otherwise."

I nod and think about this, actually having a discussion now, rather than an argument. At last I say, "I thought it would be noisier. Yelling."

"I don't have to yell to be scary," he says easily.

"Is not being scary the point of the pit and whatever?"

"Not hurting the other person is the point. The Monster Deal asks me to do things I know will cause you to suffer, and to trust that you are strong enough to withstand it."

"Huh," I say. "A wall is a wall is a wall."

"What's that?"

"I had this professor who used to say that. 'A wall is a wall is a wall.' You built a wall to keep the monster in so you wouldn't hurt people, but that same wall keeps people out, keeps them from being nice to you. You're trapped behind the wall with the monster."

He raises an eyebrow at me. "And fool that I am, I've spent the last month teaching you to climb."

A long time later I put my arms around his neck and roll on top of him.

With one hand on my butt, he finds his way inside me and then puts both arms around my waist, bracing me down. He kisses me and fucks me, and I feel more fragile than I ever have before. When I attempt to pull away from the kiss, to come up for air, he moves one of his hands to the back of my head and forces my head down beside his, my mouth on his neck, and I whimper into the heat.

"Fuck. Annie," he grinds out from between his teeth.

My body is locked against his, my arms trapped under his neck. I soften my body and relax into his thrusts, letting my body bounce against his, at his will.

Very gradually, my relaxation transforms into arousal, arousal into desire, and, very gradually, with the push of his pelvis against my clit, desire into desperation. I'm hovering at the edge, hovering there, and I recognize at last that he's doing it on purpose, holding me at that edge. He knows my body, knows how to keep me there, suspended indefinitely.

As soon as I see the trick, I smile.

"Charles, I want to come now," I say firmly into his neck.

"I know you do," he grunts back.

"So let me, you jerk!" I laugh, and he grips me harder to him with a rough noise, and fucks me harder. I groan luxuriously into his neck.

"Beg me," he says, still fucking me.

I laugh. "What? No way!"

And he stops. He just stops. He's breathing hard under me, his arms gripped like iron bands around me, but he's lying still inside me.

I squirm as much as I can against him, saying, "Hey!"

"Beg," he commands.

"No!" I say, struggling more fiercely now. With effort, I pull my arms out from under his neck.

When I get them free, he grabs my wrists and wrestles me onto my back. I laugh as he does it, but when he pins my wrists to the mattress, next to my shoulders, and slides his cock back into me, he looks into my eyes, my neck arches back, and I'm not laughing anymore.

He says, "Beg."

"No."

He fucks into me hard, once.

"Do you want to come?"

"Yes!"

"Beg me, and I'll let you."

"No."

And he slides hard into me, twice.

"Do you want to come?"

"Yes, Charles," I say in my most sex-kitten voice, but it does nothing.

"Beg."

I whine instead, and he slams his cock in me three times. Hard. I grunt with each one.

"Do you want to come?"

"Yes."

"Beg me."

I press my lips together.

Four times. Hard. Steady. I breathe, "Oh god," after each one, as my arousal seems to cross threshold after threshold without ever approaching the final edge.

"Do you want to come?"

"Yes." A broken whisper this time.

"Then say it." He fucks into me.

"Oh god, Charles."

"Beg." Again.

"I want—"

"Now."

"Please, Charles."

"Don't stop."

It comes out of me in a soft, high chant, "Please make me come, make me come, please, Charles, please, Charles, let me come," and he moves perfectly, perfectly, pressing and moving against my clit, moving inside me as I surrender and plead, until I can't breathe—but as soon as I stop, holding my breath with the approaching orgasm, he's still again.

"If you stop, I stop," he says, gasping as much as I am.

"Please," I whisper. It devolves into a desperate, wild, "Please. Please. Please," with each focused thrust, and when I come, my whole body spasms, my arms and legs wrap themselves around him, and I lift myself entirely off the bed, closing all the distance between us. I'm clinging to him, dangling from him, thrusting myself against him, rolling and gripping and half-blind.

He drops off of his elbows and presses me into the mattress, silently thrusting those three hard, sharp thrusts of his orgasm.

"Ow, my bloody elbow," he says as we lie there, panting. He kisses me cheerfully, rolls over, and laughs, while I feel shattered and raw.

It marks a change in the way Charles touches me. There is an exigency in him, and a demand. He asks more of me—more orgasms, more surrender—and I give it. There is an intensity, as well. Though he always begins tenderly, his touch escalates to real force, so that by the time I'm coming, he may slap my ass or my thigh or my breasts to a hot, stinging peak. Friday morning he finds bruises from his fingers on my arm. He kisses the marks and asks softly, "Hurt?"

"Nah."

And it doesn't. It feels like he's trusting me to be strong enough to withstand the inevitable bruisings of wide-open connection, and I feel myself earning that trust.

I will not drop him again. Not if I can help it. Not even if he drops me.

Which he does.

Chapter 24

Feeling Like Shit About Feeling Like Shit

Margaret and Reshma are sitting in front of the television when Charles and I let ourselves into the apartment on Saturday morning.

"Did you hear about what happened?" Margaret says without looking up.

"Huh?"

"In California? Some fucked-up college kid killed six people because no one would have sex with him."

"What the hell are you talking about? When?" I say.

"Last night. It just happened. Some boy killed all these people, and he left a video on the Internet saying he was going to kill a bunch of women because none of them would sleep with him. It's on the news right now."

We sit and watch the news.

"Dude," is all I can say.

"Jesus fucking Christ," Charles adds.

But it gets worse.

Reshma is reading something on her phone and finally says, "Huh. The douchebag's 'manifesto' insanity says his family is some kind of prestigious English family that lost all their money. He doesn't sound English in the video."

"I'll get the boxes from the car," Charles says.

I follow him as far as the door, then watch him go out to his car and pause, head lowered, his hand on the car door before he opens it and pulls out the flattened boxes we've brought for the move. When he comes back, his face is pale and stiff, and he sighs heavily. "Let's get this done and have a fucking drink, eh?"

"Hear, hear," Margaret calls from the living room.

We get it done. With four of us, it takes less than an hour to get all Margaret's stuff into the rented truck, and then we drive an hour up to Indianapolis and load all the stuff into Reshma's apartment.

We're done, it's noon, and the whole world is going to hell.

You bet your ass we have a fucking drink.

Maybe an hour later, Margaret and Reshma start making out in a pretty heavy-duty way, and Charles tosses his keys at me and says, "Let's get out of their way. You'll have to drive."

"Okay, let me say bye to Margaret."

"Sure."

I clear my throat at Margaret. "Hey, lady, I gotta take Momma Duck home."

She pulls her mouth away from her fiancée's and turns to look at me, frowning. "Oh my god, this is it!" she says.

"I know," I say, and my eyebrows get all worried.

She comes over and hugs me. "What am I going to do without you?"

I hug her back hard. "The same thing I'm going to do without you," I say.

We both start crying a little.

"I'll miss you so much," she says.

"Me too!"

"You'll call me. You'll e-mail. You'll text, you bitch, or I'll come to New York and fuck your shit up."

"And you'll invite me to your wedding, whether it's a legal one or not, or I'll come to Indianapolis and fuck *your* shit up."

Reshma has stood up too, and she gives me a hug.

"You take good care of this lady," I tell her.

"I will."

"Good luck in Montreal!" Margaret says, hugging me again. "You'll be awesome."

"Good luck at Pfizer," I tell her. "They're lucky to have you." And then we hug just one more time.

"Okay, I really am going now," I say with a sniff. I turn to Charles. "Ready?"

"Yep. Bye, Margaret, Reshma." He turns away without meeting my eye and without waiting for Margaret's, "Bye Momma Duck, and thanks!" and I follow him out the door. Only when he stumbles on the steps do I realize how drunk he's gotten.

I drive us home, through Charles's gloomy silence.

When we get back to his apartment, I unlock the door for him and he lays himself onto the sofa, moaning, "God, drunk in the middle of the day. Prince bloody Charming, me."

I scoot onto the couch under his ankles. I take off his shoes for him, as I've done a dozen times for Margaret.

"How now, Ophelia, what's the matter?" I ask, and he giggles morosely.

With his hands rubbing his forehead, he says, "This is what entitlement leads to. Bloody evil viciousness and remorseless cruelty."

"Are you identifying with creepo?"

"Yes, look—you don't have to hang around for this. I'm in a dark hole. I'll find my way out, but I'm pretty unpleasant to be around at the moment, and I don't want to inflict this on you."

"Okay," I sigh at his feet. I'm sad and mad and frustrated and trying to be accepting, but I think maybe it comes out passive-aggressive. I say, "I guess I was sort of hoping I wouldn't have to spend the night alone in my empty apartment, but if you'd rather . . . um . . . wallow in a drunken stupor, that's cool too. I mean, you seem kinda wrapped up in your thing, and I have to admit I'm kinda wrapped up in my thing of saying good-bye to my best friend, so . . . I mean. That's cool. I'll go home."

"Ah, young Coffey. I'm sorry. Come here." He raises an arm off the couch and beckons.

I tuck myself in next to him, and he wraps his arms around me and kisses my neck in small, precisely placed kisses.

"I think our difficulty," he says between kisses, "is that you're a hoper."

"A hoper?"

He pronounces:

> *"There is a secret medicine*
> *given only to those who hurt so hard*
> *they can't hope.*
> *The hopers would feel slighted if they knew."*

He sighs heavily, his breath boozy, and turns my face to his. With his palm on my cheek and his forehead against mine, he blinks heavily and says, "'S a poem."

"What is the secret medicine?"

"Can't tell you," he mumbles. "Secret."

"Is it shots of vodka?"

He shakes his head. "'S the opposite." He wraps his arms around me and holds me against him. "Oh, Annie. What are we going to do with you?"

I shrug and sniff and cuddle myself deeper into his arms.

"My father's brand of insanity," he says suddenly. "I've watched it turn from darkly charming to murderous in the blink of an eye. I've felt that kind of rage inside me. I know it lives inside me. There but for the grace of . . . I don't know what . . . nothing at all. There is no grace between me and that. There's only my own disgust. Oh, for fuck's sake, listen to me. I'd forgotten what a maudlin drunk I am. Ignore me.

> *"When water gets caught in habitual whirlpools,*
> *dig a way out through the bottom*
> *to the ocean."*

"What?"

"Nothing. Let's take a shower."

We do, standing under the streaming water, kissing with our tongues. He's kissing me deeply, hard, but his hand is stroking my wet hair so gently. I wrap my arms around him and let the water fall over us.

We don't have sex, though. Charles isn't that steady on his feet. And after the shower, he drops into bed and falls asleep. Passes out.

I wander into the living room and look at his book titles. I putter around the kitchen, not finding anything I want to eat. I clean the bathroom. I wish I had work to do.

I decide to go home.

I ride back to my apartment and wander around, listening to the emptiness of the spaces. Only the TV and coffee table are left in the living room—the futon was Margaret's. The kitchen table and chairs are gone too. Her bedroom is empty. Her half of the bathroom cabinet.

I sit on the living room floor and text Margaret.

MD was DA-RUNK when we left. He was pretty freaked out about the crazy dude.

She texts back after a few minutes,

He seemed weird. Not like himself.
Are you okay?

Yeah, it's fine. He kinda went to bed.
I came home to pack. I'm all sad and lonely here without you, though.

You want me to come down? I can spend the night with you. Don't be sad and lonely!

No, don't do that, it's your first night in your new place together!

I just don't know what to do about Charles.

What do you WANT to do?

1. punch him in the face for getting wasted when I wanted him to be nice to me about you moving away.

Okay, let's put a pin in that one.

2. hug him forever because he's such a good guy and he really believes he's a bad guy.

That's nice if you don't also want to punch him in the face.

3. cry in the bathtub because I'm in love with him and he's not in love with me.

I AM COMING DOWN THERE.

No, don't come down. Don't do that to Reshma.

She calls me.
I answer the phone with, "Don't come down. I'm fine."
"What do you mean, you're in love with him?"
"Yeah, I'm an idiot. I fell in love with him."
"You are leaving in, like, ten days! Why did you fall in love with him?"
"I didn't do it on purpose!"
"And what the hell is wrong with him that he's not in love with you?"
I try to explain about the monster and our agreement about The Acceptance Deal and The Monster Deal without telling too much about his family—those are not my secrets.
"He's all broken and stuff," I conclude. "And my job is to, like, be cool with that, while his job is to try to not be broken."

She says, "That is a fucking nightmare."

"Got a better plan?"

"Can't you just not see him?"

"We're going to Montreal, remember? We leave on Thursday. We're there until Sunday. I can't not see him."

"Dude, that is . . . dude."

"Anyway, I don't *want* to not see him. Just thinking about leaving—" I stop, choking on tears. "I mean, I'm definitely leaving, I'm going home, I'm going to med school, I'm leaving fucking Indiana. But it's like I'm going to have to chew off my own arm to do it, like that hiker guy. Only it's not my arm, it's my heart."

"*Ugh*," she moans.

"I know." I cry into the phone for a minute, before I say, "And he wants me to be able to just, like, enjoy the moment, right, like, to experience the pleasure without thinking about the impending doom. And he's right, right? Like, when we're together, in that moment it's amazing, it's maybe the happiest I've ever been in my life. It's when I step back from that and realize the larger situation that I'm just filled with this . . . big . . . gaping . . ."

"Annie, do you want to come up here? Come sleep on the futon, and we can go out for breakfast tomorrow and have pancakes and diner coffee."

Yes, I want to go up there. That sounds like exactly what I need.

"How'm I supposed to get to Indianapolis?" I snivel.

"We'll come and pick you up."

"I don't want you to have to drive all that way—"

"*Dude*. Shut the hell up. We're coming to get you."

I smile and take a deep breath. "Okay. Let me just call Charles and let him know."

"Okay."

"You're the best."

"I know."

I call Charles.

He picks up on the fourth ring, sounding like I've woken him up. "Yah."

"Hey, it's me."

"Annie. Hey."

"Uh, how are you feeling? Sober yet?"

"Er. Feeling pretty ashamed of myself, mostly. Not quite sober, but on an upward trajectory. May I know where you are?"

"I went home."

"Ah, fuck. I'm sorry, Annie."

"It's okay. You had a thing. Hey, listen, so Margaret invited me up to her place to spend the night."

"Right. Okay. So you're going up there?"

"Is that okay?"

"Of course. Choose whatever gives you the most pleasure."

"I *want* to choose you," I say. "But you're slightly busy accidentally being kind of a jerk. Which I realize is not the accepting thing to say, but I'm currently failing at The Acceptance Deal."

"Acceptance and forgiveness are not the same things, my harpy. Nor tolerance, nor approval. A night without you seems a just punishment for my behavior."

"So this is the accepting thing to do? Because I'm, like, working really hard on being accepting right now, and I gotta say it hurts like a motherfucker and I don't even know what's the right thing to do or feel or . . . anything."

I hear him sigh into the phone—or groan. I'm not sure. He says, "Do you believe that I feel terrible about today?"

"Yeah," I pout. "But you don't have to feel terrible, you just . . ." I stop. What does he have to do? He doesn't have to do anything.

"Yes?" he prompts.

"Nothing," I say. "You feel like shit and you also feel like shit *about* feeling like shit. I feel like shit too, but for different reasons, and I also feel frustrated that you're too busy feeling like shit to be nice to me while I feel like shit, but I also understand why you feel like shit, and I'm mad at myself for not being totally fine with you feeling however you need to feel, *and* I know that probably you feel this shitty in part because you've been trying to do the Monster Deal, which has torn down your defenses, so it's kind of my fault that you feel this shitty. Basically, this is a lot of mutually contradictory feelings all at the same time and I'm confused." I huff.

"You, Miss Annabelle Coffey, are remarkable," he says. "No one could process today better than you are currently doing."

"This is me doing it right?" I say. "I feel like a fuckup."

"You are a marvel. I am so . . . Look, go and spend the night at Margaret's, and I'll come up there tomorrow afternoon to bring you home, okay?"

"Okay," I say, pressing the phone close to my ear, my eyes closed. "I'll text you in the morning?"

"Okay."

"I love you." It just slips right out. I was trying not to say it, but the words are like a puppy squirming under a fence.

He's silent for a few long seconds. At last he says, "What would you prefer for me to say when you say that?"

"Um, anything that's true?"

"Even though the truth isn't your ideal?"

"The truth *is* my ideal. A shitty truth is better than a comfortable lie any day."

"And that, my harpy, my dear termagant, is what makes you remarkable. Okay, let's try it. Say it again."

"Say what again?"

"That you love me."

"Um, I love you."

I hear him inhale, and he says, "I know, Annie." And then he adds, "How was that for you?"

"It kind of sucked."

And he laughs. Real laughter, not bitter, not ironic. It's just funny to him that I both prefer the truth and feel like the truth sucks. I find I have a half smile on my face, listening to him. He says, "Better than a comfortable lie, though?"

I take a deep breath. "Should we try the comfortable lie?"

"You want to do that?"

"No." In fact, my entire body is contracting with dread at the idea. "But it seems like the only way to test the hypothesis that an uncomfortable truth is better than a comfortable lie."

"Okay. Go for it."

"Okay." I take another deep breath and say, "I love you."

"I love you too," he answers blankly.

I feel a hard, sharp, stabbing pain in my chest that makes me gasp. I press my hand against my forehead. "Oh god, that sucks so much worse. Fuck. Ow." I slip sideways down the wall and curl up on the floor.

"I'm sorry," he whispers urgently. "Annie, I'm sorry. I wish it were true. I do. I wish I could. I think it must be one of the great failures of my life that I can't."

"Don't ever do that again, not even if I ask you to," I say.

"I won't. I won't ever lie to you, sweetheart, not even if you want me to. I'm sorry."

Chapter 25

The Things That Need Saying

With a fancy bottle of wine and charmingly profuse apologies, Charles makes it up to Margaret and Reshma. He takes me back to Bloomington on Sunday afternoon and treats me like a princess, with dinner and reading to me in the tub—he joins me in the tub this time—and a long, slow-burning massage with oil that smells of citrus and something woody.

"Is this part of the Monster Deal?" I ask, my face half-muffled in a pillow.

"Merely the convenient meeting place of bottomless guilt and slavering lust."

"Well, gimme some monster, baby."

"Haven't you had enough to last you a while?"

I shift and snuggle deeper into the pillows. "I think you don't get that I *like* the monster. Have you not noticed that I enjoy being challenged and pushed?"

"Maybe I'm the one who's had enough for a few days, then. I'd rather be gentle," he says, "if that's all right with you."

It is. But it's heartbreaking. When he kisses me softly and slowly, as if kissing me is all he ever expects to do for the rest of his life, when he rests his hand on my forehead as he does it, when he moves inside me with the attentive, slow movements that notice every change in my arousal, every detail of my response, I feel more in love than I can contain. It brings tears to my eyes, and he kisses them away. And it feels like he loves me too, so that when I come, almost silently, his eyes watching mine and his lips touching mine, I whisper the words as low as I can, "I love you." And then he closes his eyes, and my heart tears apart just a little.

He was right. I had no idea how hard it would be to accept him when he wasn't facing the monster. Not because I don't love him then, just as much. But because when it's him and the monster, it's like he's slaying dragons for me, fighting for me, trying to get to me through the walls and the monsters and everything that stops him from keeping his eyes open and saying it back to me.

I'm crying a little after I come, and I wrap my arms around his neck, to hold him close. "This is hard," I say. And he tightens his arms around me, and it gets a little more difficult still.

We climb on Tuesday, as usual. What's great about climbing is that you forget everything else while you're doing it. It's like dancing that way.

Which is why it's only in the car on the way home from climbing that it occurs to me: this was the last time we'll climb together.

Climbing is our first "last time."

I feel doors starting to close.

And so, on the drive home, I start crying.

Again.

I put my hand over my mouth. And then I can't stop crying. When we get to his apartment, Charles parks and we sit there together.

He raises his eyebrows at me, empathetic but puzzled. "We have these few days. A week. I don't understand—we have these few days, and you're acting as if it's already over."

"I know," I sniff. "I'd stop if I could. I'd forget if I could. If I could live the next six days unaware that—" I'm choked by tears, and I just sit there, crying for a minute, without access to language for what I'm experiencing. But then I consider: if I could live the next six days unaware that they were The Last Six Days, would I appreciate them? Would I notice the glory of his skin next to mine if I weren't so acutely aware of how few times I would feel it? Would it, in fact, feel as glorious? And when I say, *glorious,* I mean *tragic.*

Charles's thoughts seem to have mirrored mine uncannily. He says, "I wonder if it isn't some kind of survival mechanism that people are almost completely oblivious to almost everything about their present experience, to the simultaneous profundity and meaninglessness. The way every moment is both a celebration and a lament."

We sit for a moment in silence and then he gets out of the car and comes around to my side, opening my door.

"Come on," he says gently. "Let's have it then. Let's go in and have an argument and get it behind us. Say all the things that need saying so we get past it."

I follow him blankly into the building and up the elevator.

"I'm not wrong!" I burst as soon as he closes the apartment door.

"Not wrong about what?" he asks calmly.

"About The Love Thing. This Thing we have is A Love Thing." I sniff and cross my arms, trying not to cry anymore.

He leans against the wall and says gently, "You're not wrong. The Thing is A Love Thing. And it's equally true that The Thing involves me, and I can't. It's not that I won't, it's that I can't. It's like . . . being able to touch your toes. For some people it comes automatically, some people can work up to it, and some people will never be able do it. Love Things come easily to you. There's never been a day in your life when you haven't been able to do it, spontaneously and without effort. But I haven't, not once in my life. I am not built that way. My body does not know how, and it does not know how to learn it."

"You won't even try," I say. I'm angry. I'm enraged. I'm actually trembling with rage. Because it's not. Fucking. Fair.

He says, very softly, "This is me trying."

"You did this on *purpose*," I snarl.

"No"—he shakes his head—"Annie. No."

"You fucking lied to me. You said—" But I can't think of one lie. Why can't I think of any lies? I feel like I've been led blindfolded into a room, with the expectation that a surprise party waits for me but actually it's a room full of snakes. "You fucking lied to me."

"You feel deceived," he answers softly. "I know that. I'm sorry."

"Don't be *sorry;* just be *honest.*"

"Honest about what?"

"About how you feel! About what you want!"

"I want to be your friend. I want to give you pleasure," he says. "And most of what I feel is self-contempt and regret."

He's not defending himself, and that only enrages me more, fuels my urge to lash out, to make him feel *something,* to *make* him react.

"Why can't you just get angry and yell? Why can't you fight back?"

"How would it help for me to yell?" he inquires.

"It would show me that you're a human being, that you give some kind of shit about me."

"My yelling is what will tell you I give a shit."

"Yes," I insist.

He sighs and rubs his forehead, then stuffs his hands into his pockets. "I forgot. You want me to lose control. Losing control is how I prove your worth to you."

"Losing control is how you prove you care more about *me* than you do about being in control, you selfish asshole."

He looks at me then like a deer in headlights. Terror. That's what I see. He's terrified, petrified. Of me.

"I do care more—" But he stops. And then—worst of all—he slides down the wall into a crumpled heap on the floor.

"Charles." I approach him and put my hand on his shoulder—and he flinches away from me.

"I'm sorry," he says in a painfully soft voice. "Annie. I'm sorry. Please," He puts his hand over his eyes, and I feel a cold flood of shame that I've caused him such pain.

I should back off and leave him alone.

I should apologize.

I should let it go, stop pushing him.

But instead I lie on the floor in front of him, so I can see his face, see the pain he doesn't want me to see, the tears he's working so hard to hold back, and I say, "What if I weren't leaving? I'm not staying—I'm definitely leaving—but hypothetically."

Ironic, dark laugh. "Don't think for one second that if you hadn't been leaving, I would have gotten into this in the first place. It was safe because you were leaving." Another quiet laugh and a shake of his head. "It was safe."

Silence. I roll onto my back and look at the ceiling, wondering idly at the range of silences I've experienced in the last few weeks, from the warm, affectionate silence after we first had sex to this . . . this cold, acid silence.

"Is this what it was like with Melissa?" I ask, unable not to. "Both of you on the floor, crying?"

"No." He sniffs. "I sulked, and she threw cushions at me."

More silence. I stare at the ceiling.

"How's that acceptance working out for you then?" he inquires. I turn my face toward him and find he's resting his cheek on his fist, his elbow on his knee, watching me with a kind of exhausted, grim, red-eyed half smile.

"It's easy when we're climbing or having sex or eating," I say. "It's hard when . . ." I pause, struggling to explain. "It's hard when my feelings get more intense and yours don't. Any feeling. Love, anger, anything."

He nods.

I ask, "How's the monster thing?"

"It's easy when we're climbing or having sex or eating," he agrees. "It's hard when you cry."

"Is that what I should be doing differently? Should I not cry?"

"There's nothing you need to do differently—though I do have one request."

"Yes. Anything."

"The actual name-calling is not so helpful."

I look at him aghast. "Did I call you names?"

He nods sadly, and his lower lip twitches as he says, " 'Selfish arsehole.' "

"I said that?"

He nods again.

"Oh my god, I don't think that about you. You're, like, the least selfish person I know. I was just mad. I didn't mean it. I—"

"I know that, Annie. But when you say it, I believe you."

"Don't believe me! I'm a fucking idiot. I'm a mean, bullying bitch. I'm—"

He interrupts, "The name-calling rule applies as much to yourself as to me."

"I suck so much at fighting!" I despair, and I flop my limbs melodramatically on the floor.

He laughs—a sweet, light, genuine laugh. "You haven't had much practice. Apparently, I can help with that."

I turn my face to him. "Is there a book I can read about how to fight?"

He shrugs. "It's not that complicated. The main thing is to remember that you like the other person enough to care about what they've done or said."

Chapter 26

I Fucking Hate You

I do not begin the day optimistically. We have ahead of us an hour-long drive to the airport, an hour of airport administrivia, four hours on the plane, and another ninety minutes of rigmarole on the other end before we're in our hotel. Eight hours in the constant, public company of the man I'm in love with, who is determinedly not in love with me.

But we weather it pretty well, considering. There is a helpful moment early in the day that helps set a mood of mutual patience. We're standing in the security line at the airport, and I'm reading the inside of my passport out of sheer desperation for something to occupy my brain.

"Good god, Coffey, was this the best you could do?" He's staring at my passport picture in mock horror.

"Okay, Mister Smartmouth, now you have to show me your passport picture, just to be fair."

"Oh no!" he says as I grab for it, and he actually puts it behind his back! Like a child!

Well. His desire not to wrestle like fools in the airport security line is greater than mine, and so I win this particular struggle. But when I open his passport, I barely notice his photo.

"'The holder is the Honourable Charles Douglas,'" I read. I look at him and grin. "The Honourable Charles."

Charles looks chagrined. He snags his passport out of my hands and puts it in his pocket. He says, "The Duke of Devonshire—the Duke of bloody Devonshire, mind—has said in public, the whole system is an anachronism; just put the thing out of its misery. It's dead. And he's right. The whole thing is cold on the slab."

"Isn't there a thing now from *Downton Abbey*, they're trying to let women inherit?"

"Pumping blood into a corpse," he says dismissively. "Or I suppose it's more like a brain-dead patient on life support. Just taking up a bed that somebody else is waiting for, but the family can't let go. The worst part is, the patient is an abusive, destructive, self-aggrandizing arsehole of monumental proportions, and still the family insist on sustaining a heartbeat for as long as they can."

We stand in silence for a few minutes before Charles quirks up the corner of his mouth and says, "The Duke of Devonshire also went to the same school as Bertie Wooster." And then he giggles, a nearly silent, shoulder-shaking giggle that makes me laugh too.

What I'm saying, I suppose, is that Charles is unpredictable, interesting to talk to, and forgiving of my crankiness, and that's pretty much the best traveling companion you can ask for. I'm reminded, as I watch him negotiate the fatiguing indignities of air travel, that long before I put any part of his body into any part of my body, I just *liked* this guy. I like him still.

And so I just let the rest of it go for now. We're going to Montreal. Montreal with Charles can only be better than Montreal on my own.

The hotel is at the upper end of beige hotels, comfortable, familiar, and anonymous. We could be in any city in North America—so I'm startled when Charles checks us in in French. We have separate rooms booked, on separate floors. This is a plan made back in February.

In the elevator Charles says, his eyes on the number panel, "Now then, young Coffey, what's your pleasure? Sleep separate? Sleep together? Your wish is my command."

"My wish is to know what your pleasure is," I say.

"You are," he says, glancing at me.

The elevator dings at the twelfth floor, and the doors open. I look at him as I hit the close doors button. Of course I'm going to spend these nights with him. I'm in love with him. I'm going to put my body in his hands and receive everything I can from him, accept all he is willing to give, give all he is willing to accept.

The elevator continues to the fifteenth floor.

"Before, at the front desk?" I say. "Checking in in French?"

"Mh?"

"That was hot."

Charles chuckles as the elevator doors open again. "If my adolescent self could have known that a woman like you would say something like that, I'd probably have studied harder."

When we get to the room, we've barely put our stuff down when Charles grins at me and says, "Let's fuck in the shower and then go have dinner."

"Okay!"

We do. Actually, we fuck in the hotel shower and on the giant hotel bed and on the woolly hotel carpet, and then we put on grown-up clothes and go down to the grown-up restaurant, both of us pink-cheeked and grinning with sex.

Eating in the fancy hotel restaurant with Charles is eye-opening. I walk into it, treating it like a joke, an awkward joke we'd have to fake our way through together. But he is not faking. I see it in the way the waiter talks to him—in French—and the way he orders. I see it, when our food arrives, in the way he uses a fork and knife. Have we ever eaten a fork-and-knife kind of meal together? Have I ever seen the way he keeps the fork upside down and in his left hand, index finger extended?

Have I ever noticed how people—strangers—respond to him? His quiet, deliberate command? He is always gentle, always calm, but always the one in control of an interaction. With the waiter, with the busser, with the woman back at the check-in desk. With me. They—we—all behave as he requires.

He's not doing it on purpose; it just happens.

I find myself self-conscious about my method of eating asparagus—a joke I didn't understand when I read it in *Right Ho, Jeeves,* but that resonates so deeply now that I stare helplessly at my plate, the asparagus arranged in unmanageably long stalks beside a piece of fish drowned in a buttery sauce that I now imagine staining the only dress I brought with me.

I watch him dexterously remove a bone from his fish with his fork and knife, and I say, "So . . . you're, like, really rich, right?"

"Hm?" He looks at me, startled by the question. "No, no, not—well, I mean, I suppose yes, by many standards."

"Because of the title thing?"

He tips his hand side to side, so-so. "It's not strictly inherited wealth. My father is, predictably, a corrupt banker, so I was raised, you know, in the one percent, but I haven't taken any money from him for years. Most of my own money comes from the patent on the blood pump. Why do you ask?"

"You own a patent?"

"Well, me and a few other people."

"So you're rich because *you're* rich, not because of your dad or the title thing." I'm relieved by this. "See, I keep saying you're a genius."

"No, honestly, I'm not. The title . . . God, you don't really want to hear the history of the British peerage."

"Of course I do! Inherited wealth," I say. "Go."

He piles a little heap of food onto the back of his fork and takes a bite, chewing and thinking. Then he takes a drink of wine. He says, "Erm," a few times.

And then he starts telling me how the system developed in an economy where land was power and wealth and the very survival of the people—land equals food equals survival. You fight for it and you pass it to your children—to your son, because it's the men who fight in wars and the women are, like the land, fertile property that you fight for. But when the economy shifted from agrarian to industrial, power and wealth shifted away from the land, so land was a liability rather than an asset.

I hope you're not snoring. I'm not. I could not be more fascinated. I'm sitting in a froufrou restaurant with a titled aristocrat (almost, anyway), and he's explaining what the hell happened between Jane Austen and *Downton Abbey*. I got a 5 on the Advanced Placement European History test four years ago, and yet I know nothing about this.

He says, "Anyway, if a family managed the transition well, they have their estates intact. The ones that didn't . . . don't."

"Does the Duke of Devonshire still have his family's stuff?"

He snorts a laugh. "Yes. He has their stuff."

"And your family doesn't?"

"No, our lot didn't do brilliantly—at first it was just our own shortsighted ill management, and then we had a reasonable share of bad luck," he says.

"Bad luck?"

"Well, not so much bad luck as bad wars. My great-grandfather was managing pretty well, but he was killed in the war—the First World War, when my grandfather was only an infant. Taxes and . . . it doesn't matter. Anyway, Hitler came along about the time my grandfather was old enough to take the reins. He had a bad time of it in the war, and when he came back, that was the end. He died in the 1950s of an accidental overdose of painkillers due to a war injury, goes the story, and that's true enough. My father paid the bulk of that price, in every sense. The estate was obliterated, nothing left by the time he inherited."

"Wait, how old is your dad?"

Charles shrugs with a thoughtful moue. "Must be seventy or so? Three generations before him didn't see forty, so he didn't have any of us until he'd crossed that threshold.

"Anyway, it doesn't matter as much as you might think about losing the stuff. The title—and the social capital that goes with being born into that class—plus some brains and no moral compunctions at all, were more than enough for my father to leverage a new fortune out of an economy that was bleeding working-class jobs. You *can't* be interested in this."

"Sure I am! Wouldn't you be interested to know my family's history?"

"Yes, I would. Tell me." He takes a sip of wine.

"Oh." That was a pretty fast change of subject. "Dude, I have no idea. All four of my grandparents were born in New York. I'm half Irish, half German. Both of my grandfathers were doctors. One grandmother was a nurse, the other was a teacher. That's all I know."

"Crikey, really?"

"Really. It never even occurred to me to wonder, until now."

"I cannot begin to imagine what that's like," he says, bemused. By now the waiter has cleared the table, and we're sitting across from each other, a few scattered glasses and utensils between us.

Charles puts a hand over mine, on the table. "Anyway, where we started with this is that I'm not a genius at all, I was born with every cultural privilege you can have, and an appalling human being for a father, who pushed some school officials into letting me skip forms until I was three years younger than everyone around me. Without the money and the title, no one would have done what he wanted."

"And then you'd just be starting your residency now?"

He nods. "I suppose that's true."

"And then I wouldn't have met you."

He gives me the warm, melting smile. "I suppose that's true too."

"Well, for that, anyway, I'm grateful to your appalling human being of a father."

"Come back to the room," he says softly. And he holds my hand as we walk to the elevator. He holds it still as we're lifted up to the fifteenth floor.

*   *   *

I'm nervous before my talk on Friday, but once I've started, it's fine. It's just like my defense—easier, actually, because the questions at the end are really simple and obvious, not like the questions from Charles and Professor Smith.

And of course Charles is sitting at the back in case I get lost. But I don't.

He comes up to me afterward, at the front of the crowd who wants to talk and ask questions. "Shrew," he says, and I know he means I did well. He toys briefly with the ends of my scarf—the same black scarf he blindfolded me with a few weeks ago—and smiles into my eyes. "Come up to the room after you're done here?"

My lips part and I nod.

When I let myself in half an hour later, he's sitting on the bed, reading, and a room service cart stands in the middle of the room.

"Hey," he says, putting his article aside.

"Hey."

"Good questions?"

"Yeah, good. One lady offered me a job."

He smiles at this. "What did you say?"

"'Thanks, but I have eight more years of school to do first.'"

"Excellent answer," he says. He gestures toward the cart. "Food."

"Oh, thank god. Just let me shower first."

"Mh." He's already reading again.

After my shower, I don a hotel bathrobe, pick up two covered plates, and join Charles on the bed.

"Nearly finished," he mumbles, still reading.

I lift a lid and find a pile of triangular sandwiches. I don't even care what kind. I pick one up, take a huge bite, then ask through the mouthful, "What are we doing tonight?"

"Mh."

He's not listening yet. So I sit and chew and watch him read.

I'm on my third triangle when I find myself counting in my head. Tonight, Saturday, Sunday, Monday. That's it.

My mouth dries out, and I put down the sandwich. I carry the plates back to the cart. I drink some water.

Enjoy the present was his hint about acceptance.

I'm standing, staring blankly at the cart, trying to enjoy the moment, when I hear Charles's teacher voice behind me. "Come here."

As I turn and approach the bed, he says, "Lie on your back with your head at the foot of the bed and your hips over mine and your feet on the headboard."

I sort out these instructions as I go, and find I'm lying with my feet on either side of his head so that he has a direct view of my whole body.

"Untie the robe."

I do, looking up at him while I do it.

"Pull it open," he says.

I do, still looking at him, running my hands over my shower-softened skin.

He takes one of my feet and puts it on the center of his chest. I curl my toes into the cotton of his shirt. He takes the other foot and begins kissing my toes, licking the tender underside of them, kissing and biting along the arch.

"Oh my god." I flex on the bed at the warm, wet pleasure of his mouth. "That's really, um . . ."

As he transitions to the other foot, he comments, "I can see you getting wet."

I put my hand on my vulva to feel what he means, but he says, "Don't touch yourself yet." So I put my hands flat on the mattress, and he drapes his legs over them, holding them down. And he continues to suck and lick and bite my foot and toes, and my hips move restlessly over his. I can feel his erection growing under me, through his clothes and the robe.

"Could you come from this?" he asks.

"You know I can't come without touching my clit," I say. This much has been evident to me since our very first night. I can get close—right to the edge—from almost anything he does to me, but until there's direct pressure, direct stimulation on my clit, I can't come. And he has used this knowledge to torture me often enough.

"Not true. You came when I touched your foot the night I tied you up," he says.

"Well, but that was, like . . ."

How can his tongue on my toes be erotic? It is, desperately so.

"Like what?"

"You know," I say, shy suddenly. I tip my knees together. "That was, like, *perfect* sex. You can't have sex like that all the time."

"Let's have sex like that now." He slides out from under me and off the bed. "Kneel on the bed."

I turn over to my hands and knees and look at him. He's standing casually, leaning against the desk chair where I draped my suit before my shower.

"Up on your knees," he corrects, and I rise up on my knees.

"Take off the robe."

I quirk my lips. "You take it off."

He shakes his head and says in his teacher voice, "Do as I tell you."

My lips part, my lungs contract, and I do as he tells me.

For a long, long minute I watch him looking at me. Just the sensation of his gaze on me is making my heart beat faster. His face is serious, like he's studying me, like he's memorizing me.

Finally he approaches me and gestures me forward too. "Edge of the bed, and turn around," he says. "More on the edge. There."

I'm facing away from him, balanced with my feet and shins off the bed.

With his lips pressed against my ear, but so softly I have to strain to hear, he says, "Put the backs of your hands on the small of your back."

I do.

"Thank you," he says into my ear.

And he ties my wrists together with, I realize, my scarf. I am still, my heart pounding as he does it. I close my eyes to focus on the sensation of his hands and the silk.

With his lips against my ear again, he says, "Is that comfortable? Blood supply okay?"

I nod.

He laces the fingers of one hand into mine, his face still close to mine. "Annie, what will you say if you want me to stop?"

"Stop."

"And slow down?"

"Wait."

"And when I tell you to beg?"

"Please," I whisper.

He runs his fingertips up my spine.

"You . . . are . . . breathtaking," he says.

And then he's gone. . . . I turn to see where he went. He's undressing, his eyes hungry on me. He grins at me but shakes his head. "Turn round," he says.

And then I feel his mouth and hands and tongue and stubble on my feet.

"Oh my god," I moan. "Why does that feel so fucking good? Oh my *god*." I drop my head and close my eyes, attending to nothing but the sensations on my feet. I point my arches and flex my toes, opening wide spaces for his tongue. "Fuck, I love that so much," I say.

He doesn't answer, just continues the soft, warm, wet exploration of hands and mouth. When he puts my big toe in his mouth and sucks and rolls his tongue around it and scrapes his teeth along it, I gasp, and my head goes back. He does the same thing to each toe, with agonizing slowness, deliberateness. The toes of my left foot point and flex as he attends to my right and I battle to keep those toes relaxed for him. The effort has me breathing like I've just sprinted a mile.

Then, leaving his warm palm over the arch of my right foot, he moves his mouth to the left, and we do it all over again.

"Oh, ffffffffuck youuuuuu," I groan, and I hear him laugh softly, feel it as his teeth scrape across my big toe. "Oh my god. Oh my god, Charles." It doesn't make any sense. Each toe is as sensitive as my clit, and he's sucking and licking and nibbling on each, and it makes me desperate beyond anything else he does to me.

As he sucks my toes, I begin trying things to make myself come. I imagine touching my clit . . . but that only makes things worse, since I can't actually touch it. I rock my pelvis, my abdomen tight. No better. I bring my knees together, press my thighs together, and move my hips.

"Knees apart," Charles says.

I groan and separate my knees, and he slides a hand between my thighs, never coming too close to my labia. "Wider than that," he says. He's standing behind me now, his mouth near my ear. With a whimper of protest, I separate my knees more.

"Just a little more," he says.

I give him a little more and then bend my knees, lowering myself onto his hand, searching out his palm.

"Ah," he scolds. "No."

"Please, Charles," I say desperately. "Let me come. I'm ready to come. Please touch my clit."

"No," he says, and he bites my earlobe, which makes me pant, but it doesn't make me come. "And I didn't tell you to beg."

"Dude, I fucking hate you," I say.

"Good," he says. "Put your shoulders on the bed."

I lower myself to my shoulders, the side of my face pressed into the hotel sheets. I feel his fingers on me, slick with lube but maddeningly far from my clit. Then he slides into me, fucking me hard and fast, his one hand roaming lightly over my skin, my back, my ass, my arms, my thighs, touching me everywhere but my clit. His other hand holds my foot in a warm, firm grip. I groan hoarsely into the mattress, biting at the sheets.

I pull at the scarf, trying to free my hands so I can touch my agonized clit, but then he stops.

"No, you don't." He turns me to my back and spreads my legs wide.

"Please." With my legs wide open and my arms pinned under me, my pelvis is rocking desperately. "*Please.*"

"You can have no idea what seeing you like this does to me," he whispers. "No idea." He kneels at the end of the bed and begins a slow—*slow*—path of kisses along the inside of my open thigh, starting at my knee. His lips and his tongue and his stubble make an agonizing combination, but he's moving closer and closer to my clit.

"Yes," I grind out.

He gets about halfway up my left thigh, and then switches to my right thigh, beginning again at my knee and working a slow, wet trail of kisses up, slowly up, again about halfway up my thigh.

And then he does it again on my left thigh, beginning at my knee.

"*Fuck you,*" I say, but he doesn't answer. He makes it about three quarters of the way up my thigh this time before switching to the right, where again he starts at my knee, licking and kissing and abrading the inside of my thigh until he's about three quarters of the way to my vulva. My whole body is lifting off the bed in waves now. I'm making fierce, gruff noises in my throat. I'm grimacing with the desperateness of my arousal.

A third time, he starts at my knee, and this time his hands are moving over my belly and breasts as my body continues to lift off the mattress in rolling waves of pleasure. His lips travel up my thigh, and he gets so close, I can feel his breath on my pussy. His mouth hovers there, and I lift myself up to him, try to press my vulva against his lips—but he pulls away.

"If you do that again, I'll stop," he says firmly. "Be still now."

"Oh my god, I fucking hate you, Charles." But I lie still. My arms are aching now, and my legs are trembling. My feet are visibly shaking. He begins once more up my right thigh from my knee, kissing and licking with a slow deliberateness that angers me, even as it tantalizes me. When at last his mouth is at the top

HOW NOT TO FALL   249

of my thigh, he just barely touches his parted lips to my vulva. My breath shudders, but I stay still as much as I can, struggling to breathe slowly against the desperate contractions of my belly.

"Good," he says, and I feel the lightest brush of his lips on my clit. "Now beg."

"Please," I say instantly. "Please let me come. Please, Charles, please put your mouth on my clit and let me come. Please lick my clit. Please."

"And what will you do for me?" he says softly, and again I feel his breath, his lips.

"I'll come for you," I sigh. "I'll come for you. Please let me come for you."

He moves away, and I whimper desperately. And then he's pulling my foot in close to my vulva with one hand, his mouth on the arch, licking and kissing and sucking at the tender skin . . . and then his other hand brushes like a cat's tail over my labia.

I burst like a supernova, like a bolt of lightning has split me open. A thought passes vaguely through my mind that our neighbors must think something is wrong; I'm making noises like he's killing me. But I can't stop. I don't want to stop. I only want to let the full flood wash through me.

He kisses my foot and strokes my vulva until the throbbing eases to sporadic jolts, then he puts his mouth on my clit, sucks and flicks his tongue in just the way my body has taught him to, and all at once a second wave hits me, a peak and a cascade of contractions that almost hurt in their intensity. I wrap my legs around him, my arms still trapped under me.

"*Ffffffffuck*, god, oh my god, Charles, I can't—it's too—I can't, please."

He lifts his head and says, "Shall I stop?"

"Yes."

So he comes up and lies beside me, folds me into his arms, holds me, kisses me, calls me sweetheart, and all at once I'm crying quietly against his chest.

"It's all right," he says, and he holds me closer, undoing the knot at my wrists. "Sweetheart, it's all right." As soon as my hands are free, I put them around his neck, moving delicately against the stiffness.

"I don't hate you," I whisper.

"I know," he whispers back.

"I'm in love with you," I say.

"I know," he says. "It's all right."

"I don't know how I'm going to leave on Tuesday," I say.

"I know," he says. "Don't think about it. Just be here with me right now."

"I am. I'm here. I'm here." I hold him as close as I can and I say, "I'm such an idiot."

"Me too," he says, and he kisses my forehead.

We lie wrapped around each other for long minutes.

I don't remember getting under the covers or falling asleep or Charles getting out of bed, but when I open my eyes, I find myself warm under blankets, and the room is dark except for the glow of Charles's computer at the desk and the reflection of his screen on his glasses.

Into the silence, I say, "Charles."

He turns my way. "Mh."

"Tomorrow after the last session, I want to take you to this place I heard about. Will you go?"

"Anywhere you like," he says softly.

"I love you."

"I know, Annie."

And I sigh and relax back into sleep. Because he always tells me the truth.

Chapter 27

The Fundamental Unreliability of the Universe

It's just a few blocks from the hotel. We stroll through the narrow park, and Charles reads each row of letters, bowed like shockwaves traveling away from the nearby college campus.

"Who are the names?" he asks, pointing at the markers. "Where are we?"

I try the French, pronouncing it sort of like it's Spanish, since that's all I know.

He looks at me, puzzled. "The nose for fourteen whats?"

"The nave for fourteen queens," I say.

"Ah," he says. "*Nef pour quatorze reines.*"

"Yes. What's a nave?"

"It's the part of a church where you sit. And who are the fourteen queens?"

"Most of them were students at the École Polytechnique, mostly right around my age. In 1989 a guy went on a shooting spree and killed them. Most of them were women who wanted to be engineers," I say. "And they died for it."

"Jesus," Charles says.

We sit together on a park bench. I say, "I thought there might be something here that would help me understand."

"Understand what?"

"Why people do horrible things?" I shrug. "The nature of evil, I guess? But what this shows me is how much people loved these women."

Charles nods and says, "Fear. The nature of evil is fear."

I look at him and nod too, as if I understand. "Everyone feels fear, though. Not everyone—"

"Hits his wife and tells her it's her fault?"

I nod again, and consider what else it takes. Eventually I say, "It doesn't seem to matter whether a person has money or an education or social status or anything. The world just seems to . . . break some people."

"Though most people in the world don't have any of those things, and nothing can break them."

"So fear," I conclude, "plus fragility."

"Mh," Charles says.

We sit together in the darkening evening, and I think about how hard I was on Charles the night we fought, how hard I pushed him, how he looked at me with fear in his face and then collapsed against the wall. I watch now as the breeze ruffles his hair delicately against his temple.

"What do you fear, my termagant?" Charles asks the grass.

I think carefully for a few minutes, discarding my earliest thoughts—I only fear what I'm not certain I could survive, and I'm pretty certain I can survive most things—before I say, "Two things, at least. I'm afraid of not living up to my potential."

"Ah," he says. "Alas, fearing something like that is the perfect way to create the thing itself. Trust me, I know."

"And I'm afraid of hurting you," I say, and he looks at me, stunned. "Also, heights," I feel compelled to add, for full honesty. "What do you fear?"

He doesn't answer at first. He looks everywhere but at me. He says, "I think people don't fear heights. They fear the fall—and not even that. They fear the consequence of the fall." Then he folds and unfolds his hands in his lap and finally says, "I fear I have already failed my most essential test."

"Your mom," I say, and he nods, still not looking at me.

"And I fear losing your respect."

A month ago—a week ago—I might have said, *Well, fearing something like that is the perfect way to create the thing itself,* or offered a list of all the people who are fragile. To prove I'm smart. To make sure he sees the same thing I see. But I don't need to prove anything with Charles. And I know he sees what I see. So I just lace my fingers between his.

I tilt my head against his shoulder and ask, "What made your senior year hard?"

"Mh?" He's still looking at the grass.

"Back in April you said your senior year was hard. You alternated between data analysis and weeping."

"Ah." He clears his throat, opens his mouth, hesitates . . . and then says, "My mother came to visit me. She was depressed. Eventually I got it out of her that she had miscarried—again, though she thought I didn't know about the first one. She was over forty, but she was twenty-two weeks along, and everything was fine. It was a girl. Mum was calling her Marianne.

"She didn't tell me what my father did. I think he might have pushed her down the stairs or hit her and she fell down the stairs or . . . I don't know. She told me she fell. She told me it was her fault. I knew better by then." His hand is gripping and regripping mine.

"What's it like to miscarry that far along?"

"It's like giving birth," he says. "The heart had stopped beating. She went to hospital, and they induced labor. She wanted a funeral, but he—my father—wouldn't let her. So she came to visit me instead."

What do you say to a story like that? *I'm sorry? That's too bad? Wow, your father really is a total horror show?* We just sit in silence together for a long time.

I sit up and begin, "I was nine . . . ," This is a story I avoid telling, generally. No one in Indiana really understands, so why would a guy from England?

But then I realize: yes. I've found something I don't share. So I'll share it.

So I start again. "I was nine in 2001, and we lived in Greenwich Village, which is—"

"Oh my god," Charles says. He gets it instantly.

"I was in school at the time. It was this amazing sunny day. Blue sky. We were doing fractions. We . . . My parents, I mean, they're doctors, right? They came and got me from school and walked me back to the apartment, and by then everything was gray and the air was dusty, everything was covered in ash. The air tasted like ash and burning. I didn't know what was going on. They left me with Miss Rocío, our housekeeper. She had brought her kids with her. They taught me the names of colors in Spanish. Mom and Dad didn't get home until late, but they came to kiss me good night. They smelled like smoke. When it turned out there wasn't that much need for doctors at the hospital, they just went right to ground zero, but . . . When they got home, they hugged me and kissed me and tried to answer my questions, but it's just one of those things, you know, where there aren't any answers."

"The fundamental unreliability of the universe," Charles says quietly. "What will we do if the sun never comes out again."

I look at him, taken aback. "Oh yeah. I didn't . . . I guess that's how it started."

He sandwiches my hand between his two, and we sit, silent, as the sun begins to go down. And it dawns on me that it doesn't matter if he can't love me the way I need him to; I don't love him because of the way he loves me. I love him because our inner worlds map onto each other. When he shows me more of himself, he is illuminating a new place inside me, and when I give him more of myself, I am showing him a hidden place inside himself.

It's not about him giving me what I need no matter what. It's about him *being* what I need, no matter what. Because he's a mirror, and he shows me the version of myself I most want to be. And I think maybe I do the same for him.

And that's what will hold us together, whatever comes next.

I shiver a little with the chill of the evening, and at last Charles looks at me. We stand up at the same time and walk back to the hotel slowly, our fingers laced together.

We make love that night, lost in the sensation of each other's skin against our own, in the pleasure of two bodies brushing up against each other with affection and a celebration of life. In the dark, I feel like I can read his mind—read his heart—through the tension in his muscles, the flexion of his tendons and joints. So it's no surprise to me at all when, in the quiet rest before sleep, he says brokenly into the darkness, "Annie."

"Hm?"

"You're not wrong." And he kisses my hair.

"I love you too," I say. And I kiss his mouth, and he kisses me back, brushing his palm over my forehead, over my cheek, over my hair.

Taxi, airport, plane, airport, car. Some people enjoy traveling; I've never been one of them. I've always hated flying, especially— though I've suddenly realized why that might be true. Duh. Planes.

Anyway, we have two more nights together.

And, because I'm a fucking idiot, we spend this one fighting.

"Some part of this has to be my fault!" I shout. I can hardly remember how the argument started, but blood is pounding in my ears, and I am desperate for Charles to criticize me, correct me, yell at me, anything. But he won't. He sits at his end of the sofa, and he listens empathically and takes all the blame. I yell, "Just tell me what I've done wrong! If I could see my own mistakes, I wouldn't need you to point them out to me!"

"You've done nothing wrong. I'm—"

"What, I'm perfect and you're the fuckup? That is the most infuriating part about this! There has to be *something* I can do differently, some part of this I can change and control, instead of just accepting things the way they are!"

"Instead of accepting *me* the way I am," he says with an edge of frustration—at last. He makes a frustrated sound and gets up, his hands on his head. With his back to me, he takes several deep breaths and then rubs his hands over his face.

I stand up and follow him. "You can't make things better by accepting them the way they are," I insist. I'm trembling with helpless frustration, my hands fisting and unfisting, my jaw clenched in fury.

"Well, you're wrong about that," he says, turning to face me.

"I'm not. You have to be dissatisfied, you have to *work* and *fight* and *push*." I step forward. He steps back.

"You don't."

"Yes, you do! How can you say that? How can you just *stand there*?" I step forward again, gesturing at his relaxed posture, his calm face. He steps back and puts his hands into his pockets. I'm mortifyingly aware of the difference in our postures. I can hear my own breath, fast and shallow, and I can feel my eyebrows raised, my eyes wide and desperate. I feel the clock ticking, and it fills me with wild panic—and yet he's acting like he's coaching me through a little academic puzzle.

"Is criticizing you really how I show you I care?" he says.

"*Yes!*" I shriek. "Tell me what's wrong so I can *fix it!*" I step forward.

He steps back and raises his eyebrows at me. Quietly and slowly, he says, "Then I tell you now you're angrier than is helpful, and I'd like you to calm down a bit."

" 'Calm down'?" I shout. "That's how I can fix things? *By caring less?*" I step forward, my hands fisted so hard, my nails are digging impotently into my palms. There isn't any time, and he won't help me. How do I make him help me? He has to *help me.*

He steps back and looks at the floor. "That's not what I said—"

"Yes, it is!"

And I shove him, once, hard, both hands on his shoulders.

Charles staggers backward two steps under the force of my push and holds his hands up by his shoulders. He isn't looking at me. He's breathing hard through his nose.

I clap my hands over my mouth, appalled at myself. "I'm sorry, Charles."

"I know. It's all right."

"Oh my god."

"Don't worry about it. Just go."

"Go?"

"Please, Annie."

"But I—"

"*For god's sake,*" he says through his teeth, and then he puts his hands over his face. I see his fingers trembling.

So I go. I walk out the door, close it behind me, and sit in the hallway, my arms wrapped around my head.

I hear Charles moving. I hear water run through the pipes. Is he making coffee? No, it must be the shower. He's taking a shower.

I sit there in the hall, ashamed, crying as quietly as I can manage. After about twenty minutes he texts me—my phone bleeps.

And then the door opens.

"Heard your phone out here," Charles says. His hair is wet over his forehead, and he's smiling a little. "Do you want to come in?"

I nod and rise and go in, and as soon as the door is closed, I throw my arms around his waist and burst into noisy tears and apologies. He puts his arms around me and tells me it's all right, I'm all right, we're all right, everything will be fine. It's all nonsense. I will never be fine again.

"I love you so much," I say. "I'm so sorry."

"It's all right."

"I hurt you."

"I'm all right."

"I pushed you."

At this, he actually laughs, "My harpy, you've been pushing me since the day you kissed me."

"I mean I physically pushed you!"

"I know what you mean, sweetheart, and it doesn't matter."

"How can it not matter?"

He steps back and holds my face in his hands. "Will you ever do it again, to me or anyone else?"

"Oh my god, no!"

"And that's why it doesn't matter."

I put my arms around him again. "I love you. I'm sorry. I love you so much."

"I know, Annie. It's all right."

"And I get the monster thing better now."

He kisses the top of my head. And he starts laughing lightly.

I squeeze him. "How can you laugh?"

"It's just so awful and ridiculous," he says through a chuckle. "Here we are, with hardly any time together left, and we can't even enjoy it for what it is, because we're so wrapped up in what it's not."

"Why is that funny? It's awful."

"Oh, my termagant, my shrew." He pulls away enough to put his hand on my cheek, and he smiles into my eyes. "It's not genocide or famine or disease. It's just the two of us, in a comfortable room, in our comfortable lives, with everything anyone could want except one tiny, immaterial thing. And all either of us is thinking about is the one thing we don't have. That is fucking *hilarious*."

He hugs me again, laughing still, and says, "Let's go to bed, sweetheart."

So we do.

The sex that night is amazing to me. He leads me by the hand to the bedroom, takes off our clothes methodically, and then lays me on the bed and kisses and caresses every inch of my body— every inch, the webbing of my fingers, the soft curve under my toes, the hidden, tender spot behind the top of my ear—and talks to me the whole time, telling me what I feel like, what he likes about my body. He doesn't make me come; he doesn't even try. He touches me almost worshipfully, and I'm left in a haze of pleasure.

Then he tells me I'm in charge, so I do the same to him,

touching and kissing his beautiful body and talking to him, and I find I've made myself feel so in love with him, I can hardly stand it.

I shift gears, wrangle us so I'm on top. I grab his wrists and pin them above his head, thrust my tongue into his mouth. When I feel him smiling through the kiss, I stop.

"Can I try something?" I say.

"Anything," he answers, grinning.

I sit up, turn around, and straddle him, facing his feet. I lean forward with one hand on his shin and I reach between my legs to position his cock.

"Brace yourself, Bridget," I say, and he laughs out loud.

"Don't laugh!" I say, laughing myself as I press down and he pushes into me. "Oh, that's interesting. That is very interesting." All my attention turns to the sensation of him inside me at this new angle. I can touch my clit as much as I want, exactly the way I want, this way. I move on him, one hand on my clit, one at his ankle, and ride him slowly.

"I really, really like this," I say. I sit up to use both hands on my clit.

"That is magnificent," he says, and I feel his hands on the backs of my thighs, on my ass. "You are magnificent."

"I feel magnificent," I say, eyes closed, all my attention focused on how it feels. I make myself come—a surprisingly solitary experience, considering his cock is inside me and his hands are on me. But it's my hands on my clit and breasts. He can't see my face; all he can see is how, when I come, my head tilts back.

As the pulsing fades, I lean back and lie over him, my back to his chest as I breathe in recovery. He wraps his arm around me. "You are spectacular," he says into my ear, and he fucks me that way. He knits his fingers between mine and uses my hands to touch me, my breasts, my clit, my belly. When he's using one hand to press steadily against my clit, he moves the other hand to wrap around my throat.

All the while, he's murmuring into my ear, "You are so fucking amazing. I could never have enough of you. You're the most beautiful woman, the sweetest, funniest, sexiest woman I'll ever know. The way your body moves when you come, god, Annie. Touching you. Tasting you. I love the taste of you."

And that, I think, is as close as I'll ever get to hearing him say it.

I turn my head to kiss him, he grunts in pleasure, and I come again, thrusting against our entangled hands.

Chapter 28

It Hurts

People who say, "Live every day as if it's your last," have not taken into account the fact that if it's your last day, you may very well be too miserable with grief about the impending loss to enjoy what you still have. I bet a "last meal" doesn't taste like anything.

But maybe it's a kind of, I don't know, educational experience. A "teachable moment," my mom would call it. It will make me a better person to walk through this day, aware that it is what it is, and just let it be hard. Not try to make it anything it isn't inclined to be.

I spend Monday packing my rented moving truck while Charles is at work. That afternoon I clean my apartment for the last time, leave my key at the desk, and drive the truck up to Charles's place.

We have twelve hours, and I have to sleep for some of them. So maybe four hours together? Six? Not more.

I let myself in and shower off the sweat and grime of packing, then lie on the couch with *Right Ho, Jeeves*. Predictably, I'm asleep when he gets home. I wake to the sound of the door opening and then sit up.

He doesn't come over to me, but leans against the wall, look-ing at me with that soft, warm smile that tears me inside out.

"What would you like to do tonight?" he says. "What can I give you that will please you?"

"Your heart," I answer without thinking.

"Oh, Annie." He comes forward and kneels in front of me by the couch. "Is it selfish of me to say I need my heart more than you do?"

I shake my head, and my chin wobbles.

Charles sits beside me then and pulls me against him, wraps me up in his arms. "I've been trying to find the moment when I could have prevented this," he says. "Maybe if . . . that first night, when I found out how inexperienced you were, if I had lis-tened to the part of me that said stop. If I had known, that night, that it would end like this, Annie, please believe me, I would have sent you home."

I roll my eyes. "Do you honestly think I'd have just accepted that and gone away? Have you met me?"

He kisses my temple and tucks me into the crook of his shoul-der. "Maybe the day you came to practice your defense and you kissed me. I should have said you were wrong about The Thing."

"But I wasn't wrong, and you don't lie to me."

"No."

"I'm not wrong now, either."

He's silent.

"Why did you come to the lab that night with the veggie burger?" I ask.

"Why did I come?" Charles sighs massively. "I'd begun think-ing about you differently. I'd begun to see—I hope this doesn't sound arrogant—but I saw myself, a bit, in you. And I recognized that you're about to launch into the world and you'd be joining the same field, and I wanted a stronger connection with you than just being your research supervisor. I suppose I was thinking about it as mentorship.

"I've always liked you, Annie. You were the most competent of the ducklings when I arrived in the lab, and you were funny, and then it turned out you weren't just competent, you were brilliant—I have worked with brilliant people and you are . . . It's slightly terrifying how clever you are. I had been, er, harboring lustful thoughts, as you know, but I had no doubt I could keep them in check. That day in Soma when—"

"The Bread Fiasco."

"Yes. I wanted to say, 'Yes, we have A Thing, so please, yes, let me make you come six times, and then we'll go our separate ways.' But I didn't."

"Because you're a responsible adult."

"I am. Then you came in that day to practice your defense and you kissed me and you were *determined* to have me acknowledge The Thing. I wanted to lay you out on my desk and—well.

"But never, never did it occur to me—not even when it turned out you had no experience at all—not until Diana brought it up, did I consider the possibility that there would be emotional risk for you. It really never occurred to me that you might fall in love."

"Or that you might."

He's silent.

"For fuck's sake, Charles." I rest my forehead on his chest and sigh.

He's silent for a moment, and then he says, "I know."

I look up at him. "That's it? You know?"

"This is always what it was going to be. You were always going to leave. You knew that as well as I."

"Well, I didn't know it would feel like this."

"And I let myself be selfish." He puts his hand on my face. "Even after . . . even after you said you loved me, I thought it might be all right, that it could just be a learning experience for us both and a lot of pleasure, with memories you could take with you, rather than regrets. In fairness, I confess it's not . . . that is . . ." He stops. He's embarrassed. "It's difficult for me too. I feel like . . . the lights are going out."

I grab on to his shirt, then notice what I'm doing and let go. Then I think, *Fuck it*, and I grab it again.

Charles says, "It's the family bloody motto, you know? Has your family got a motto? Mine's '*par la souffrance, la vertu.*' 'Virtue through suffering.' But whose suffering, and whose virtue? Questions the motto does not see fit to address."

"Doesn't anyone have the motto 'Virtue through pleasure'? Why isn't feeling good just as noble and valiant as feeling like shit? I mean, god knows there are plenty of times when it's easy to feel like shit and really difficult to experience pleasure."

"Perhaps that's what it means after all. Virtue is finding something worth liking in the swamp of human experience." He pauses, his lips on my temple, then whispers, "Will you spend tonight with me, Annie?"

"Of course."

Of course. How could I do anything else?

We make love sitting up, my legs wrapped around his waist and his arms wrapped around my waist and my arms wrapped around his neck. He's as deep inside me as it's possible to be. I let him all the way in. And I'm as deep inside him as he'll let me.

The word for this hovers at my lips, between our mouths, inside our kiss. I can taste it. *Love.*

It's hard to stop touching. He makes me come, over and over, until I cry, and then holds me and murmurs wordlessly into my hair. I fall asleep on his chest and wake in the middle of the night, with him curled along my back. I wake him with kisses and say, "Please."

In the thick darkness, he's ready for me. He turns me onto my stomach and pins me to the bed by my wrists, outstretched. He fucks me hard in the dark, from behind, almost without noise. My head is turned toward him and he kisses me, never letting my wrists go. He wants to make me come this way and it's not going to happen—not because I'm holding anything back, not because I haven't utterly surrendered to him, but because I am not built that way.

He takes my hand in his and tucks our fingers between my legs, where his thrusting moves my pelvis over our hands. I'm slippery and sensitive. His other hand tugs at my hair, turns my face fiercely to the side so he can kiss me more deeply, his tongue in my mouth. My arousal rises quickly with the friction of our two hands against my clit, and I begin to rock my pelvis into the rhythm of his thrusts, into the pressure of my own palm pressed against my vulva. As I approach the threshold, I give a sharp high gasp—and he pulls out, away from me.

"I want—"

"I know what you want," he says.

With a grunt, he turns me over and fucks me again, his pubic bone grinding deliberately against mine. His hands are on either side of my face, I can feel his breath on my cheek, and he's fucking me hard, touching me exactly the way I like. He can read the tension of my body, he feels me sprung around him, and he lets it grow slowly. In a month, he has learned every nuance of my body's rhythms, every tremble of muscle, every suspension of breath.

I relax my body into his, surrendering again, surrendering always, and he fucks me in a fast, steady rhythm that presses on my clit, growing the arousal inside me, slow and massive, to an expansive scale that bottlenecks inside me.

He grips both fists in my hair and says, "Look at me."

When I do, I find him watching my face, a wrinkle of concentration between his eyebrows.

When I finally peak, with agonizing slowness, I kiss him, my eyes still open, watching him watch me, and I clutch my arms around his shoulders as I breathe against his mouth, "Don't let go, please." And he says, "I won't let go," and I'm rocked with thunderous, slow waves of spasms that won't end and I'm kissing him with my eyes open and then begging him, "Don't let go, not yet, please not yet," and he keeps saying, "I won't let go, Annie, I won't let go." His forehead is against mine, his eyes watching mine, and I'm still there, suspended in the dark, shuddering, as if the aperture of my orgasm is too small to release all the tension inside me. I dig my nails into his back, panting, "I can't stop, god. Fuck, I can't stop it."

"Don't stop," he says, and my entire world is his eyes on mine and the slow explosion happening inside my body. "Don't stop."

"I can't stop."

"Don't stop."

"Charles. It hurts."

"God." His eyes close and he lowers his face to my ear. He says, "Hurt me, Annie."

I close my eyes and bite into his shoulder, still coming, and dig my nails into his shoulders. I scratch hard, wanting to make him bleed. I beat on his back with my fists, and I scream, I actually scream.

"More," he says into my ear, and then I'm wild and flailing around him, hitting and scratching, and he's holding fast, inside me, all around me, my entire universe is Charles, and then he's coming too, coming inside me with a cry just as vicious as my own. Only then does my release widen and break into soft, rolling waves, and we rock against each other, break against each other, rolling and pushing and wetness and kisses.

Our bodies gradually soften together, still clinging to each other.

"I fucking hate you," I whisper, and I caress and kiss the spot where my teeth made dents in his shoulder. I wrap my arms tight around his neck and say, "I love you so much. I love you."

He's holding me so tight and close, his arms are shaking. He whispers my name. I kiss his ear. He shudders against me, tightens his arms even closer around me, and says into my shoulder, "I can't."

And I murmur nonsense into his hair—it's okay, you're okay,

we're okay, everything is going to be fine. Nonsense. He kisses my neck and my ear and then my mouth very softly, so softly.

And then he withdraws, pulls away to his side of the bed. He pulls me with him, spooning me to him, his arm around me.

"Don't let go yet," I say.

"I won't let go," he whispers, and he tightens his arms around me.

Charles is asleep when my phone alarm vibrates at six. In his sleep, he has turned onto his back and let me go. I've been lying here, feeling him breathe and making a to-do list in my head. Get out of bed. Put on clothes. Get your bag. Leave the book and the key. Get out.

Go. Go now.

I get out of bed. I put on my clothes. I stand in the bedroom doorway, watching the rise and fall of Charles's chest. He's sleeping on his back, one arm over his head, one on his belly. The gold hair on his abdomen glints in the bare light of early dawn.

Get your bag. Leave the book and the key. Get out. Go.

I get my bag and retrieve the book and the key. I press the book to my lips and feel my eyes burn with tears. I don't want to get the book wet. I put it on the coffee table. For less than a second I watch the gilt lettering in the early dawn light, and then I walk away, out of the apartment, locking it behind me.

I drop the key into an envelope, together with a note, and I leave it in his mailbox.

I get in my rented truck and I drive away, into the sunrise.

There's how you feel about someone. And there's what relationship you can have with them.

Maybe this is all it was ever going to be. Maybe this is what there is for us. A few weeks in May.

I think . . . You guys, I've tried to be honest this whole time, but I think I may have been ignoring some things. I think maybe I've been in love with Charles all along—I mean *all* along, like all two years, yes, but *always*, like maybe his heart and my heart were built from the very beginning to fit neatly together, but people were careless with his, they damaged it, knocked it out of alignment, and so now we don't fit, when we should have. We should have.

My heart was treated with care my whole life. There are bruised places now, little tears and sore spots where I tried to jam it into a fit with his jagged edges. And we've both bled.

In principle, I know mine will heal.

People don't fear heights. They don't even fear the fall. They fear the consequences of the fall. The greater the height, the greater the consequences, and so the greater the fear.

How not to fall is to not mind falling; and how not to mind falling, is to fall a lot.

It's about a twelve-hour drive from Bloomington to Manhattan.

How can you know for sure the sun will come out again?

How can you *know?*

And what would you do, how could you live, if the rain never stopped?

Epilogue

Hey, Charles,
So three things, I guess:

*1. Thank you for the most beautiful month of
my life.*
*2. You are the best man I know. You are the best
man I know. You are the best man I know.*
3. Please don't call or write for a while.

Love,

Annie

*PS I looked up that poem you were quoting.
You left out this part:*

*Look as long as you can at the friend you love,
no matter whether that friend is moving away from
you or coming back toward you.*

It's not over! Catch up with Annie and Charles in

How Not to Let Go

Coming in 2017

Chapter 1

Everybody's Got
to Learn Sometime

I've never driven a moving truck before, but I drive this one for twelve hours, Indiana to New York, sobbing off and on the whole way. I listen to Beck's version of "Everybody's Got to Learn Sometime" on repeat. The sky is gray and it spits rain all day, like there's a rain cloud following me east.

By the time I pull up in front of my parents' building on Fifth Avenue, opposite the park, the sky is thundery and dark, too dark for an evening in June. My parents meet me under the green awning and hug me in happy greeting. If they notice my blotchy, tear-stained face, they don't mention it. If they wonder why, when I say I'm so glad to be home, I instantly burst into tears, they don't ask.

The super finds a couple of guys to move my stuff into the library, and Mom and Dad feed me dinner while the guys bring it all in. I take a shower and wash away last night's sex, and then my parents and I sit on the living room couch and celebrate my homecoming by binge-watching *Gilmore Girls*, which was one of my favorite shows when I was little.

And then I go to bed alone. I lie there, wondering what Charles is doing, how he feels, how he felt when he woke up and I wasn't there.

The swamping shame of sneaking out like that is too much. I curl up in a ball, teeth gritted, and try to soothe myself by making lists in my head of the many valuable things I've learned recently:

- How you feel about a person doesn't necessarily match the kind of relationship you can have with them.
- When you and your partner laugh while you're fucking, you can feel the laughter inside your body.
- If a baby monkey's mother starts abusively rejecting the baby, it will abandon all its friends and obsessively try to make its mother love it again.

I cry myself to sleep.

I wake up, cry a little more, go for a run, take a nap, eat dinner with my parents and watch a movie with them, and then cry myself to sleep again.

This is most of how I spend my month at home before I leave for medical school.

At my parents' suggestion, I start attending the drop-in ballet classes for adults at Joffrey a few times a week. They think the discipline and the community will do me good. They're right. I rip the shanks out of some old, dead pointe shoes and stop eating sugar and kick my own ass three nights a week, and it keeps my bleeding heart tethered to the rest of my body. I enjoy being in a group of "adults." Which is apparently what I am now.

And every night, for a month, I lie in bed, staring at my Alan Turing poster—"We can only see a short distance ahead, but we can see plenty there that needs to be done"—and I make lists in my head, to remind myself of all the important things I'm learning:

- The death of hope is like the death of a parent, the permanent loss of the place you would return to when life is at its worst.

- When you sob until you can't breathe, you don't die, even though it feels like you might. All that happens is you stop sobbing and you start breathing.
- My mom is really, really, really fucking smart.

I knew that last one already, but about ten days into my cry/run/nap/ballet/dinner/cry/sleep routine, she follows me into my room after we watch *Groundhog Day*, sits on the bed, and pats the spot next to her. "Tell me what's going on, girl."

"Nothing."

"Yeah," she says, rolling her eyes, and she pats the bed again.

So I sit beside her and bunch my lips together against the trembling that they've learned to associate with lying in this bed: If on bed, then cry until asleep. Ugh.

"Charles," I say, suppressing my tears. I stare at my hands.

"What did he do?"

"He didn't—" I stop and hold my breath, and then whimper, "He just didn't love me." I feel like a six-year-old confessing that another kid at school didn't want to be my friend.

She sighs heavily and brushes her hand softly over my hair. "Annabelle Frances Coffey." She only uses my whole name when she's about to say something she feels self-conscious about saying.

"Yeah." I sniff.

"I'm only going to say this once. Are you really listening?"

"Yeah," I huff into my knees.

"Your heart. Is too wise. To love someone. Who doesn't deserve it. So either: He's a superb human being who has earned your friendship. Or else you will stop loving him altogether, and soon. I don't know which it is, but I know it's one or the other. This thing you're experiencing right now is the chaos as your heart decides whether to let go of the love or . . . hold on to it in a new way."

I wipe my nose on my sleeve and try to breathe. I ask, "How do you know?"

"How do I know what?"

"How do you know my heart will figure out what to do?"

"That's what hearts do, when you let them."

I sigh and sniff again, and I believe her. "Okay."

And she's right. That's what mine does.

Slowly, painfully, like a hand uncurling from a fist to an open palm, my heart opens up, exploring ways to hold Charles differently.

But.

I'm not out of the chaos yet when Margaret calls me, barely three weeks after I left Indiana, and says in an urgent voice, "I know the answer is probably no, but you're my best friend and I have to ask: Can you fly to Indiana *tomorrow* to attend my wedding?"

"What?!"

"The district court overturned the ban on same-sex marriage today. We want to go get a license right away because you *know* that shit is going to be stopped within a matter of days."

"Oh my god, yes! Oh my god!"

Margaret and Reshma pick me up at the airport the next morning and take me to Reshma's moms' house and we clean and decorate and cook and hug and laugh. I mow the lawn while Margaret and Reshma weed the flower beds, which seems to be mostly an excuse to roll around in the dirt, tickling each other. The moms are inside moving furniture around to create space and "flow." They're getting married too—a double wedding in the backyard— and I feel so, so lucky to be here with these amazing people on this amazing day.

I also feel like I'm a one-hour drive away from Charles. I don't know if he's coming, and I can't bring myself to ask. I just do what I'm instructed to do, being as helpful as I can until it's my turn to take a shower and put on a dress, and then I start meeting guests at the back fence. My job is to let people in without letting the dog out. (The dog has no interest in getting out. He's a twelve-year-old bulldog with an underbite and casual attitude about licking his penis in public.)

Eventually Margaret's and my research supervisor, Professor Smith—"*Diana*," she insists—arrives with her husband. I hug her hello. She's so pregnant I worry she might pop like a balloon if I squeeze her, but I hug her as hard as I dare.

"Hey, is Charles coming?" I ask casually. The impression I want to give is that this isn't something I've been obsessing about more or less nonstop since Margaret called.

Professor Smith—Diana—looks at me suspiciously, but only says, "He's here—we drove up together."

"Oh." Something cold drops into my stomach, even as my heart starts fluttering.

All of our heads turn back to the driveway, and there he is.

Chapter 2

Tell Me What to Do

I've hardly ever seen her in a dress. Mostly it's skinny jeans and novelty T-shirts; you'd mistake her for an awkward fourteen-year-old boy if it weren't for the way she moves—not awkward, not a boy. But she stands at the fence now in the same red silk thing she wore under her academic regalia at commencement and to dinner in Montreal. At commencement, she looked pretty and happy. In Montreal, she looked fucking gorgeous, tousled and pink-cheeked from sex. Now, though, she looks pale and sick and much too thin, with exhaustion in her eyes.

That's my fault.

There's a look of dread on her face as her eyes find mine.

That's my fault, too.

I wouldn't have come if I had known. When the e-mail from Margaret came yesterday, and Diana asked if I would drive her and her husband up, I said yes easily, thinking there was no chance Annie would fly back for one day. No chance.

But she is a better friend than I gave her credit for, and now I am imposing myself on her, at her best friend's wedding. Fuck. I am a waste of skin and oxygen, and she—god. Brilliant. Strong. Sane, so sane, I felt like an escaped convict with his face turned toward raw winter sunlight when I talked to her. Clear. Vivid. Luminescent and illuminating.

I made her cry. I made her hurt.

I tuck the crate of wine bottles and presents under my arm, put on my sunglasses, and go to the fence.

"Hey," she says, not quite looking at me.

"Hey," I answer.

"Need help with that?" she asks, squinting against the sun.

"Just point me to the food table."

"In the house." She closes the gate behind us and waves us to the back door. "Living room. It's easy to find."

I make for the house, planning tactics for staying out of Annie's way for the next couple of hours.

Reshma and Margaret are married in the backyard, right after Reshma's parents. Annie cries becomingly through both ceremonies, standing beside Margaret and handing over the rings when it's her turn. I watch her the whole time; I can't take my eyes off her. She looks so obviously unwell—can anyone see her and not see the grief, the loss of appetite, the disrupted sleep? They're all my fault.

And at the same time . . . her feet are bare, her bare toes in the grass. Can anyone see Annie's long, bony bare feet in the grass and not imagine the dirty, cool soles pressing into the backs of their thighs as she laughs and wriggles under them? I want to make love with Annie outside. I've never done that.

I never will do that.

Just stay out of her way, you arse.

During the reception, I occupy myself with noticing when Annie comes into the room so that I can leave it—trying to give her space, trying to do what she asked. The third time this happens, Diana comes over and asks me what the hell is going on, and I look at the floor and the wall and the furniture as I confess, "Er, it's awkward. Annie told you that she and I had, as she put it,

'A Thing,' but it ended rather messily when she left Indiana and she asked for space. I'm trying to give her that space."

Diana pats my arm and gives me a sympathetic smile. "We'll go," she says. "I'm hot and tired, and my feet are swelling anyway. Let me just say good-bye to Margaret."

I nod—then I notice Annie watching us, and I walk out the front door. I put on my sunglasses and sit on the porch swing to wait for Diana.

After just a minute the door opens and I look up, expecting Diana, but instead . . . there's Annie.